BUFF: A COLLIE

ALBERT PAYSON TERHUNE

BUFF: A COLLIE

AND OTHER DOG-STORIES

By

Albert Payson Terhune

Author of LOCHINVAR LUCK,

LAD OF SUNNYBANK,

TREVE, BRUCE, etc.

jT272 4

GROSSET & DUNLAP

Publishers *New York*

BY ARRANGEMENT WITH DOUBLEDAY, DORAN & COMPANY, INC.

PRINTED IN THE UNITED STATES OF AMERICA

FOREWORD

A swirl of gold-and-white and gray and black,—
Rackety, vibrant, glad with life's hot zest,—
Sunnybank collies, gaily surging pack,—
These are my chums; the chums that love me best.

Not chums alone, but courtiers, zealots, too,—
Clean-white of soul, too wise for fraud or sham;
Yet senseless in their worship ever new.
These are the friendly folk whose god I am.

A blatant, foolish, stumbling, purblind god,—
A pinchbeck idol, clogged with feet of clay!
Yet, eager at my lightest word or nod,
They crave but leave to follow and obey.

We humans are so slow to understand!
Swift in our wrath, deaf to the justice-plea,
Meting out punishment with lavish hand!
What, but a dog, would serve such gods as we?

Heaven gave them souls, I'm sure; but dulled the brain,
Lest they should sadden at so brief a span
Of heedless, honest life as they sustain;
Or doubt the godhead of their master, Man.

Today a pup; tomorrow at life's prime;
Then old and fragile;—dead at fourteen years.

At best a meagre little inch of time.
Oblivion then, sans mourners, memories, **tears!**

Service that asks no price; forgiveness **free**
For injury or for injustice hard.
Stanch friendship, wanting neither thanks nor **fee**
Save privilege to worship and to guard:—

That is their creed. They know no shrewder **way**
To travel through their hour of lifetime here.
Would Man but deign to serve his God as **they,**
Millennium must dawn within the **year.**

CONTENTS

vii

CONTENTS

BUFF: A COLLIE

BUFF: A COLLIE

CHAPTER ONE: THE FIGHTING STRAIN

SHE was a mixture of the unmixable. Not one expert in eighty could have guessed at her breed or breeds.

Her coat was like a chow's, except that it was black and white and tan—as is no chow's between here and the Chinese Wall. Her deep chest was as wide as a bulldog's; her queer little eyes slanted like a collie's; her foreface was like a Great Dane's, with its barrel muzzle and dewlaps. She was as big as a mastiff.

She was Nina, and she belonged to a well-to-do farmer named Shawe, a man who went in for registered cattle, and, as a side line, for prize collies.

To clear up, in a handful of words, the mystery of Nina's breeding, her dam was Shawe's long-pedigreed and registered and prize-winning tri-colour collie, Shawemere Queen. Her sire was Upstreet Butcherboy, the fiercest and gamest and strongest and most murderous pit-terrier ever loosed upon a doomed opponent.

Shawe had decided not to breed Shawemere

Queen that season. Shawemere Queen had decided differently. Wherefore, she had broken from her enclosure by the simple method of gnawing for three hours at the rotting wood that held a rusty lock-staple.

This had chanced to befall on a night when Tug McManus had deputed the evening exercising of Upstreet Butcherboy to a new handyman. The handy-man did not know Butcherboy's odd trick of going slack on the chain for a moment and then flinging himself forward with all his surpassing speed and still more surpassing strength.

As a result, the man came back to McManus's alone, noisily nursing three chain-torn fingers. Butcherboy trotted home to his kennel at dawn, stolidly taking the whaling which McManus saw fit to administer.

When Shawemere Queen's six bullet-headed pups came into the world, sixty-three days later, there was loud and lurid blasphemy, at her master's kennels. Shawe, as soon as he could speak with any degree of coherence, bade his kennelman drown five of the pups at once, and to give like treatment to the sixth as soon as its mother should have no further need of the youngster.

At random the kennelman scooped up five-sixths of the litter and strolled off to the horse-pond.

As a result of this monopoly the sixth puppy throve apace. When she was eight weeks old, fate intervened once more to save her from the horse-pond. Mrs. Shawe's sister had come, with her two children, to spend the summer at the farm. The children, after a glimpse of the pure-breed collie litters gambolling in the shaded puppy-run, had clamoured loudly for a pup of their own to play with.

Shawe knew the ways of a child with a puppy. He was of no mind to risk chorea or rickets or fits or other ailments, for any of his priceless collie babies; from such Teddy Bear handling as the two youngsters would probably give it. Yet the clamour of the pair grew the more plangently insistent.

Then it was that the bothered man bethought him of the illegitimate offspring of Shawemere Queen, the nondescript pup he had planned to drown within the next few days. The problem was solved.

Once more, peace reigned at Shawemere. And the two children were deliriously happy in the possession of a shaggy and shapeless morsel of puppyhood, in whose veins coursed the ancient royal blood of pure colliedom and the riotously battling strain of the pit-warriors.

They named their pet "Nina," after a Pomeranian they had mauled and harassed into con-

vulsions. And they prepared to give like treatment to their present puppy.

But a cross-breed is ever prone to be super-
sturdy. The roughly affectionate manhandling
which had torn the Pom's hair-trigger nerves and
tenuous vitality to shreds had no effect at all
upon Nina. On the contrary, she waxed fat
under the dual caresses and yankings of her new
owners.

Which was lucky. For, while a puppy is an
ideal playmate for a child, the average child is a
horrible playmate for a puppy. With no consciousness of cruelty, children maul or neglect or
otherwise ill-treat thousands of friendly and helpless puppies to death, every year. And fond parents look on, with fatuous smiles, at their playful offsprings' barbarity.

Strong and vigorous from birth, Nina began
to take on size at an amazing rate. Before she
was eight months old she stood higher at the
shoulder than any collie at Shawemere. She
looked like no other dog on earth, and she was
larger by far than either of her parents.

The cleverest breeder cannot always breed his
best stock true to type. And when it comes to
crossbreeding—especially with dogs—nothing
short of Mother Nature herself can predict the
outcome.

Nina was a freak. She resembled outwardly

neither collie nor pit bull-terrier. Withal, she was not ill to look on. There was a compact symmetry and an impression of latent power to her. And the nondescript coat was thick and fine. In spite of all this, she probably would have met with a swift and reasonably merciful death, on the departure of the two children, that autumn, had not Shawe realised that the youngsters had been invited to the farm for the following summer, and that the presence of their adored Nina would save some thoroughbred pup from sacrifice as a pet.

So the crossbreed was permitted to stay on, living at Shawemere on sufferance, well enough fed and housed in the stables, permitted to wander pretty much at will, but unpetted and unnoticed. The folk at the farm believed in breeding true to form. A nondescript did not interest them.

And the loss was theirs. For the gigantic young mongrel was worth cultivating. Clever, lovable, obedient, brave, she was an ideal farm dog. And wistfully she sought to win friends from among these indifferent humans. Sadly she missed the petting and the mauling of the children.

These so-called mongrels, by the way, are prone to be cleverer and stronger than any thoroughbred. Rightly trained, they are ideal chums and pets and guards—a truth too little known.

If the farm people had troubled to give Nina one-fiftieth of the attention they lavished on the kennel dogs, they would have seen to it that she did not set forth, one icy moonlight night in late November, on a restless gallop over the hills beyond the farm. And this story would not have been written.

Champion Shawemere King was one of the four greatest collies in America—perhaps on earth. He was such a dog as is bred perhaps twice in a generation—flawless in show qualities and in beauty and in mind. He had annexed the needful "fifteen points" for his championship at the first six shows to which Shawe had taken him. Everywhere, he had swept his way to "Winners" with ridiculous ease. He was the sensation of every show he went to.

Wisely, Shawe had withdrawn him from the ring while King was still in his glory. And, a few years later, the champion had been taken permanently from the kennels and had been promoted (or retired) to the rank of chief house-dog. As perfect in the home as in the ring, he was the pride and ornament of the big farmhouse.

On this particular November night of ice and moonlight, King had turned his back on the warmth of the living-room fire and the disreputable old fur rug that was his resting-place, and had stretched himself upon the veranda mat, head between forepaws; his deep-set dark eyes fixed on the highroad leading from town. Shawe had gone to town for the evening. He had forbidden King to go with him. But, collie-like, the champion had preferred waiting on the cold porch for a first glimpse of his returning master, rather than to lie in smug comfort indoors.

As he lay there he lifted his head suddenly from between his white forepaws and sniffed the dead-cold air. At the same moment the patter of running feet on the icy ground caught his ear. Scent and sound came from the direction of the distant stables.

Then, athwart his gaze, loomed something big and bulky, that flashed in the white moonlight, cantering past him with an inviting backward lilt of the head as it made for the hills.

At once, on the invitation, King forgot his accruing years and his dignity. With a bound he was at Nina's side. Together the two raced madly across the yard and across the yellow road and on up into the hills.

It was a wonderful night for such a wild run. Pure-breed and cross-breed were obsessed by the urge of it all. Forgotten was King's stolidly loyal intent to lie on the chilly mat until Shawe should return. Forgotten was the wistful loneliness that had saddened Nina since the departure of the two children.

As the dogs bounded across the bright road, the kennelman, returning from a stroll, caught sight of them and recognised them. He shouted to King to come to heel. The champion did not so much as look back. At Shawe's call he would have obeyed—though with vast reluctance. But this man was a hireling. And no dog knows better than a collie the wide difference in the loyal obedience due to a master and the negligible civility due to an employee. So King kept on, at the shoulder of his galloping new mate.

When Shawe, late in January, followed the kennelman into the corner of a disused stall and stared down at Nina, his face was creased in a frown of disgust.

There, deep in a pile of bedding, lay the big young cross-bred dog. She looked up at the visitors with a welcoming glint of her round brown eyes and a thumping wag of her bushy tail. She was happy at their notice. She was inordinately proud of what they had come to see.

Snuggled close against her side squirmed seven puppies. They were three days old. A more motley collection could not have been found in dogdom.

Two were short-haired and bullet-headed, and were white except for a brindle spot or two on head and hip.   Throwbacks, these, to their war-like grandsire, Upstreet Butcherboy.   Three more were intermediate of aspect, and might or might not be going to have long coats.   A sixth was enough like a thoroughbred collie to have passed muster in almost any newborn collie litter.

Over this harlequin sextette Shawe's contemptuous glance strayed.   Then his gaze focused on the seventh pup.   And the frown was merged into a look of blank incredulity.

The pup was lying an inch or two away from his dam, and several inches from the huddle of brothers and sisters.   Every line of him was clearly visible and distinct from the rest.

To a layman, he looked like any three-day-old collie.   To Shawe he did not.   Any collie expert will tell you that at the age of three days a pup gives far truer promise of his future appearance —to the trained eye—than he gives at three months.   To the man who knows, there is a look— to the head, especially—that foreshadows the lines of maturity.

Later, all this foreshadowing vanishes.   At two or three months it is next to impossible to predict what the pup is going to turn into.   But in that one brief phase of babyhood the future often is writ clear.

Shawe noticed the coffin-shaped skull, the square muzzle, the full foreface, the set of the tiny ears, the general conformation. Unbelieving, he stared. He picked up the wiggling morsel of fur and flesh and looked more closely at those prophetic head-lines.

"Good Lord!" he mumbled, bewildered, "why, —why, that's a—a DOG! He's the living image of what King was, at three days. And I picked out King for a great collie when he was this youngster's age. I've never known it to fail. Never, up to now. What's this measly mongrel doing with the head and build of a winner?"

"Well," ruminated the kennelman, "we know he's three-quarter bred, don't we? King's his sire. And Shawemere Queen was his dam's mother. Best blood anywhere in colliedom, ain't it? And it had to come out, somewheres, didn't it? Cross-breeding ain't like mixing feed. You don't get the same mixture, every measureful you dip out. Some is all one kind and some is all another, and some ain't neither. Look at them two white fellows! They're straight bull-pup. (Wherever they got it!) Not a trace of collie to 'em. It's got to be av'raged up, somewheres. And it's av'raged up in that little cuss you're holding there. He's all collie. Just like the two whitish ones is all bull. It's——"

"I've—I've heard of such cases," muttered Shawe wonderingly, as he laid the tiny pup back at the mother's side. "But—oh, he'll most likely

develop a body that'll give him away! Or else
the head won't live up to its promise. Well, leave
him, anyhow, when you drown the rest. That
can't do any harm."

Sheepishly, he gave the order. Still more
sheepishly, as he left the stall, he stooped and
patted Nina's lovingly upraised head—the first caress he had ever wasted on the lonely cross-breed.

Thus it was that a great dog was born; and that
his promise of greatness was discovered barely
in time to save him from death in earliest babyhood. For the collie—or near-collie—pup was
destined to greatness, both of body and of brain.

Shawe named him "Buff." This, of course,
without the honorary prefix of the kennel name,
"Shawemere." For Buff could never be registered. His spotty pedigree could never be certi-
fied. He could claim no line in the American
Kennel Club's Studbook. He was without recognised lineage; without the right to wear a number
after his name.

A dog, to be registered, must come of registered parents. These parents, in turn, must come
of registered stock; since no dog, ordinarily, is
eligible to registration unless both his sire and
dam have been registered. That means his race
must have been pure and his blood of unmingled
azure since the beginning of his breed's recog-
nition by the studbooks.

Buff's sire could have traced his genealogy back, in an unbroken line, for centuries. King's nearer ancestors had been the peerless noblemen of dogdom. Nina's sire and dam—though of widely different stock—were born to the purple. Despite all this, their descendant was a mongrel, and barred by kennel law from any bench show.

The nameless pup grew to beautiful doghood. To all outward appearance, he was a pure-bred collie of the very highest type. The head was classic in its perfection. The body had the long, wolf-like lines of the true collie. The coat was a marvel. The chest was deep and broad, the body powerfully graceful. No collie judge, unhung, could have detected the bar-sinister.

The mind and the soul and the heart, too, were of the true collie sort. But, blended with the fiery gaiety and dash of his predominant breed, ran unseen the steadfastness, the calm, the grimness, the stark warrior spirit of the pit-bull terrier.

This same strain ran, equally unseen, through the physique as well; giving un-collielike staunchness and iron strength and endurance to the graceful frame; imparting an added depth of chest, a gripping and rending quality to the jaw muscles; a mystic battling genius to body and to spirit.

Yes, old Upstreet Butcherboy was present **in**

this collie grandson of his. So were a hundred mighty bull-terrier ancestors. It was a strange blend. Yet it was a blend; not a mixture. Nature, for once, had been kind, and had sought to atone for the cruel joke she had played in the making of poor, neglected Nina.

The first half year or more of Buff's life passed pleasantly enough at Shawemere. At the age of three months he was moved from the stables and put in one of the puppy runs. Nina was miserable at her baby's abduction. Whenever she was loose she would rush up to the puppy-runs and canter whimperingly around their wire boundaries, seeking to attract her little son's attention.

And always, at first sight or sound or scent of her, Buff would leave his fellow pups and come hurrying to the wire to greet her. Through the wide meshes their noses would meet in a sniffing kiss; and with wagging tails they would stand in apparent converse for minutes at a time. It was a pretty sight, this greeting and talk between the young aristocrat and his mongrel mother. But, at Shawemere, dogs were bred for points and for sale; not for sentiment.

At first, Buff was wretchedly lonely for Nina. In the daytime it was not so bad. For there was much to amuse and excite him in the populous puppy-run. But at night, when the rest were asleep, he missed his mother's warm fur and her loving companionship. To some extent, this homesickness for her wore off. But never entirely. Always Buff sought means to get back to her. And their frequent meetings, on opposite sides of the wire meshes, kept the impulse alive in his heart.

The run contained a nine-pup litter, a couple of months older than little Buff. The biggest pup of the litter, on the hour of Buff's arrival, undertook to teach the lonesome baby his place. This he did by falling unexpectedly upon Buff as the latter stood disconsolately at the fence looking for his absent mother. The bully attacked the small newcomer with much bluster and growling and show of youthful ferocity.

It was Buff's first encounter with an enemy— his first hint that the world was not made up wholly of friendliness. And it staggered him. Making no resistance at all, he crouched humbly under the fierce attack. The bully, at this sign of humility, proceeded to follow up his advantage by digging his milk teeth into Buff's soft ear.

The bite stung, and with the sting came a swirl of wholesome indignation into the exiled baby's hitherto peace-loving brain. Away back in his cosmos snarled the spirit of Upstreet Butcherboy. Scarce knowing what he did, he flashed from under the larger body and made a lightning lunge for the bully's throat.

Subconscious fighting skill guided the counter-assault and lent zest to the grappling youngster's onset. As a result, some five seconds later, the bully was on his back, squalling right piteously for mercy from the opponent that was barely two-thirds his size, and half his age.

By this time, Buff had shifted his vise-like grip from throat to forelegs, and thence to stomach. For, along with the pit terrier's instinct for biting hard and holding on, he had inherited his collie forbears' knack of being everywhere at once in a fight; and of changing one hold for a better at an instant's notice. Which unusual combination would have delighted the soul of any professional dogfighter.

Yet, the moment the bully was cowed into subjection, Buff let him up. Nor did he—at food trough or elsewhere—seek to take advantage of his new position as boss of the run. He did not care to harass and terrorize lesser pups. He preferred to be friends with all the world, as he had been with his dear and friendly mother.

And so time wore on—time that shaped the roly-poly Buff into a leggy but handsome six-months' pup. And now the promise of the three-day baby was fulfilled, more and more every hour. With puzzled pride Shawe used to stand and in-

spect him. The pup was shaping into a true winner. But what could be done with him—minus
pedigree and plus bar-sinister as he was? If
Buff had been a thoroughbred he would have
been worth a small fortune to his owner. But
now——

Again fate settled the problem—once and for
all.

It was the night after the kennelman had put
collars for the first time on all the pups in Buff's
yard. These collars were of a rudimentary sort,
and for use only long enough to accustom the
young necks to such burden. Each collar was a
circle of clothesline, with buckle and tongue attached, and with its wearer's "kennel name"—a
very different title from the lofty "pedigree
name"—scribbled on a tag attached to the steel
tongue.

Buff did not like his collar at all. It fidgeted
him and made him nervous. The name-tag
flapped tantalisingly just beneath the reach of
his jaws; which added to the annoyance. That
was one reason why Buff could not sleep. After
a time he gave up the effort at slumber, and came
out of the sleeping quarters where his companions
were snoozing in furry comfort.

He made a few futile attempts to get the flut-
tering tag between his teeth and to rub off the
collar against the wire meshes. Then, with a

sigh of annoyance, he stretched himself out on the ground near the yard's gate.

He was still lying there when the kennelman came to fill the yard's water-pans before going to bed. As all the pups, presumably, were asleep in their houses, the man did not bother to shut the wire gate behind him as he entered the yard.

Buff saw the open portal. Beyond, somewhere in the dense darkness, were the stables where his mother lived. His mother had always been able to solve his few perplexities and soothe his hurts in the days when he still had lived with her. Doubtless she could help him worry off this miserable collar and tag.

On the instant, the pup trotted out, through the swinging gate, without so much as a glance at the dimly seen man who was bending over the row of pans. And in another second the truant was in the road, sniffing to locate the stables.

But the wind set strong from the opposite direction that night. It brought to Buff a faint whiff of stables, it is true; but they were the stables of a farm a mile down the turnpike.

Now, though stable scents had been Buff's earliest memory, yet he did not know there were any other stables extant besides those in which he had been born. So, locating the odour, he ambled eagerly off down the road in search of his mother.

Perhaps the length of the journey puzzled him, but, as every step brought the scent stronger, he kept on. At a bend in the road, a half-mile below, he struck off into the fields and woods, taking the shortest cut to the source of the ever-increasing odour.

A furlong from the road, his way led through a thick copse. Into it he galloped merrily. In its exact centre his run was halted with much abruptness. Something touched him on the chest, and, in the same instant, tightened painfully about his neck.

Buff snorted with scared anger and lunged forward. The thing about his neck promptly cut off his breathing apparatus, and dug deep into his soft flesh. Resisting the panic impulse, Buff ceased to plunge and roll, and sought to find out what had caught him.

He had run full into the middle of one of several nooses, cunningly strung through the copse, for foxes.

Twisting his head, he seized the noose's taut end between his jaws and fell to gnawing. But he had his labour for his pains. The thin rope was braided with strands of copper wire, against just such a move on the part of some fox.

At gray dawn, the hired man of the farm, toward which Buff had been faring, came out to look at his traps. All the nooses but one hung limp. In one writhed and struggled a very tired little collie. At sight of the farmhand, Buff stopped struggling and wagged his tail. All humans, so far as he knew, were friendly to dogs. Here, presumably, was a rescuer. And Buff greeted him with warm cordiality.

The man stood gaping at him for a space. Then a slow grin began to crease his leathery mouth. This was no fox he had caught. But it was something that might well prove as valuable. He knew Shawemere, and had often seen the Shawemere collies. He had heard that the Shawemere pups brought big prices. Here, evidently, was one of those pups—a Shawemere collie that had strayed in the night and had been noosed.

By taking the dog back to its home he might, perhaps, annex a five-dollar reward; but scarcely more. There seemed better ways of capitalising his treasure trove. Paying no heed to Buff's friendly advances the man left him there, hurried home, received grudging permission for a half-day off, to visit the dentist in town, and presently returned to the copse, with a pig-crate over his shoulder.

It was market-day at the near-by town. And this would not be the first or the tenth time a dog had been exhibited for sale in the market enclosure. So, a hundred yards from his destination, the man lifted the pup from the too-tight

crate and fastened a rope to his collar. Then he
prepared to lead his prize across to the market.

But a dog that has never before been led has to
be trained to follow at the gentle tug of the leash.
This training sometimes takes only a few minutes, it is true. But it is needful. Now, never
before had Buff been on the end of a leash. He
did not know what to do. He had lost, moreover, his early liking for his captor, and he
wanted to go home.

At first tug of the rope the puppy braced all
four feet, and pulled back. A tired-looking man,
passing, in a still more tired-looking motor run-
about, slowed his car at sight of the puppy's resistance, and scanned Buff appraisingly.

A second and more vehement yank of the rope,
accompanied by a mouthful of profanity from
the hired man, brought renewed resistance from
Buff, and brought the stranger's slowing car to a
complete stop.

Buff braced his feet and sought in vain to get
some sort of purchase for his claws on the stone
pavement. His conductor gave the rope a vicious
jerk and struck the puppy over the side of the
head.

This was the first blow received by Buff in all
his short life. He did not at all grasp its meaning. But it hurt like the mischief, and it set his
delicate ears to ringing. Incidentally, it brought

the stranger, at one jump, out of his car and on to the narrow pathway.

"You idiot!" exhorted he, striding up to the farm-hand. "Don't you know any better than to hit a collie over the head? It might——"

"Don't you know no better'n to butt in?" retorted the wrathful hired man. "I'll make this mangy cuss mind me, if I have to bust ev'ry bone in his wuthless carcass!"

By way of emphasising his intention, he lifted the amazed Buff clean off the ground on the end of the rope, and drew back one large-booted foot for a drop-kick at the swinging youngster that had dared to disobey him. The kick might well have smashed every rib in the soft young body, besides rupturing its victim. But it did not reach its mark.

The tired-looking man did two things, and he did them in practically the same gesture. With his left hand he jerked the rope from the calloused hand that held it, and lowered Buff gently to earth. With his right he caught the farm-hand deftly by the nape of the neck, spun him around, and bestowed upon him two swift but effective kicks.

Both kicks smote the amazed labourer approximately at the point where his short jacket's hem met the seat of his trousers. As his assailant at the same time released his hold of the shirt-collar, his victim collapsed in a blasphemous heap at the gutter-edge.

Buff had been watching the brief exhibition with keen interest. Gradually it had been dawning on his unsophisticated mind that his escort was trying in some way to harm him, and that the stranger had not only averted the harm, but was punishing the aggressor.

So, in his babyhood, had Nina flown at a stable cat which had scratched Buff's too-inquisitive nose. Once more the puppy knew the glad thrill of having a protector.

As the fallen man scrambled to his feet, the stranger felt a cold and grateful little nose thrust into his palm. Instinctively—and with unconscious proprietorship—his hand dropped lightly on the silken head of the dog. But he kept his tired eyes unwaveringly on the man whom he had assaulted.

The latter was on his feet again, swearing and gesticulating. But, all at once, in the middle of a contemplated rush at his antagonist, he checked himself and looked worriedly up and down the deserted lane. In case of interference—in case of court proceedings—he might have trouble in explaining his possession of the dog. A dozen persons in court might well recognise the puppy as belonging to Shawemere. And there would be difficulties—all manner of difficulties—perhaps a jail term. Decidedly it was a moment for wile, rather than for force. There were worse things than a kick. Jail was one of them.

"If you're so stuck on the pup, why don't you buy him?" he whined. " 'Stead of pickin' on a poor man what's got a livin' to earn? He's for sale."

"I'm not buying livestock——" began the stranger.

Then he paused. The silken head under his hand shifted, and the cold little nose again nuzzled his palm.

"If you ain't buyin'," retorted the farm-hand, "give him back to me, and I'll take him to where I c'n git an offer on him."

He snatched the rope before the tired-looking man was aware of the intention. But Buff was aware of it—well aware of it. As the rough fingers grabbed at his collar, the youngster growled fiercely and launched himself at the tyrant.

"Good!" applauded the stranger, catching the angry puppy in mid-air and holding him under one arm. "He's got pluck! That means you haven't had him long. If you had, you'd have cowed or killed him, or made him mean and savage. He's thoroughbred, too. What do you want for him? If the price is fair, I'll buy. If it isn't, I'll carry him to the nearest police-station. Which is it to be?"

Out of a volley of indignant denial, punctuated by such stock phrases as, "I'm an honest man!" and the like, came at last the grunted words:

"Thutty dollars. He's wuth a sight more. But he b'longs to my boy, and we're movin', so I gotta sell him, an——"

"Here's the cash," interrupted the stranger, taking out some greasy notes. "But, next time you steal a dog of this kind, just remember that thirty dollars is a fool's offer. It proves the dog is stolen. There's no use asking whom you stole him from. If there were, I might be able to return him. I had no idea of cluttering my life with anything again—even with a dog. But if I don't, you'll maltreat him. And he's too good for that. There are easier ways, you know, of showing how much inferior you are to a dog, than by kicking him."

The stranger was doling out bill after bill from his thin roll. Finishing, he stuck the rest of his money back into his pocket, picked up Buff, and started for his car. Midway, he hesitated; and looked back at the gaping and muttering farmhand.

"By the way," he said carelessly, "think twice before you steal again. Not for the sake of your alleged soul, but because it's liable to land you in a cell. Nothing is valuable enough to steal. A cell isn't a pleasant place to live in, either. I know," he added as an afterthought, "because I've just come out of one."

He lifted Buff into the car, cranked the muddy and battered little vehicle, and climbed aboard. Then, as the farm-hand still gaped at him with a new respect in the bulgingly bloodshot eyes, the stranger called back:

"If you decide to tell this dog's owner what has become of him, my name is Trent—Michael Trent. And I live at Boone Lake, about fifty miles south of here. At least, I used to—and I'm on my way back there."

It was Buff's first ride. For a few minutes it startled him to see the countryside running backwards on either side of him, and to feel the bumping vibration and throb of the car under his feet. But almost at once he felt the joy of the new sensation, as does the average dog that gets a chance to motor.

Besides, this rescuer of his was a most interesting person, a man whose latent strength appealed to Buff's canine hero-worship; a man, too, who was unhappy. And, with true collie perception, Buff realised and warmed to the human's unhappiness.

Added to all this, Trent had a delightful way of taking one hand from the steering-wheel from time to time and patting or rumpling the puppy's head. Once the strong slender fingers found the name tag.

" 'Buff,' hey?" murmured Trent. "Is that your name or the colour of the goods that were marked by this tag? How about it, Buff?"

He accented the last word. In response, Buff's tail began to wag, and one forepaw went up to the man's knee.

" 'Buff' it is," nodded Trent. "And a good little name at that. A good little name for a good little dog. And now that I've gone broke, in buying you, will you please tell me what I'm going to do with you? I'm an outcast, you know, Buff. An Ishmaelite. And I'm on my way back to my home-place to live things down. It'll be a tough job, Buff. All kinds of rotten times ahead. Want to face it with me?"

Much did Trent talk to the dog during that long and bumpy drive. His voice was pleasant, to his little chum. And it was the first time in Buff's six months of life that a human had troubled to waste three sentences of speech on him. The attention tickled the lonely pup. His heart was warming more and more to this tired-eyed, quiet-voiced new master of his.

Closer he cuddled to the man's knee, looking up into the prison-pale face with growing eagerness and interest. There was a wistfulness in Buff's deep-set eyes as he gazed. With tense effort he was trying to grasp the meaning of the un-known words wherewith from time to time Trent favoured him. The man noted the pathetic eager-ness of look, and his own desolate heart warmed to this first interested listener he had encoun-tered in more than a year. He expanded under the flattering attention, and his talk waxed less disjointed.

"Yes," he said presently, stroking the puppy's head as it rested against his knee, "we've a tough row to hoe, you and I, Buff. Just as I told you. Since you're so different from two-footed curs, that you're willing to associate with a jail-bird, perhaps it'd amuse you to hear how I came to be one. Eh, Buff?"

At each repetition of his name, Buff wagged his tail in delight at hearing at least one word whose meaning he knew.

"Not to take up too much of your time, Buff," proceeded Trent, trying to negotiate a rutted bit of road with one hand while with the other he sought to ease the bumping of the car for the dog, "here's the main idea: I'd just got that farm of mine on a paying basis, and changed it from a liability to something like an asset, when the smash-up came. Just because I chose to play the fool. It was down at the Boone Lake store one night. I had walked into town for the mail. It was being sorted. And on the mail stage had come two biggish boxes of goods for Corney Fales. He's the storekeeper and postmaster there, Buff."

Again, at his name, Buff wagged his tail and thrust his cold nose into Trent's free hand.

"The boxes were left on the store porch while Fales sorted the mail," went on Trent. "It struck me it would be a corking joke to carry them out behind a clump of lilacs to one side of the store, where it was black dark that night. I hid them there for the fun of hearing old Fales swear when he found them gone. Well, he swore, good and plenty. And by the time he'd sworn himself out, I'd had about enough of the joke. And I was just going to tell him about it and help him carry the boxes back to the store, when a couple of chaps—that I'd ordered off my land the week before—stepped up and told him they'd seen me lug the boxes away in the dark. So I went out to the lilac clump to get the stuff and carry it back to Fales.

"And, Buff, the boxes weren't there. They'd been stolen in dead earnest while I had been standing in the store laughing at Fales's red-hot language. It had been a silly joke, at best, for a grown man to play, Buff.

"And, anyhow, nobody but a born fool ever plays practical jokes. Always remember that, Buff. But you know how a fellow will limber up sometimes after a lonely day's work, and how he'll do silly things. Well, that's how it happened, Buff.

"Of course I owned up, and offered to pay the sixty dollars Fales said the goods were worth. But he wouldn't have it that way. It seemed he'd been missing things for quite a while. And his pig-headed brain got full of the idea I had taken them all, and that I'd pretended it was a joke when I was caught at last. So he prosecuted. And the county attorney was looking for a record. And he got it, Buff. He sure got it.

"I was sent up for eighteen months. Just for being a fool. And perhaps I'm a fool to go back now and pick up life again in a place where everyone thinks I'm a thief. But that's what I'm going to do, Buff. I'm going to win through. It'll take a heap of time and a heap more nerve to do it. But—well, we're headed for Boone Lake. The sooner we begin the fight the sooner we'll win it."

He paused, half ashamed of his babbling, yet half relieved at being able to speak out at last to some listener who did not greet the tale with a grin of incredulity. Buff snuggled the closer to him, and licked his clenched hand as the pain underlying the light speech struck upon the collie's sensitive perceptions.

"Good little pal!" approved Trent, touched

at the wordless sympathy and feeling somehow
less desolate and miserable than he had felt for
many a long month.

It was mid-afternoon when they drove through
the edge of a rambling village and on for a mile
or so to a lane that led into a neglected farm.

"This is home, Buff!" announced Trent, his
eyes dwelling with sharp unhappiness upon the
tumbledown aspect of the deserted place. "Home
—including the mortgage that went on to it to
pay for my lawyer. Did you notice how those
village people stared at us, and how they nudged
each other? Well, that's just the first dose. A
sort of sample package. Are you game to stand
for the rest of it? I am, if you are."

Running the battered car into a shed, Trent
lifted Buff to the ground and set off towards the
closed and forbidding house. Buff capered on
ahead of him, trotting back at every ten paces to
make sure his master was following.

Trent paused for a moment in the dooryard,
to grope in his pocket for a key. Buff had gained
the summit of the low veranda. As Trent halted,
the pup took advantage of the delay to rest his
car-cramped muscles by stretching out at full
length on the narrow strip of porch. Trent took
a step forward, then stopped again; this time
to stare in bewildered surprise at the collie. For
he noted that Buff was lying like a couchant lion,

so far as his forequarters were concerned, but that his hind-legs were both stretched out straight behind him.

Now, as Trent's dog-lore told him, that is a position in which no collie lies. Nor does any dog lie with his hind legs out behind him, unless he has in his make-up a strong admixture of bull-dog blood. Yet, Trent's dog-knowledge also told him that this was apparently a pure-bred collie; perfect in every point. Wherefore, he stared in wonder at the phenomenon of Buff's position.

Then, giving up the problem, he advanced into the house. Buff, springing up at once, followed Trent inquisitively through the doorway, as the key turned noiselessly in the lock and the front door swung open under the pressure of the man's knee. Out gushed the musty odour that haunts unused country houses. It filled Trent's nostrils and deepened his sense of desolation. But, mingled with the smell of emptiness and disuse, another and more definite scent assailed Trent's nose. It was the reek of tobacco—of rank pipe tobacco, at that. Nor was it stale.

At the whiff of it Trent stiffened like a pointing dog. His lips had been parted in a careless word to Buff. Now he choked back the unborn syllables.

Treading on tiptoe, he made his way from room to room. Buff, sensing the other's efforts at silence, padded quietly at his heels. As they moved along, Trent paused from time to time, to sniff the heavy air.

Presently he flung open a door, with no caution whatever, and sprang into a room beyond. It was the kitchen he entered in this whirlwind fashion. And he saw, as his nose had told him, that it was already occupied. A mattress had been hauled hither from one of the bedrooms. Sprawled thereon were two men. One of them was snoring, the other was puffing at a clay pipe.

On the floor beside them lay a full sack. Piled in a corner of the room was a heterogeneous stack of household articles—a clock, a silver candlestick, three gilt picture-frames, a plated soup-tureen, some spoons, and similar loot. Trent had scarce time to note these facts and a heap of empty bottles in another corner, before the smoker had dropped his pipe with a grunt and sprung scramblingly to his feet. The sleeping man, roused by his companion's noise, sat up and blinked.

"H'm!" mused Trent, as the two stared owlishly at him. "I see. You boys didn't reckon on my time off for good behaviour, eh? Thought I wasn't due home for another month or so; and in the meantime this was a dandy place to hide in and to keep the stuff you steal? Clever lads! H'm!"

The two still blinked dully at him. Evidently their density was intensified by the contents of some of the empty bottles lying near the mattress.

"I'm beginning to understand things," pursued Trent evenly. "You two testified you saw me take away those boxes from Fales' store. I went to prison on your testimony. You had lived hereabouts all your lives, and there was nothing known against either of you. So your word was good enough to send me up—while you pinched the boxes, and plenty of other things. Since then"—with a glance at the plunder—"you seem to have gone into the business pretty extensively. And you picked the safest place to keep it in. Now, suppose you both——"

He got no further. By tacit consent, the two lurched to their feet and flung themselves upon him.

But, careless as had been his pose and his tone, Trent had not been napping. Even as he spoke, he realised what a stroke of cleverness it would be for the men to overpower him and to claim that they had found him in his own house surrounded by these stolen goods. It would be so easy a way to fix the blame of such recent robberies as had scourged Boone Lake on some unknown accomplice of Trent's! The craft that had once made them take advantage of his joke on Fales would readily serve them again.

But as they flung themselves on Trent, he was no longer there. In fact, he was nowhere in particular. Also he was everywhere. Agile as a lynx, he was springing aside from their clumsy rush, then dashing in and striking with all his whalebone strength; dodging, blocking, eluding, attacking; all in the same dazzlingly swift set of motions. It was a pretty sight.

A prolonged carouse on raw whisky is not the best training for body or for mind in an impromptu fight. And the two trespassers speedily discovered this. Their man was all over them, yet ever out of reach. Too stupidly besotted to use teamwork, they impeded rather than reinforced each other. Up and down the broad kitchen raged the trio.

Then, ducking a wild swing, Trent darted in and uppercut one of his antagonists. The man's own momentum, in the swing, added fifty per cent. to the impetus of Trent's blow. Trent's left fist caught his enemy flush on the jaw-point. The man's knees turned to tallow. He slumped to the floor in a huddled heap.

Not so much as waiting to note the effect of his uppercut, Trent was at the other thief; rushing him off his feet and across the room with a lightning series of short-arm blows that crashed through the awkward defence and landed thuddingly on heart and wind. In another few seconds the fight must have ended—and ended with a second clean knock-out—had not one of Trent's dancing toes chanced to light on a smear of bacon fat on the smooth floor.

Up went both of his feet. He struck ground on the back of his head, after the manner of a novice skater. And, half stunned, he strove to rise. But the impact had, for the moment, knocked the speed and the vigour out of him. Before he could stagger half-way to his feet his opponent had taken dizzy advantage of the slip. Snatching up one of the big bottles by the neck, the thief swung it aloft, measuring with his eye the distance and force needful to a blow over the head of the reeling and dazed Trent.

Then the blow fell. But it did not fall upon Trent. It missed him by an inch or more, and the bottle smashed into many pieces on the boards. This through no awkwardness of the assailant, but because a new warrior had entered the fray.

A flash of gold and white spun through the air, as the bottle was brandished aloft; and a double set of white teeth buried themselves in the striking arm.

Buff, from the doorway, had been watching the battle with quivering excitement. In his brief life he had never before seen prolonged strife among humans. And he did not understand it. To him it seemed these men must be romping, as he and the other inmates of the puppy run had been wont to romp. And he watched the wild performance in breathless interest.

But, all at once, his master was down. And, above him, his foe was brandishing something. Thus menacingly had been raised the farm-hand's arm when Buff was struck. Surely this was not a romp! His master was threatened. And into the fight gallant young Buff hurled him-self—attacking the arm that menaced the quiet-voiced man he was learning to adore.

Just below the elbow he found his grip. Deep drove the sharp white teeth; not slashing, collie fashion, but with the grim holding power that had won a score of battles for old Upstreet Butcher-boy. On the swung canvas strip, a hundred of his bull-terrier ancestors had been made to strengthen the crushingly powerful jaw muscles they had bequeathed to Buff.

The pup's forty pounds of squirming weight deflected the blow's aim, and saved Trent's skull from certain fracture.

The thief, in pain and terror, tore at the cling-ing furry body in frantic rage. But the bulldog jaws were locked, and the fearless collie spirit refused to unlock them at the yells and the ham-merings of the panic-stricken thief.

All this for the merest second. Then, still

dizzy, but himself again, Trent was up and at his foe.

The rest was conquest.

Hampered by the ferocious beast that clung to his right arm—weak from pain and exertion —the man was ridiculously easy to overcome.

"You've won your welcome, Buff, old chum!" panted Trent, as he trussed up his prisoners, before marching them to the village. "And you've saved a life I don't value overmuch. But you've done a lot more. You've let me clear myself of the other charge. These men will have to talk when the police sweat them. And that will make life worth while for me again. Yes, you've paid your way, all right! Something tells me you and I are going to be the best pals ever. But— where in blue blazes did a thoroughbred collie ever pick up that bulldog grip?"

CHAPTER TWO: "THE HUNT IS UP!"

MICHAEL TRENT stood knee-deep in a grey-white drift that eddied and surged about him in tumultuous, soft waves, almost threatening to engulf him.

The grey-white drift filled the tiny field in whose centre Trent was standing. Its ragged edges were spilling in irregular driblets into the adjoining fields and the road, scattering thence athwart the nearer countryside.

To descend to bare fact, Michael Trent was in the middle of a milling and unruly flock of merino sheep; and he was, incidentally, in more or less of a fix.

Of these sheep, seventy had belonged to his farm for months. And he had just added to them two additional flocks, new-bought, of thirty and of twenty-five each; making a grand total of one hundred and twenty-five.

This morning he had undertaken to pasture the three groups together in a single paddock-field while he should assort from the full flock a detachment of forty which he planned to drive to Boone Lake the following morning for the rural metropolis' monthly market day.

It had seemed a simple thing, this opening of the gates from two fields and driving into a third field the occupants of the other two. So simple had it appeared that Trent had not even enlisted the services of his beautiful collie Buff in the petty task.

Buff had been sent, a half-hour earlier, to drive the farm's little bunch of cattle to the "forest pasture," a mile to the east; and he was not yet back. Trent had not bothered to wait for the collie's return before herding the three flocks of sheep into one. He had merely opened the gates leading into the central field where were pastured his original flock, and had driven the newer occupants of those two fields into the middle one.

Then trouble had set in—as trouble is forever waiting to do, where sheep are concerned.

One of the two new flocks had stampeded at sight and scent of the strange flocks, and of the still more strange man. The stampeding flock had ploughed straight into and through the thick of the others, jostling and shoving them roughly, and communicating to them the stampede impulse.

That had been quite enough, and all at once there were a hundred and twenty-five crazy sheep surging around Trent and radiating away in every direction. Their fear-driven bodies had found a weak panel in the hurdle fence that bordered the road. Down flapped the hurdle, and through the gap the nearest sheep began to dribble. The remainder were in great and ever-increasing danger of injury from the mad plungings of their companions.

Another accidental shove had loosed the half-fastened latch on the centre field's gate, which Trent had neglected to clamp when he came into the paddock; and another leakage seeped out through that opening.

Helpless, wrathful, Trent waded through the turmoil, trying in vain to restore quiet, and to make his way to one or both of the apertures before a wholesale stampede should empty the field through gate or hurdle, bruising and perhaps killing some of the weaker sheep against the sides of the gap.

In his extremity, the farmer put his fingers to his lips and sent forth a whistle agonisingly piercing and shrill. Then he turned back to his futile labours of calming the stampede. Because he turned back thus, he missed a sight really worth seeing.

Over the brow of a ridge, across the winding high road, flashed a tawny and white shape that was silhouetted for an instant on the pulsing sky-line—the shape of a large collie running as no dog but a collie or a greyhound can run. Close to earth, in his sweeping stride, Buff was coming at full speed in response to the far-heard whistle.

As he breasted the ridge-crest, the dog took in the scene below him in a single glance. He saw the milling and straggling sheep, and his distracted master in the centre of the panic throng. Thus, he did not wait, as usual, for the signals Trent had taught him in "working" sheep. Instead, he went into action on his own account.

Through the waves of greyish-white a tawny and wedge-shaped head clove its way at express-train speed. With seeming aimlessness, Buff swirled through the mass, sheering now to right, now to left, now wheeling, now halting with a menace of thundered barks. Yet not one move was thrown away, not one step was without definite purpose.

As by miracle, the charging sheep began to shape up, in the field's centre; and while they were still following this centrifugal impulse, Buff was gone from among them. Out into the high road he flew, not waiting to find either of the openings; but taking the tall hurdles in his stride.

And in another second or so he had caught up with the rearmost of the stragglers, had passed it and flashed on toward the more distant strays. Before the sheep in the paddock had shaken off their Buff-given impulse to crowd to the centre of the enclosure, the collie had rounded up the scampering and bleating strays and was driving them in a reluctant huddle through the gateway and in among their fellows once more.

Then, without resting, he swung shut the gate —an easy trick long since taught to him, as to many another working collie—and was guarding with his body the gap made by the overset hurdle.

Trent ran up, fixed the hurdle in place, and then turned to pet and praise his exultant dog.

"Buff," he declared, taking the collie's fluffy head between his two gnarled hands, "you're worth ten times your weight in hired men, and you're the best side-partner and chum a lonely chap ever had!"

Buff grinned, licked his master's hand in quick friendliness, then lay down at Trent's feet for an instant's rest. And, for the thousandth time in the past three years the man noted something in the collie's pose that baffled him.

For, though Buff was lying upright and not on his side, both hind legs were stretched straight out behind him. Normally no collie lies thus, nor does any other canine that is not the possessor of a strong strain of bulldog. It was Buff's favourite posture. And Buff had every point of a pure-bred collie—indeed, of the highest type of "show collie."

The man's bewilderment was roused, thus, from time to time, by the dog's various bulldog traits, such as lying with hindlegs out behind him, or of holding a grip with the grim stubbornness of a pit terrier rather than with the fiery dash of a true collie, or of diving for the heels of driven cattle instead of for nose and ear.

Waiting only for a moment, while Buff was breathing himself after his hard run across country, and his harder rounding up of the flock, Trent chirped to the collie, and prepared to shut the two new consignments of merinos back in their respective pens. The mingling of the three flocks had been a mistake. Until their forthcoming drive to market, the three bunches would fare better among their own acquaintances than among strange sheep.

But the task was no easy one. To a casual eye all the milling sheep looked just alike. Trent could distinguish by his personal red mark his original flock. But the two sets of strangers were unmarked. Wherefore his chirp to Buff.

The moment the collie was made to see what was required of him, he was in the thick of the jostling turmoil again, flashing in and out like a streak of tawny fire, seeming to have no objective, but to be scampering without any special purpose.

Yet within fifty seconds he had headed a scared sheep through the gateway into the right-hand paddock where stood his master. Then another and yet another sheep, then a huddled half-dozen of them cantered bleatingly into the paddock. While Trent looked on in wonder, Buff proceeded to segregate, until the entire twenty-five that belonged in this particular field were back within its boundaries.

Trent shifted to the opposite paddock, whence he had turned the second flock of thirty into the central enclosure. And here Buff repeated his unerring performance.

Though Trent was filled with amazed admiration at his pet's discernment, yet he recognised there was nothing miraculous in it. Buff had herded both these new flocks into the paddocks at least three times before, on their way from pasture, during the few days Trent had owned them. He had become familiar with their scents and their separate identities, after the uncanny fashion of the best sort of working collie.

As the job ended, and Trent started homeward, with Buff trotting chummily beside him, a slender black saddle-horse came single-footing around the bend of the road between the paddocks and the farmhouse. Astride the black, sat a figure as slender and highbred as the mount's own.

The rider was a girl of perhaps twenty, clad in crash and booted. At sight of the man and the collie she waved her crop gaily at them, and put her horse to a lope by a shift of the snaffle-rein.

Trent's bronzed face went red with surprised pleasure at the equestrian vision bearing down on him. Buff, after a single doubtful glance, recognised horse and rider, and set off at a run to welcome them.

"Why, I didn't know you were at home yet, Ruth!" exclaimed Trent, reaching up to take the gauntleted little hand extended to greet him. "Your father said you'd be in the city another month. I saw him at the store last evening, and he said——"

"Yes," she interrupted, "I know. He hadn't got my telegram, then. Aunt Hester had to go out West to take care of her son—my cousin, Dick Clinton, you remember? He has a ranch in Idaho. She had a letter from him yesterday morning, saying he'd broken his leg. So she packed up, right away; and took the night train, West. And I came home."

"Oh!" said Trent, in an effort at sympathy. "And you had to cut your visit in half? What a shame!"

"No," she denied guiltily, "it wasn't a shame. It was a blessing. I oughtn't to say so, but it was. She did everything to give me a good time. And I enjoyed it, too, ever so much. But all the while I was homesick for these dear hills.

And I'm so glad to get back to them! It's queer," she added, "how I've grown to love this Boone Lake region; when dad and I have lived here barely eighteen months."

"Eighteen months and nine days," gravely corrected Trent. "I remember. I had gone to town that evening to get the mail. And when I passed by the old Brander house I saw lights in it. At the post-office they told me a New York man and his daughter—'some people named Hammerton'—had moved in, that day, and that they'd come here for Mr. Hammerton's health. It wasn't more than a week—just six days, to be exact—after that, when your father stopped here to ask me about the commission people I was dealing with in the city. He spent the morning, and he asked me to come and see him. It was the next evening I called. That was when I met you. So——"

"Do you keep a diary?" she asked, in an amusement that seemed tinged with embarrassment. "Or have you a genius for remembering dates?"

"And," pursued Trent, "it was just sixteen days after that when we went horseback riding the first time. It—it may be a bit of silly superstition," he went on reluctantly, "but I've always dated the start of this farm toward real success from the time you people moved to Boone Lake. Ever since then I've prospered. Another six

months will find me in shape to install the last
lot of up-to-date machinery and to take over that
eighty-acre tract of Holden's that I've got the
option on. Then I can begin to call my soul my
own and live like real people. And, the first
day I can do that, I am going to put my whole
fortune and my life, too, to the biggest test in
the world. A test I hadn't any right to put it
to while I was staggering along on the edge of
bankruptcy and with the future all so hazy. In
six months I'll be able to ask a question that will
show me whether all my luck is Dead Sea fruit
or—or the greatest thing that ever happened."

He talked on, ramblingly, with an effort at
unconcern; avoiding her eyes. But his gaze was
on her little gloved hand as it lay athwart the
horse's mane. And he saw it tremble and clench.
Trent was half glad, half frightened that she
had caught the drift of his blundering words.

Before he could continue, Buff created a diversion by routing a large and terrified rabbit
out of a fence corner and charging down the road
toward them in noisy pursuit of his prey. Bunny
fled in blind panic straight between the nervous
horse's forefeet. The mount snorted and reared.
As Ruth skilfully mastered the plunging steed,
Trent caught the bridle, close to the bit, and at
the same time whistled Buff to heel. Unwilling-
ly, but instantly, the collie abandoned his delight-

ful chase and trotted obediently back to his master.

"Don't scold him!" begged Ruth. "It wasn't his fault!"

"I'm not going to scold him!" laughed Trent, ruffling the dog's ears. "It's many a long month since Buff needed a scolding. He didn't drive the rabbit this way. The rabbit drove itself, before Buff could choose the direction. He——"

"Buff is splendid protection for you, isn't he?" she broke in, a tinge of nervousness in her soft voice.

"Why, personally, I don't stand in any great need of protection," he smiled. "I'm not exactly a timid little flower. But he protects the farm and the house and the livestock as efficiently as a machine-gun company could. He's a born watchdog."

Buff, realising he was under discussion, sat down in the road between the man and the girl. He was wriggling with self-consciousness and fanning the dust into a little whirlwind with the lightning sweeps of his plumy tail; as he grinned expectantly from one to the other of the speakers. But the collie's grin found no answer on Ruth Hammerton's flower-tinted face. The girl's eyes had grown grave, and there was a tinge of uneasiness in them.

"I hope you're right," she began, hesitantly,

"in saying you don't need any protection. And probably I'm foolish. But that's why I rode out here this morning."

"To protect me?" he asked quizzically, yet perplexed at her new bearing.

"To risk your thinking me impertinent," she evaded, "by mixing into something that doesn't concern me."

"Anything that concerns me," he said as she hesitated again, "concerns you, too; so far as you'll let it. What's the matter?"

She drew a long breath, knit her dark brows, and plunged into the distasteful mission that had brought her to the Trent farm.

"In the first place," she began, "do you know two men named Con Hegan and Billy Gates?"

In stark surprise Trent stared up at her.

"Why, yes!" he made answer. "Of course I do. I have good reason to know them. I've told you the story. I told it to your father, too, before I accepted his invitation to come and see him. They were the two men I found in my kitchen when I——"

"Yes, yes," she interposed hastily, as though trying to shield him from memories that must be painful. "I know. Of course, I remember. But—but you never told me their names. I'm certain you didn't. Or they'd have been familiar to me when I heard them this morning."

"This morning?" echoed Trent, puzzled. "I don't——"

"I was at the store, doing the marketing," she explained. "Some men were loafing on the steps, just outside the window. And one of them said, 'A fellow from down Logan-way told me just now that Con Hegan and Billy Gates are due to be turned loose to-morrow.' And one of the other men said, 'Then Trent had better hire a special cop and take out another life insurance policy. Both of 'em swore they'd get him, if they was to go to the chair for it. And that's one kind of an oath neither of 'em's liable to break. I wouldn't like to be in his shoes just now!' That was all I could hear. But it worried me. I didn't associate the names with those men you had told me about. Perhaps because the phrase 'turned loose' didn't mean anything to me. But I came out here to tell you, just the same. It wasn't so much what the fellow on the store steps said, as the scared way he said it, that frightened me. Oh, is there any real danger of——"

"Nonsense!" laughed Trent. "There's no danger at all. And you're not to give the matter another minute of your precious thought. But it was bully of you to come out here to warn me—to care enough to——"

"You're making light of it, just to make me

stop worrying!" she accused. "I know you are! Won't you please notify the police about their threat? Won't you go armed? Won't you lock your house ever so carefully and keep indoors after dark? And——"

"And wear warm flannels next to my skin, all summer?" supplemented Trent, with vast solemnity. "And carry an umbrella and wear rubbers if the day is at all stormy? And——"

"Stop!" she commanded, a hint of tears in her troubled young voice. "You're making fun of me!"

"Heaven forbid!" he disclaimed, piously.

"You are!" she accused. "And you're doing it to lead me to think you aren't in any danger; so that I won't worry. But there *is* danger! And I know it. I'm positive of it, now that you've told me who those men really are. Oh, can't you——"

"Listen!" he begged. "You're getting all wrought up over nothing, Ruth. It's wonderful to have you bother your head over my safety. But I'm not going to let you do it. Here's the idea: Hegan and Gates belonged to the 'Riverside Gang,' over in South Boone. The gang was cleared out some years ago. Some of its members went to jail. The police had nothing definite on those two; so they let them alone. They picked up a living by their wits, as semi-stationary tramps and they kept their petty thefts from being found out. Then, when they'd sent me to prison—they'd had it in for me ever since the time I caught them near my hen-roost and ordered them off my land, to the accompaniment of a stray kick or so—they went into the business on a larger scale, using my house as a place to store their plunder and to hide out in, when the neighbours might be suspecting them of a share in the robberies. When Buff and I collared them they went all to pieces and confessed everything. Just as I told you, before. Now, I leave it to you if two such pitifully cowardly sneak thieves are likely to risk another jail sentence by trying to harm me. It's ridiculous. Just the same, I'm as much your debtor for warning me, as if the danger were real."

Ruth had dismounted, during the talk. Now, turning to the horse, she prepared to get into the saddle once more. But first she bent down and laid her soft cheek against the delighted Buff's head. Under cover of the collie's glad whimper of friendliness she whispered very low:

"Take care of him, Buff! Oh, take care of him—for *me*."

Then, with assumed lightness, she said, as Trent lifted her to the saddle:

"Probably you're right. But it didn't do any harm to warn you. I'm sorry if I've seemed foolish. Good-bye!"

The little black horse cantered away. Michael Trent and Buff stood in the middle of the road watching the girl out of sight. Then Trent turned slowly to his chum.

"Buff, old man," said he, "we made a good bluff of it just now, you and I. All the same, it's up to us both to keep our eyes open for a while. Hegan and Gates were soaked with cheap whisky and sodden and jumpy after a week's carouse, when the chief of police 'sweated' them. And he sure did 'sweat' them good and hard. It smashed their nerve. Because they were in prime shape to have it smashed. And that's how he got them to go all to pieces and confess. That and the goods he found on them. And, besides, he told each of them separately that the other one had squealed; and made them sore on each other that way.

"But that wasn't like either Gates or Hegan to give in. When they were normal, they were as tough a pair of birds as I care to see. They've had nearly three years to sober up in and get back their nerve by hard work and plain food and no drink, Buff. And unless I've got them both sized up all wrong, they've been spending most of that three years in planning how to get back at the man who spoiled their game and thrashed them and got them put away.

"They've had plenty of time to store up venom,

Buff. And plenty of venom to store up. Yes, and a good alibi, too, to clear them if anything happens to me. Buff, we aren't going to be fools enough to worry. But we'll keep awake, just the same. And, Lord, but wasn't it glorious of her to care enough about me to come 'way out here and warn me! Buff, she knew what I meant, too, when I told her about having the right pretty soon to 'ask a question.' I wonder if I'm pig-headed not to have asked it long ago instead of waiting till I had something besides my measly self to offer?"

During his mumbled address to the wistfully listening dog he had been moving homeward. Now, standing on his neat porch, the man looked about him, over his well-kept farm and its trim buildings; with a little throb of pride as he contrasted it with the way the home had looked on his return from prison three years earlier. The world, all at once, seemed to him a wonderful place to live in, and life seemed unbelievably sweet. His glance strayed down the long, yellow road toward the old Brander place, and his lean face softened with a glow that transfigured it.

Early the following morning Michael Trent set off down the same yellow road toward Boone Lake for the monthly market day. But the patch of road directly in front of him was no longer yellow. It was filled with jogging and tossing billows of greyish-white.

Forty sheep, consigned to the market, were moving in close formation in front of their staff-swinging master. For one reason alone did they keep this close formation or, indeed, keep to the narrow road at all.

That one reason was Buff. The collie, with calm generalship, was herding and driving them. And he was doing it to such perfection as to make Trent's rearguard task a sinecure.

For more than thirty months now Buff had been the lonely Trent's closest chum and almost his only companion. With true collie efficiency, the dog had learned his hard and confusing farm lessons from the master, who never lost his temper with him and who never dealt unjustly by him. The bond between the two had sharpened and increased Buff's naturally "human" tendencies, and had brought out in him the great soul and uncanny brain wherewith nature had endowed him. A one-man dog, he idolised Trent and served him with joyous zeal.

Trent and Buff guided their woolly charges through the single winding street of Boone Lake, now beginning to fill with market day traffic, and on to the fenced-in market square. There they herded the forty silly sheep in one corner of the livestock enclosure, a rod or two distant from a second and much larger flock.

The owner of this second flock—a drover named Bayne—had no dog to reinforce his shepherding. Instead, three of his hired men were busily running and shouting along the wabbly borders of the hemmed-in flock.

Trent observed that they were not keeping their sheep in the best order, and that they seemed to be wilfully exciting instead of calming the big flock. At this he wondered, even as he had wondered when these same shepherds had been equally awkward at two former market days— days whereon Trent himself had had no sheep to sell.

He had heard rumours—odd, unconfirmed gossip—about this Bayne's methods. And, when he was not watching the antics of the three clumsy shepherds, he observed Bayne's craggy and shifty-eyed face with covert interest.

A half-hour later, as a third huddle of sheep were driven into the enclosure, there was a new commotion among Bayne's flock.

All three shepherds dashed into the jostling mass as in an effort to calm the pestered beasts. Instead, the noisy move stampeded the entire flock. They scattered broadcast through the entire enclosure.

The new arrival saw the panic. He jumped

ahead of his own bunch of sheep as they were filing in, and drove them precipitately out of the square, standing at the opening to see that none of Bayne's stampeding flock should follow. Thus, by rare presence of mind—and perhaps having also had experience with Bayne—he avoided any chance of his sheep mingling with the runaways.

Michael Trent was less fortunate. Full tilt into the very midst of his orderly flock charged some fifty of Bayne's stampeders, a shepherd at their heels yelling to them to stop. The shepherd's voice and excitement had merely the effect of urging them on. Trent, watching, wondered wrathfully why so stupid a man should be placed in charge of any market consignment.

Ragged and lean were the newcomers, of mixed blood and in bad condition; as was the way with Bayne's livestock. They were not to be compared to Trent's fine merinos, either in blood or in condition—assuredly not in value.

Into and through the Trent flock swarmed the invaders. In ten seconds the two flocks were inextricably intertangled. In vain did Buff seek to restore order. He could do nothing against three men—four now, for Bayne had joined the bedlam—whose yells and crazy rushes frustrated his every movement. The dog looked up in angry bewilderment at Trent, mutely begging for advice as to how the snarl might be straightened out.

But Trent did not see the appealing glance. His mind and eyes were too completely taken up in staring at Bayne and the latter's three men.

For in a flash the quartet had changed from impotently roaring and running idiots, to swiftly certain and efficient shepherds. With splendid skill and speed they were quelling the stampede, separating the two flocks and driving their own sheep to their allotted corner of the enclosure. Their command of the situation was something to admire.

Presently the Bayne flock was in its place, orderly and safe, with two shepherds in front of it to prevent further panic flight. Trent glanced back at his own flock, attracted to them by a sudden stir among the forty.

Buff, leaving his master, had plunged into the flock and was busily at work, but for what purpose Trent could not guess. Then, almost at once, he was out of the compact flock again, driving in front of him six sheep, which he detached from the remaining thirty-four, and sent helter skelter out into the middle of the square.

Still wondering if his wise dog had lost his wits, Trent chanced to take special note of the six sheep as they hurtled past him. And his face went blank. The six were dirty, thin, undersized, sparse of wool. They were as different from his own plump flock as a scavenger horse from a Derby winner.

Before Trent could speak or move, Buff had deserted the six ragged specimens, leaving them bleating forlornly in the centre of the square.

And he had bounded straight at Bayne's close-huddled flock. At one leap he was on the backs of the sheep which formed the outer wall of the mass. He did not even waste time to plough through their tight-held front rank.

Over their backs he ran; and on until he vanished into the milling sea of wool.

Then, while Bayne and his three shepherds still shouted in uncomprehending dismay, the dog appeared again on one edge of the flock. Moving slowly, by reason of the press around and ahead of him, he emerged from the bunch, driving two sheep. Fat they were and of heavy wool, undoubted merinos both. Across the narrow space Buff headed them and drove them into his master's flock. Then, on the instant, he was in the Bayne flock again, running once more over the scared backs of many sheep and dropping to earth in the middle of the throng.

A second time he emerged from the huddle, again with two fat and woolly merinos ahead of him. Eluding Bayne, who rushed down on him with staff upraised, Buff galloped the two into his master's corner, and was back again, without pausing, in front of Bayne's flock.

But this time his self-imposed job was no sinecure. Bayne and the three shepherds had shaken off their amaze and were ready for him. Shouting and threatening they advanced on the eager dog.

Trent, leaving his sheep in care of an official of the market, sprang to Buff's aid. But the dog did not wait for him. Instead, the collie made a growling dash at Bayne's booted legs.

Bayne jumped aside to guard his endangered shanks, and smote at the attacking collie with his staff. The blow did not land;—Buff was no longer there. Eluding the swung cudgel with wolfish agility, he darted into the gap in the line —the gap made by Bayne's sideways jump—and was at the fiercely guarded flock once more.

As Buff reappeared, after an interval, with another pair of sheep herded ahead of him, Bayne and the shepherds were waiting for him. But so was Trent. A shepherd made a lunging rush at the two salvaged sheep. Bayne aimed a murderous blow at the dog.

Trent, with ludicrous ease, tripped the awkwardly charging shepherd and sent him asprawl on the ground. Trent's staff met the descending stick of Bayne, and the latter's weapon was shattered by the impact.

In practically the same gesture, Trent leaped between his dog and the two remaining shepherds, menacing them with staff and voice, and holding them in check while the collie cantered the rescued sheep back into Trent's flock.

Bayne, swearing and mouthing, strode in pursuit. He was met by a crouching collie, who faced him with an expression that looked like a smile and which was not a smile.

Bayne hesitated, whirling on the tranquil Trent.

"Your cur's stolen six of my sheep!" he thundered in righteous indignation. "I'll——"

"No, you won't, Mr. Bayne," gently contradicted Trent, his pleasant voice slow and drawling. "Stop a second and cool off, and you'll let the matter drop. You'll let it go as a mistake of your men's in separating the two flocks. Men often make mistakes, you know. Buff never does. There are six sheep straying over yonder—six thin, cross-bred sheep. Not merinos. They are yours."

"I tell you——" spluttered Bayne, though visibly uneasy at Trent's manner and at the crowd that was collecting three deep around them.

"No," intervened Trent. "Don't tell me, Mr. Bayne; don't bother to. I see it was a mistake. Just as you are beginning to see it. There's no sin in a mistake. Though there's always sure to be a mistake in a sin. My sheep are safe. So are yours. Let the matter drop. I've seen stampedes of your flocks before. And I've heard of them, too. This time no harm's done. That's all, I think."

"I'll get a court order for my sheep your cur run off!" flared Bayne in a last rally; and he turned to his shepherds, commanding:

"Here, boys, go and get them sheep he run into that bunch. Get 'em!"

"Speaking of court orders," said Trent, still in the same cool, slow tones of indifference and interposing his own lithe body beside the bristling Buff's to the hesitant advance of the shepherds—"speaking of court orders, Mr. Bayne, when you get yours, be sure to tell the judge that I'm ready to show him the secret mark on each and every one of my sheep, to prove they're mine. Now, if your men care to keep on edging toward my flock, Buff and I will try to entertain them as best we can till the police come up."

Bayne glowered horribly into the smilingly level eyes that met his glare so tranquilly. Then, with a grunt, he turned back to his own corner, the three shepherds trailing after him.

Behind his calm exterior Michael Trent drew a long breath of relief. These forty sheep of his were culled from the two new flocks he had so recently purchased. None of them bore a mark.

The only "secret mark" on them was Buff's unerring knowledge of their identity. Trent stooped and petted the collie lovingly on the head and stroked the massive ruff.

"That's how Mr. Bayne makes money, old man," he whispered. "One of his several hundred ways. We couldn't have proved he didn't have six fat merinos in that mangy bunch of sheep. And his shepherds would have sworn to them. Figure out the price-difference between six of our best sheep and six of Bayne's scarecrows, and you'll know to a penny how much cash you've saved me to-day, Buff."

The collie did not get the sense of one word in five. But he realised he had somehow made Trent very proud of him and that he was being praised. So for a moment he forgot to be stately and aloof. He wagged his tail wildly and caught Trent's caressing hand between his mighty jaws in well-simulated savageness, pretending to bite it ferociously, while not exerting the pressure of a fraction of an ounce. Which was one of Buff's many modes of showing affection for the pleasant-voiced man who was his master and his god.

Dusk had fallen when Trent and Buff turned in at the gate of the silent farmhouse. The day had been prosperous. The merinos had brought a well-nigh record price—the whole forty having been bought by an up-country stock farm man. Thus, Trent's investment in them had turned into an unexpectedly quick and large profit.

Also, he had been congratulated by a dozen fellow sheep raisers on his victory over Bayne. He had banked his market cheque—the Boone Lake Bank remaining open until seven in the evening on market days—and had spent a blissful half-hour on the Hammerton porch with Ruth on the way home. Now, comfortably tired and buoyed by an equally comfortable sense of well-being, he lounged up the short path leading from the road to his house. As he reached the fence gate he had bidden Buff fetch the cows from their upland pasturage and drive them to the barn. He himself went around to the side door, for the milk pails that were kept in the kitchen during the day.

He unlocked and opened the door and stepped in. As he did so a bag was thrown over his head, and the upper part of his body—a bag whose bottom was soaked in something that smelt like crushed apples. A rope was flung about his arms at the same moment and its noose ran tight.

Vainly, Trent stamped and writhed to free himself. His wiry strength was pinioned and cramped by the noose and the impeding bag. More of the apple-smelling liquid was dashed

into his face through the sack's loose meshes.
Then, as he still struggled and choked, something
crashed down upon his skull.

Buff trotted obediently across the road toward
the hill pasture.   Like his master, Buff had had
a happy and busy day.   He had been praised
much and petted much by Trent, and had had a
truly marvellous dinner at the Boone Lake Hotel.
He was complacently at peace with the world.

Then all at once he was not at peace with anything.   For, far behind him, he heard the noise
of scuffling feet and of a loud, choking gasp.
And his weird sixth sense told him his master
was in trouble.

Wheeling, he set off for the house at a tearing
run.   Excited as he was, he was aware of a
strange and vaguely remembered foot-scent as
he whirled in through the gate and up the path.
His faint memory of the scent was hostile.   He
could not remember why.

At a bound he reached the open kitchen door.
Trent was lying inert and crumpled on the floor.
Two men were bending over him.   And, as he
charged, Buff caught their scent.

Like a rabid wolf he hurled himself upon the
nearest of the men.   His teeth closed in Hegan's
shoulder with the bone-crushing grip of his pit
terrier ancestors.   At the same moment Gates

drew a pistol and fired point blank at the leaping dog.

Buff's muscles collapsed. He slumped to the floor and lay lifelessly across the body of his master.

"What'd you shoot for, you chucklehead!" panted Hegan, nursing his rent shoulder. "Want to bring all Boone Lake down on us?"

"Only way to get him!" retorted Gates. "He'd 'a' chewed us both into Hamburg steak if I hadn't."

Quickly and deftly the two worked. First assuring themselves that no one had heard the shot, they went through the house and through Trent's clothes. Then, their loot gathered, they carried it to the barn and stowed it in Trent's new car. After which, under cover of darkness and carrying Trent between them, they loaded their victim into the tonneau, covering him with a blanket. Then, while Hegan groaningly and laboriously cleaned away the tell-tale blood spots and other marks of struggle, Gates scowled down at the motionless huddle of tawny soft fur.

"Got to lug him along with us, too, I s'pose?" he grunted. "Can't leave him here."

"Get a stone," commanded Hegan—"a big one. Tie it around his neck. Then drop him down the well."

Gates groped around the steps until he found

one of the old-time door stones, and in another minute or so this was firmly affixed to Buff's collar by a stout rope. As Gates picked up the heavy dog and carried him puffingly to the well the telephone bell rung.

Tossing dog and stone over the well curb, Gates bolted for the house in sudden fright. Hegan had already gone into the hall, and was lifting the instrument from its table.

"Hallo!" he grunted in a stifled voice as he motioned Gates to silence.

His face cleared, and he made answer to the query at the far end:

"Yep, this is Michael Trent. Yes? No, I won't be here. Nope. I'm just starting off on a motor trip up country. I may go a couple of thousand miles before I get back. Maybe I won't ever come back. I'm dead sick of this hole. Yep. Good-bye."

He hung up the receiver.

"Corking good alibi!" he chuckled gleefully. "Some feller that Trent sold some sheep to to-day. Don't seem to know Trent well. Didn't suspicion the voice. Now, when Trent and his car are missing, nobody'll ask nosey questions. Come along!"

They hurried to the barn, backed the laden car out, and drove away into the night.

Not for some minutes did Buff recover con-

sciousness from the bullet graze that had rapped
his skull so hard as to stun him and to gash the
silken fur above his eye.

He woke in decided discomfort; his head was
still in dire pain, and he was fastened securely in
one spot.

When Michael Trent had had his farm drinking water tested, a year earlier, he had learned
that the well showed strong traces of stable drain-
age. Wherefore, the well had been filled up, to
within two yards of the surface, and a new well
had been dug on higher ground behind the house.

Thus it was that Buff woke to find himself
sprawling on a pile of rubble, with a short rope
attaching him to a large stone.

Indignantly the collie set to work gnawing the
rope in two. This accomplished, he got dizzily
to his feet. A rush and a scramble, and he was
up the stone-lined wall of the well and on firm
ground above.

Straight to the house he ran, his teeth gleaming, his ruff abristle. At the kitchen door he
halted. The door was shut; he could not get in.
But his scent told him Trent was no longer there.
His scent told him more—much more. It confirmed his memory of his master's two assailants,
and stamped their odour for ever in his mind.
Their steps led him to the barn whither they
had carried Trent. The senseless man's clothing

had brushed the lintel of the barn door as they had lifted him into the car. Buff looked wildly about him, sniffing the air, his tense brain telling him much.

Then a red light began to smoulder in his deep-set eyes. Out into the high road he dashed, not running now like a collie, but like a timber wolf. As he ran he paused but once, and then he waited only long enough to throw his head aloft and shatter the night silences with a howl as hideous and discordant as it was ear-splitting.

A mile away a drowsy farmer dropped his weekly paper with a shiver.

"If I was back on the frontier," he mused to his startled wife, "I'd say that was a mad wolf a-howlin'—and I'd say the hunt was up!"

CHAPTER THREE: MASTERLESS!

NOW this is the story of the masterless wanderings of Buff.

Long and unavailingly did Buff follow the
track of the car which had borne away the man
who was his god. Dizzy from his wound, faint
from loss of blood, heart-broken and frantic at
the vanishing of his master, the collie sped in
pursuit. The scent was fresh in his nostrils—
the scent of the kidnapped man and of his ab-
ductors, and the familiar odour of Trent's car.

Mile after mile galloped Buff through the summer night; trusting wholly to his sense of smell.
With the peculiar mile-eating canter of his wolf-
ancestors, he stuck to the trail, even when the
car's track ceased to furrow the dusty country
road and passed clean through a busy little city.

Though the city's myriad odours and distrac-
tions, Buff stuck to the scent of his master's car.
Other cars—hundreds of them—had laced the
trail. The asphalt's smell of gasoline and grease
was sickeningly acute in the dog's nostrils, confusing and sometimes all but blotting out the
scent he was following. Yet never quite did Buff
lose the track.

Under the lamps of motor-trucks and trolley cars he flashed, swerving barely far enough out of their way to save himself from death; then ever picking up the scent again.

Once a troop of small boys gave chase, realising the chances of reward that lay in the capture of so fine a dog. But Buff, with that odd and choppy wolf-stride of his, soon out-distanced them. And they threw stones, futilely, in the wake of the flying tawny shape.

Again, a Great Dane whirled out of a dooryard and pursued the passing collie. Buff was aware of the larger dog's presence only when a spring and a snarl warned him to wheel, in bare time to avoid the full shock of the Dane's charge.

Buff had no time for fighting. Paying no further heed to the attacking giant, he swerved from the assault, caught the trail again, and increased his pace. But the Great Dane would not have it so. His instincts of a bully were aroused by the meek flight of this stranger dog from his onset. And he pursued at top speed.

A motor-bus, whirring out from a side street, checked Buff's flight for an instant, by barring the way. Before he could get into his stride again, the Dane had hurled himself upon the fugitive, bearing him to the ground, in the slime and mud of the greasy street.

By the time Buff's tawny back smote the asphalt, he was master of the situation. Furious at this abominable delay he reverted to type—or to two types.

It was his wolf-ancestry that lent him the wit and the nimbleness to spin to his feet, under the big assailant's lunging body, and to find by instinct the hind leg tendon of the lumbering brute. All this, in one lightning swirl, and before the Dane could slacken his own pace.

But it was his pit terrier strain that made him set his curved eye-teeth deep and firmly in that all-important tendon, and to hold his grip with a vise-like steadfastness and might, while he ground his jaws slowly together.

Almost before the smitten mongrel could shriek forth his agony and fear, before the toppling gigantic body could crash to the ground, the fierce-grinding jaws had met in the centre of the thing they gripped. And, leaving behind him the crippled and howling bully, Buff slipped through the human crowd that had begun to collect; and was casting about once more for the ever-fainter trail of Trent's car.

In a moment he had found it. And he sped along in renewed zest.

Through the city and out into its straggling suburbs galloped Buff. There, a mile beyond, was a wayside garage, with one or two ram-

shackle buildings on either side of it. Behind
them a rotting dock nosed its way out into the
river. Here, at times, tugs and tenders and light-
ers touched; on their way between the city and
the ocean harbour, eight miles to southward.

At the garage the trail ended. Here had halted
Michael Trent's car.

Buff ran twice around the closed garage. His
nostrils told him the car was inside that dark
and deserted building. He had followed it twenty
miles or more. He was worn out from the run.
Yet here the scent of his adored master was
stronger than it had been anywhere along the
way.

The dog scratched imperiously at the garage
door. The sagging wood shook and grumbled
under the impact. But it held firm. Nor did anyone come from inside to answer the summons.
Frightened at the silence, yet certain of the scent
he sought, Buff circled the building once more,
nose to earth, steps uncertain, head darting from
side to side.

The quest did not bring to his senses any trace
of Trent. But it did bring to him a dual odour
that set the dog's ruff to bristling, and his teeth
to glinting from under his uncurled lip. For here,
side by side, had trodden Hegan and Gates. Not
more than an hour earlier they had walked here,
their heels striking deep in the dirt, as though they

carried between them some heavy weight. They had walked thus to the dock and to its outer edge.

Baffled, the collie made his way back to the garage. There, distinct through the reek of gas and oil and dead tobacco and dried grease, he caught again the scent of his master. With a little whimper of eagerness, Buff paused beneath a shut and locked window, some three feet from the ground. He gathered his waning strength for one more effort, and sprang upward.

Through the thin and cracked glass and the rotting sash he clove his way, alighting on the slimy concrete floor of the garage amid a shower of window particles.

The glass, by some minor miracle, scarce cut the dog. Apart from a scratch or two on his pads and a shallow cut on the nose, he was none the worse for his dive through the shaky casement.

The instant he touched ground, Buff was in new search of his master's scent. And at once he found it.

There were three cars in the garage. Two of them were old and battered and in parlous condition. The third was still new. And to this new car Buff ran.

It was Michael Trent's car. Empty as it was now—even of cushions and dashboard equipments, and shorn of its license numbers—Buff knew it at a single sniff. He knew more. He knew that in this car's muddied tonneau, little over half an hour ago, Trent had been lying. Yes, and that Gates and Hegan had been occupying the front seat. Also that the nasty smell of some medicine or drug was strong in the tonneau.

But the one thing that interested Buff was Michael Trent's recent presence there. Being only a real-life dog and not a story-book detective, it occurred quite naturally to Buff that where Trent had so lately been, he would in time be again.

Trent had left the car. That was evident. But doubtless he would return to it. Every day he used this car. And, of course, he would come back to it, soon or late. Wherefore, as Trent's trail led no farther, there seemed nothing for Buff to do but to wait for him here.

Accordingly, the collie stepped up on the running board, and through the open doorway of the tonneau. Stretching himself out there, as close as possible to the space where Trent had lain, Buff began his vigil—waiting in worried patience for the return of the man whom he had chosen as his deity.

And so in time he fell asleep; worn-out nature renewing itself in his tired body and building up again the strong young tissues and the wonted vigour of frame and of brain.

Fast as the dog had run, and with as few delays, yet he had arrived far too late to ameliorate or even share his master's doom. Fast as a collie can run—and no dog but the greyhound can outstrip him—yet a new and desperately driven motor-car can cover thrice the same ground in far less time than can he.

Moreover, Buff had wasted many precious minutes in senselessness, in the waterless well, and many more in gnawing through the rope, and in casting about the farmhouse and in the yard for Trent's trail. More than an hour ahead of him, Gates and Hegan had reached their destination. They had disposed of the stolen car, borne off the valuables they had taken from Trent's home and from his body, and did all else they had planned in advance to do. The only creature with a clue to the victim's whereabouts had come up an hour too late.

It was daylight when Buff awoke. He was stiff and drowsy. The bullet graze and the glass cut on his head were throbbing. He was thirsty, too, and hungry. He did not wake, of his own accord, but through force of habit, as the crunching of human feet reached his sleeping senses.

He lifted his head. Steps were clumping up

to the garage door, and a key was at work in the padlock. Buff was keenly interested.

A dog awakens instantly and with all his faculties acute. With him there is none of the owlish stupidity and dazedness which marks the transition from sleep to awake, among humans. At one instant he is fast asleep; at the next he is wide awake. And so it was with Buff.

He was interested now at the sound of steps, because he hoped one of the two men whose tread he heard might be Michael Trent. But at once he knew it was not. Trent's step was as familiar to Buff as was Trent's scent. And neither of these two approaching persons had a semblance to Trent's light, springy stride. Indeed, before the garage door opened more than an inch, Buff's nostrils told him that these newcomers were total strangers to him.

One of the two men was elderly and disreputable. The other, a mere boy, had not lived long enough to look as thoroughly disreputable as did his companion, but very evidently he had done his best along that line in the few years allotted him.

The older man was approaching Trent's car, talking over his shoulder to the youth.

"Put them new license plates on this, first thing you do," he commanded. "Then get a chisel and see what you can do with the motor number. And we'll have to——"

He stopped with much abruptness. As he had been speaking he had advanced to Trent's car and had laid a careless hand on the swinging tonneau door. At the same moment he was aware of a tawny shape, bloody of head, that arose from the depths of the tonneau; teeth bared and eyes menacing.

This car belonged to Michael Trent as much as did the Trent farmhouse. Long since, Buff had learned that it was his sacred duty to guard the one as rigidly as the other. And here this stranger was laying an impious hand on the machine!

At the apparition of the threatening head and at the sound of the equally threatening growl, the man recoiled from the car, jerking back his dirty hand from the door as suddenly as if the latter had turned into a snake.

Open-mouthed, the two men surveyed Buff. Quietly, but not at all friendlily, the collie returned their stare. He had no quarrel with either of them. For all he knew or cared, this might be their rightful home. So long as they should abstain from touching or otherwise molesting Trent's car, he was content to let them alone. But his pose and expression made it very clear that he expected the same sort of treatment from them and that he was calmly ready to enforce such treatment.

"It's—it's—why, it's a dog!" cleverly observed the youth, breaking the momentary silence of surprise. "It's——"

"It's a collie," amended his senior, finding his voice, and his wits together. "A top-notcher, at that. Must have sneaked in here while we was closin' up last night. A dog like that is worth a big heap of cash. And most likely there'll be a reward offered for him. See, he's got a good collar on. And he's chawed his rope through. He's worth keepin' till called for. Go, catch him, sonny. And tie him up yonder, till we c'n take him over to the house."

The man spoke wheedlingly to his young companion. But the lad had noted his sire's own reception from Buff. And, modestly, he hung back. At the other's repeated and sterner mandate, the youth remarked:

"Think I'll run up home for breakfast. I'll be back in ten minutes. You might tie him up, yourself, while I'm gone. I ain't much used to dogs."

The older man scowled; then his brow cleared.

"We'll both go up to breakfast," he decreed. "We'll lock this feller in here while we're gone. On the way back I'll stop for Joe Stears. He's got a passel of dogs; and he und'stands handlin' 'em. Come on."

Compromising thus, they departed, closing and locking the garage door behind them. Neither of them having gone to the far side of the room, they did not see the broken sash and the mess of glass on the floor—a bit of wreckage hidden from their view by the three cars.

For a few minutes after they left him, Buff lay still. Then he got up, stretched fore and aft, collie fashion, and stepped down to the concrete floor. Making his way across to a water-tub, he drank long and deep. Then he stood irresolute.

He had been in this ill-smelling place for many hours. Michael Trent had not returned to his car. Michael Trent's odour had grown faint—almost imperceptible. There was no reason, after all, to believe that Trent would come back here. A few months ago he had taken his old car to a garage and had never gone back for it. Perhaps that was what he would do in the present case.

Meanwhile, Buff was bitterly homesick for his master. And Buff was worried, to the depths of his soul, as to what might have befallen Trent at the hands of the two men with whom the dog associated his master's departure—the men he was learning to hate with a mortal hatred because he knew them for his master's enemies.

By loitering here, he could get no trace of Trent, nor of the men who had carried him away.

Refreshed and once more alert, he prepared to take up his quest again.

An easy leap carried Buff out through the smashed window, and to freedom. As he stood in the road, hesitant, he saw bearing down toward him at a run the two men who had just left the garage, and with them a third man, who carried a rope and a club.

As the trio very evidently meant to seize him, and as he had no reason for staying there in the road to be caught, the collie set off across the nearest field at a hand-gallop, heading for a distant patch of woods. The men gave chase. But, without bothering to increase his speed, he soon left them panting and swearing, far in the rear. Presently, they gave up the pursuit.

Midway in the field, Buff scared up an unwary young rabbit. At sight of the pneumatically bouncing cottontail, the collie remembered he himself had eaten nothing in nearly twenty-four hours. Like a furry whirlwind, he was after the rabbit. Fifty yards on, a swirl in the long grass and a few red-stained leaves marked the abrupt end of the race. And Buff found himself supplied with a toothsome breakfast.

Thus began the collie's first day of utter loneliness; a day of bleak misery and bewilderment, of biting grief. He ranged the country for miles on either side for a trace of his master. He followed several motor-cars, on various highways, because of their vague resemblance to Trent's.

Once he ran rapturously for a quarter-mile, in pursuit of a well-set-up man who was taking a cross-country tramp; and whom, in the distance, his near-sighted eyes mistook for his master. The wind being in the wrong direction, Buff was not aware of his error until he had careered to within fifty feet of the stranger. Then, head and brush drooping, he slunk away, heavy of heart and heedless of the man's kindly hail.

Under cover of darkness, that evening, the collie made a detour that brought him back to the garage where last he had seen Trent's car. Whether he hoped Trent might have come back there, or whether perhaps the desolate dog craved the faint scent of his master on the tonneau door and flooring—in any event, he leaped in through the unmended window of the garage, and sought to locate the stolen car.

The car was no longer there. After the deft underground method employed by professional automobile thieves and receivers of such booty, the car had already been passed along the line to its next resting-place.

A boy, coming home late from the near-by city, chanced to be passing the unlit garage. From the cavernous depths of the building burst forth into the still night a hideous sound—the anguish howl of a wolf or of a masterless and wretched collie.

While the boy still stood shivering in terror at the eerie sound, a dark shape hurtled out through the window and vanished into the surrounding blackness.

And now began Buff's tortured experience as a stray—as a leal one-man dog whose master is gone. Goaded on ever by that vague hope of somewhere finding Trent, and the scarce lesser hope of finding and wreaking vengeance on the men he associated with Trent's disappearance, the great collie wandered aimlessly over the face of the countryside.

Unhappiness and the nerve-wrack of his endless quest lent him a strange furtiveness, and made him revert in a measure to the wild. Always searching—always avoiding his own kind and humans—he grew gaunt and lean. Living by his wits, in summer the forests gave him enough food to support life. He became craftily adept in catching rabbits and squirrels, and even occasional young birds. He did not starve, for the wolf-brain lent him the gift of foraging; although his farm training held him aloof from hen-roost and stall and fold, in his food-hunts.

Almost at once he skirted the city and guided himself back to Boone Lake, nearly thirty miles from where the trail had ended. The feat was not difficult, and he consumed less than a single night on the journey.

Reaching his master's farm at grey of dawn, Buff found the house and outbuildings deserted. The weeds had crept thick among the once trim crops, and there was an air of desolation brooding over the land.

Buff could not know that of all Boone Lake, Ruth Hammerton alone had refused to accept as true the report that Michael Trent had left home of his own accord. She had visited the deserted farm with her father, as soon as the story had been repeated to her, and had prevailed on Mr. Hammerton to send one of his farm-hands to transfer to the Hammertons' place Trent's suffering livestock for safe-keeping.

It was enough for the collie to know his master was not at home, and that he had not been at home since the night of his kidnapping. Buff did not belong to the silly and professionally loyal type of dog that curls itself on its owner's vacant doorstep and starves to death.

There was no time to think of such selfish matters as death, while Michael Trent remained to be found and his two enemies to be tracked down.

So, aimlessly, he took up his search.

That night he circled Boone Lake, investigating every house and path that Trent had been wont to frequent, visiting first the Hammerton place and last the market square—the scene of his triumph over Bayne, the drover.

Dawn found him miles away, ever seeking, ever wandering, living on slain forest creatures, obsessed and haunted by his overmastering impulse to find Trent.

Once, as he trotted along the ridge of a wooded hill, Buff saw in the valley below a farmer trying with pitiable ill-success to round up a flock of sixty sheep that had bolted through the pasture gate and were scattering over the surrounding fields and woods; instead of marching toward their distant fold, whose gate stood invitingly open.

Moved by an instinct he did not stay to define or to resist, the collie swept down the ridge and into the valley below. The harassed farmer beheld descending on his stampeded flock a bolt of tawny-and-white lightning that whirled in and out among the galloping strays as if bent on their wholesale destruction.

While the man was yelling his lungs out and seeking a stone wherewith to brain the marauder, he suddenly came to a foolish halt, and stood gaping at the spectacle before him.

The supposedly rabid and murderous dog was rounding up the scattered flock with uncanny skill and speed, marshalling them into the narrow road, driving strays back into the column and moving the whole woolly throng steadily and decorously toward the fold.

Arrived at the gate, one wether bolted past it, and ten other sheep followed his lead. The wether did not go forty feet before he and his fellow-truants found themselves confronted by a large and indignant collie, who forced them with gentle relentlessness to wheel in their tracks and rejoin the flock.

Tongue out, tail wagging, Buff stood at the gate of the fold, holding his prisoners from passing out again until the puffing and marvelling farmer came running up.

The man paused to fasten the gate before turning his full attention on the wonderful collie. But by the time the gate was made fast the dog was a hundred yards down the road, trotting lazily back toward the ridge. Not by so much as a turn of his classic head did he show he heard the frantic and cajoling shouts the farmer sent after him.

On another late afternoon, ten miles from there, a farmer's child was piloting her father's eleven cows and two calves home along the road from pasture. Three men, passing in a small motor-truck, halted, jumped to the ground, seized the pair of calves and prepared to sling them into the truck.

The child screamed in terrified appeal, and

caught hold of one of the men by the arm, while the herd of cows ran in panic through fields and woods.

The man shook off the child's convulsive hold with a vehemence that sent her flat in the dust of the road.

And on the same instant a huge and lean and hairy beast burst through a roadside thicket and flung himself on the man, bearing him to earth by the sheer weight of his assault.

By the time the thief had landed, rolling and yelling, in the roadway, Buff had deserted him, and was at another of the trio. And this was the collie of it. A bulldog secures his grip and holds it till doomsday. A collie, fighting, is everywhere at once. The collie strain in Buff told him his opponents were three, and that there was no sense in devoting himself over-long to any one of them at the expense of the rest. So he was raging at the second man's throat before the first fairly realised what had attacked him.

The third man, however, had a trifle more time on his hands than had either of his companions. And, wisely, he utilised that second of time in dropping the calf he had caught and in making one flying leap for the seat of the truck.

There, as fast as they could beat off the furry demon that was rending their flesh and clothes, the two others joined him. Leaving the calves to run free, the men set the machine into rapid motion and rattled off down the road.

Buff did not follow. Already he was in the thickets again, rounding up the gawkily galloping cows. And presently he had them back in the highway, in orderly alignment and walking stolidly homeward.

Dropping back beside the still weeping child, Buff licked her frightened face with his pink tongue, wagged his tail and his entire body reassuringly, and then thrust his muzzle into her trembling little hand. Thus, her father, having witnessed the scene from afar, came hurrying up, to find his cattle safe and in the road, and his erstwhile terrified daughter hugging a huge collie frantically and kissing the silken crest of the dog's head in an agony of gratitude and love.

But, as the farmer himself sought to catch hold of the dog, Buff showed his white teeth in a wild-beast snarl that made the man start back.

Taking advantage of this momentary check, the collie bounded off into the bushes and was gone.

Buff himself could not have explained the unwonted wildness and ferocity that seemed to have taken hold of him in his wanderings. For the first three years or so of his life—indeed, until Gates's pistol shot had stunned him—he had known nothing but friendliness and good treatment. And, except toward tramps and like prowlers, he had never felt hatred. Though he had always been a one-man dog, he had shown no illtemper toward those who sought to make friends with him.

Yet now, as evidenced by his snarl at the father of the child who was caressing him, he had neither lot nor part with mankind at large. His every hope and yearning were centred on the finding of his master. And the wolf strain in his make-up thrilled almost as keenly to his longing to encounter the men with whom he associated the disappearance of Trent.

For the rest of humanity he felt no interest. Not even toward Ruth Hammerton, who had reigned second to Trent in his heart.

Twice during his months as a tramp dog, Buff revisited Boone Lake—casting about the farm, trotting at midnight through the village, hanging wistfully around the Hammerton place for nearly an hour. But before dawn he was far away again.

Most of his travelling was done by night or in dusk and at grey daybreak. For experience had taught him that the open ways are not safe for an unattached dog by sunlight.

A lesser dog might readily have attached himself to one of the various friendly folk who chanced to meet him and to give him a kindly word or call. A lesser dog, too, might have chosen a home at one of the farms scattered through the broad stretch of country Buff traversed. At any of a dozen places his beauty and his prowess at herding would have won for the collie a warm and lasting welcome.

But none of this was for Buff. He had known but one master. Losing Trent, he was fated to be forever masterless, unless he should chance to find the man he had lost. And, being only a dog, he knew no better way of finding him than by this everlasting and aimless search.

On a late September afternoon, he was roused from a troubled nap in the long grass and bushes at the verge of a field, by the sound of a mad-galloping horse and of a woman's brave yet frightened calls to the runaway. Looking over the fringe of grass, towards the road, a furlong distant, he saw a fast-moving cloud of yellow-grey dust, which resolved itself into a hazy screen for a horse and light buggy.

The horse—a young and nervous brute—had taken fright at the running of a woodchuck across the road under his feet, and had sprung forward with a suddenness that snapped his check-rein. The swinging check smote him resoundingly again and again, on the neck and across the face, turning his first fright into panic, and making useless the efforts of the driver to bring him down.

A woman was driving. She was neither young nor beautiful. She had self-possession, and she had a more than tolerable set of driving hands. She was keeping the maddened horse more or less in the road, and was sawing with valorous strength on one rein while she held the other steady. Which was all the good it did her. For the brute had the bit between his teeth.

Buff arrived at the road-edge just as one of the two light reins broke under the undue strain put on it.

Before the driver could lighten the pull on the remaining rein its impulse had jerked the horse's low-laid head far to one side. His rushing body prepared to follow the lead of his head towards a steep roadside bank some ten feet deep, with a scattering of broken rock at the bottom.

Then it was that the horse became dimly aware of a furry shape which whizzed in front of him on that side, and of a flying head that struck for his nose. A stinging slash on the left nostril sent the runaway veering from the bank-edge, and plunging toward the telegraph pole on the other side of the road. He was met and turned again by a second slash from one of the collie's curved eye-teeth. On the same moment Buff stopped slashing and let his bulldog ancestry take control.

Thus the horse was assailed by a full double set of teeth that buried themselves in his bleeding nostrils, and that hung on.

The wild steed sought to fling up his head to shake off this anguishing weight of seventy odd pounds. But he could not shake himself free. He checked his furious pace and reared, striking out with his forefeet, and threatening to pitch backward into the buggy.

But a fierce wrench of the hanging jaws and a wriggle of the intolerable weight brought him down on all fours again. At once Buff released his grip and stood in front of the trembling horse. The runaway made as though to plunge forward. But he flinched at the memory of the dog's attack and at the threat of its renewal.

While he hesitated, dancing, pawing, and in momentary cessation of his run, the woman slipped from the seat to the ground and ran to his head. With practised strength she shook the bit into place and held fast. The horse jerked back. Buff nipped his heel, and instantly was at his bloody nose, again.

The runaway, conquered and shivering, lashed out with one foreleg in a last hopeless display of terrified anger. His shod hoof smote the unprepared collie in the side. With a gasping sound, Buff rolled over into the ditch, two ribs broken and a foot crushed.

Tying the horse to a telegraph pole, the woman went over to where the wounded collie lay. In strong, capable arms, that were wondrous gentle, she lifted him and bore him to the buggy. Laying him tenderly on the floor of the vehicle, she returned to the horse's head, untied the cowed and trembling steed, and began to lead him homeward.

Ten minutes later she turned in at a lane leading to a rambling, low farmhouse. And in another five minutes Buff was reclining on the kitchen floor, the woman's husband working skilfully over his injuries, while the matron poured out the tale of his heroism and cleverness.

"I know what dog this is, too," she finished. "I'm sure I know. It must be the same one that fought those thieves away from Sol Gilbert's cows over to Pompton, last week, when Sol's girl was driving them home. Mrs. Gilbert told me about it at the Grange, Monday. And he's likely the dog that rounded up those sheep for Parkins— or whatever his name was—at Revere. You read me about it in the *Bulletin*, don't you remember? The letter Parkins wrote to the editor about it? I know it must be the same one. It isn't likely there's more than one dog in Passaic County with the sense to do all three of those things. He must be like those knight-errant folks in Sylvia's school book, who used to go through the country rescuing folks that were in distress. The best in the house isn't any too good for him."

"He'll get it," curtly promised her husband, without looking up from his task. "It's lucky I've had experience, though, in patching up busted critters. Because this one is needing a lot of patching. Say! Notice how he don't even let a whimper out of him? This rib-setting must hurt like fury, too. Acts more like a bulldog than a collie. I'm going to advertise him. And if the owner shows up, I'll offer him a hundred dollars for the dog. He'll be worth it, and a heap more, to me, herding and such. *So,* old feller! Now for the smashed foot. Don't seem to be any big bones broke there."

The weeks that followed were more nearly pleasant to Buff than had been any space of time since Trent's disappearance. He was perforce at rest, while his fractured ribs and then his broken foot slowly mended. And all that time he was fed up and petted and made much of, in a way that would have turned most invalids' heads.

It was well, after his months of restless searchings, to come to a halt here in this abode of comfort and kindliness; to be petted again by a woman's soft hand, to eat cooked food once more, to be praised and to feel himself gloriously welcome.

Buff's craving ambition, to find Trent and to

run to earth his two enemies, was less acute in these drowsy days of convalescence. His sick soul seemed to be returning to normal along with his sick body.

By the time Buff could walk with any degree of comfort again, the morning frost lay heavy on the fields. The dog went out for a brief stroll with the farmer and his wife. To their delight, he did not try to run away, but accompanied them home and lay down contentedly on the doorstep.

After that, no further guard was kept over him. It was understood that he would stay with the people who had succoured and healed him.

One cold night in late autumn the dog accompanied his host, as usual, on the evening rounds of barns and outbuildings. As they were returning towards the warm red glow of the lamplit kitchen windows, Buff came to a dead stop.

A slight shudder ran through him. He lifted his delicate nose and sniffed the frosty air. He smelt nothing. He sniffed merely in an effort to corroborate in some way by scent the strange impulse which was taking possession of him—an impulse he could not resist.

"Come along, Shep, old boy!" coaxed the farmer, arriving at the doorstep and turning back towards the collie. "Supper's ready. What's the matter?"

Slowly, very slowly, Buff approached the man.

Timidly, almost remorsefully, he licked the outstretched hand. Then, throwing back his magnificent head, he made the frost-chilled stillnesses of the autumn night re-echo with a hideously discordant and ear-torturing wolf-howl.

"Why, Shep," exclaimed the farmer in amaze, "whatever ails you? What's——"

He broke off in the midst of his bewildered query and raised his voice in a shout of summons to the dog. For, like a streak of tawny light, Buff had whirled out of the dooryard and was fleeing up the road.

He heard the eager call of the man who had cured him and befriended him and given him a happy home. But he heard—far more clearly—a soundless call that urged him forward.

Guided only by mystic collie instinct and by that weird impulse which had taken possession of him, he fled through the night at breakneck speed, headed unswervingly for Boone Lake, full thirty miles away.

On the same night—after a cautious absence of several months—Con Hegan and Billy Gates ventured to return to their former homes in the Boone Lake suburbs.

RUTH HAMMERTON hurried into her father's study on her return from the post-office, whither she had fared for the evening mail.

Her dark face was aglow with a colour that had been foreign to it for many a long week—a colour that softened and mellowed the new lines of leanness and of sorrow in cheek and brow. Her eyes were alight with nervous eagerness.

Mr. Hammerton looked up in surprise from a heap of papers on his desk, as his daughter burst so unceremoniously in upon him. A month earlier he had been appointed local justice of the peace. His new duties still called for much night work, in the way of study and preparation for the next day's court duties. So it was with a slight frown that he greeted this sudden interruption of his labours.

"I've just come from the post-office!" began Ruth eagerly. "As I was coming out two men almost bumped into me. I looked back, as they slouched into the store and sat down by the stove. They had a huge bulldog at their heels. I heard one of the loafers there hail them by name. They were Con Hegan and Billy Gates.

A boy told me they had come back to Boone Lake to-day. He said it was their first visit here since they got out of prison. He——"

"Pshaw!" fumed Hammerton. "So those two crooks are back here, are they? That means more lawlessness! Just as I was congratulating myself that it was becoming a law-abiding and decent community at last! I wish——"

"You don't understand!" broke in the girl. "You don't see what I mean. You don't get the significance of it. And yet I've been all over it with you so often! I——"

"Over what?" demanded Hammerton, nettled by her air of excited mystery. "Please explain what you're driving at. I'm tremendously busy to-night and——"

"Michael Trent was the means of Hegan and Gates going to prison," she hurried on. "They swore they would get him for it. We have proof of that. The very night after they were set free Michael disappeared. And now they are back here again, after four months! Don't you see——"

"I see you are trying to lure me into that same endless old argument again," returned Hammerton with a glance of regret at his piled-up work. "But really, I can't see why these two jailbirds' appearance in town to-night should have flustered you so. There was no foul play connected with Trent's disappearance. I've explained that to you, over and over. Calvin Greer called him up on the telephone that evening. Trent told Calvin he was sick of Boone Lake and that he was starting off on a long motor tour up country. He said if he liked it up there he'd settle somewhere in the north counties and never come back. Next day he and his automobile were gone. Where is the mystery?"

"Where?" she repeated miserably. "Why, everywhere! The whole thing is a mystery. In the first place, I rode over to see Calvin Greer, at his stock farm. He had never met Michael till that day, and he wasn't at all familiar with Michael's voice. But he told me it sounded rougher and hoarser over the phone than when he talked to him face to face. And he——"

"That's no proof. Many people's voices sound altogether different over the phone. Or Trent may have had a cold. There's no mystery about it, I tell you. Most assuredly there's nothing to connect Hegan and Gates with the affair. As to——"

"You knew Michael," she went on. "You knew him well and you liked him. Tell me, was he the sort of man to go away like that and not have the courtesy to say good-bye to us? Was he? He stopped here—he and Buff—you remember, on his way home from the market square that

evening. He sat and chatted with us for half an
hour or so. He didn't say a word about going
away. Instead, he arranged to go horseback
riding with me the next day. Yet less than half
an hour later, apparently, he tells Calvin Greer
he's leaving Boone Lake—perhaps forever. Is
that——"

"Men do queer things," said Hammerton, turning back to his papers. "I can't agree with you
that there's any mystery about it, daughter. Certainly no mystery that would justify the law in
suspecting——"

"You know what care he took of his livestock,"
pursued Ruth. "Is it likely—is it possible—that
he would have left his sheep and cattle to starve,
his cows unmilked and his horses with empty
mangers? Would he have gone away like that, of
his own accord, and let all his livestock starve to
death? For they would have starved to death
out there on that solitary farm if you and I hadn't
gone to get them and bring them here."

"That's the only part of the whole thing that I
can't understand," assented Hammerton. "He
treated his livestock as other people treat their
pets. It wasn't like him to leave them to starve.
Out there they might have gone hungry till they
died before any neighbour would have been likely
to happen in and find them. Even if he hadn't
been so fond of them, it doesn't make sense for

a man to leave such valuable property to die of neglect. To say nothing of the ruin of his year's crops through his absence. Why, if you hadn't wheedled me into having his crops looked after, the year would have been a total loss to his farm. As it is——"

"Then," she declared triumphantly, "since you admit he wouldn't have done such a thing of his own accord——"

"I don't admit it. I only say I can't understand it. But it happened. We have proof of that. He went away in his car. And he took Buff along with him. If he had left Buff there I could have seen, perhaps, where the mystery came in. For he and that collie were chums. But he took Buff with him. And he took along everything of portable value in his house, too. No, that doesn't look like foul play. He did it deliberately, whatever his motive may have been. Took along his dog and his valuables and drove away in his own car. The car couldn't have been stolen, either. For he told Greer over the phone——"

"If it was Michael who told——"

"We don't know his motive," summed up Hammerton. "But we do know he went of his own accord. There is ample proof of that. As for connecting Gates and Hegan with——"

"He did not go of his own accord!" announced the girl, deathly white, her eyes ablaze, as she towered over her wondering father. "And I have every reason to know he didn't. I don't want to tell why I know it. But I must, if I want you to get the truth out of those two assassins. I know Michael Trent did not leave here of his own accord. I know it because he loved me. A man doesn't run away like that from——"

"What?" shouted Hammerton in astonishment. "He—you say he——"

"I say he loved me," reiterated the girl, her sweet voice held steady by a great effort. "And no man will go away willingly from a woman he loves as Michael loved me. Most of all, he won't go away and fail to send any kind of word."

"You never told me!" accused her father indignantly. "You never——"

"Michael never told me," she retorted.

"Then how——"

"He never told me in so many words," she went on. "Yet I knew it. A woman always knows. He loved me. And he was waiting until he could put his farm on a better paying basis before he told me of it. Now, perhaps, you'll believe me when I say he'd never have gone away like that unless he had been kidnapped or killed."

Long and silently Hammerton stared at his daughter, dazed by the revelation. Then he said, hesitantly:

"If I'd known—if you had told me—but——"

"But now that you do know," she persisted, "you'll get the truth from Hegan and Gates? You'll start the machinery of the law to working; and——"

"Dear," he said gently, "there's nothing I can do. There is no shadow of proof that either of those men was concerned in——"

"As you choose!" she exclaimed, turning to leave the room. "Since you won't interrogate them, I am going to. I'm going back to the post-office to find them. If they aren't there, I'm going to find where they live and go——"

"Are you crazy?" stormed Hammerton, jumping up to bar her way. "You surely can't mean to do an insane thing like that! I won't permit it!"

"Then interrogate them yourself, as a magistrate of this county!" she bade him. "Because if you don't do it, I shall. If it is insane, let it be insane. In these past months I have had enough to drive a wiser woman insane. I love Michael Trent. I *love* him, I tell you! And if he is on earth I shall find him, now that I have a clue."

Hammerton stared wonderingly down upon his wontedly placid daughter. Then he caught her into his arms and held her close to his heart for a moment. Releasing her, he crossed to the telephone and called up Roy Saunders, the Boone Lake chief of police.

"Saunders?" he queried. Then: "Judge Hammerton speaking. Hegan and Gates are in town again. I want a talk with them. You'll find them at the post-office. Will you bring them up here to my study? As soon as you can, please? No, there's no warrant out for them. But I don't think they'll be fools enough to refuse to come here. Thanks."

He set down the telephone and passed his arm again round the girl. Ruth, her self-control giving way, wept convulsively on his breast.

"There! There!" Hammerton murmured. "Try to get hold of yourself, darling! They'll be here in a few minutes. And our one chance is to keep cool. I—I haven't much faith in our success with them. It's only fair to tell you that, Ruth. And I've no legal right to question them at all. I'm doing it to save *you* from doing it. Try to be brave, if nothing comes of our talk with them."

Airily, not to say jauntily, Con Hegan and Billy Gates strolled up the village street and into the highroad leading to the Hammerton place. To one side of the unconcerned pair strode Saunders, the truculent but puzzled chief of police.

The men had grinned mirthfully at Saunders' command that they accompany him to the magistrate's home. They had complied without a single demur. And they lightened the tedium of the walk by guying the pompous police chief in a way that reduced him to sullen homicidal yearnings.

Marshalled by Saunders, they lounged through the doorway in the wake of a servant and were ushered into Hammerton's study at the extreme rear of the house.

They found Hammerton seated at his desk, looking very magisterial indeed. At a far end of the room, her face in the shadows, sat Ruth.

"Here they are, Your Honour!" proclaimed the chief of police, ranging his two grinning charges side by side in front of the desk.

"Yep," cheerily assented Hegan. "Here we are, Judge. We was planning to bolt. But this vigilant chief kind of overawed us. We was afraid he might cry if we stood him on his head and lit out."

"Or," supplemented Gates, "he'd maybe have hit one of us a crool slap on the wrist as we run past him. Or he might go to where we live and bust one of our umbrellas, to punish us. So we stuck."

"The judge looks pretty near as terrifyin' as the chief," confided Hegan to his companion in a loud whisper and shaking with simulated awe. "Most likely he keeps a 'lectric chair in his kitchen. We'd best be p'lite to him."

Hammerton checked an angry forward movement on the part of Saunders and addressed the grinning prisoners.

"I have no legal right to enforce replies to the questions I am going to ask you," he said quietly. "But it is only fair to tell you what rights I do possess. It is within my jurisdiction to commit you both, here and now, for vagrancy, since you have no visible means of support in this village. And before the thirty-day vagrancy term can expire there will be some new charge. So, to avoid these annoyances, I advise you to wipe those grins off your faces and to drop the attempt to insult anyone here and to answer the questions I shall put to you. Otherwise, you will leave here with handcuffs on and will proceed to the lock-up; thence to come before me in the morning on a vagrancy charge."

The men looked at each other uncertainly. Gates seemed to be measuring the distance to the study door. Unobtrusively, Hammerton took a pistol from the drawer of his desk and laid it in his lap. Instantly the two men stiffened and lost their jauntily insolent manner.

"There's no call to threaten us, Judge," said Hegan, nervously. "We're glad to answer any questions you care to spring on us. As for vagrancy—well, we're no vags. We just got home to-day and, of course, we haven't had time to look round us for any steady work yet. But——"

"You were let out of Logan Prison on the twenty-sixth of last July," interposed Hammerton. "Where did you go from there? I mean as soon as you were let out."

"We went straight to Paterson," returned Hegan. "We got out of Logan at ten, on the morning of the twenty-sixth. We took the noon train to Paterson. We got work there and we stayed on the job till yesterday, when the works shut down for the winter. Then we come back here."

"You hadn't been here since you were sent to prison?"

"Not till we got here this morning from Paterson. No, Judge."

"H'm! You were not here on the twenty-seventh of July? You are certain of that?"

"Certain sure, Judge!" declared Gates. "We wouldn't be likely to forget if we had. This is our home town. We was kind of ashamed to come back, right off, after they turned us loose from the hoosgow. So we——"

"You have not been in or near Boone Lake since you were released from prison—until to-day?" insisted Hammerton.

"No, Your Honour, we ain't. And we c'n prove

it. We went straight to Paterson; and there we——":

"Then," spoke up Ruth, coming forward, "how did two reputable witnesses happen to see you at Mr. Michael Trent's farm late on the afternoon of July twenty-seventh?"

Hegan gulped. Gates, however, answered suavely:

"Flash your witnesses on us, ma'am. If they seen us here or in this county that day they sure got good eyes. They——"

"Yep!" supplemented Hegan. "Who's your witnesses? Who are they?"

Hammerton and Saunders were looking at the troubled girl in surprise. With true feminine quibble for truth, she had put the statement in the form of a query in speaking of the witnesses whose identity she had just invented. The failure of her ruse distressed her keenly, even while the memory of Hegan's start and his scared gulp made her doubly certain she was on the right track.

"Guess you never took a course of poker playing, at school, ma'am," chuckled Gates, reading her face with all the trained skill of a true panhandler.

"Shut up, you!" grunted Saunders in wrath.

He glowered upon the suave Gates, who promptly turned his respectful gaze to the mag-

ıstrate's face. Hammerton, frowning per-
plexedly, opened his lips for further query, even
while he realised the utter uselessness of trying
to catch such skilled offenders by any questions
he might have the wit to frame.

Before he could speak a maid rushed wildly
into the room. With a manifest effort, she came
to a halt inside the doorway and stood as though
trying to announce some guest. But the guest
himself entered the room, close at her heels.

Steadily, through the gathering darkness, Buff
had run, his first mad pace settling down into
the choppy little mile-eating stride of the trotting
wolf pack. And so he kept on, ever headed for
Boone Lake, moving swervelessly and with deceptive quickness.

Stars came out. A fat moon began to butt
its way up over the eastern horizon mists. Here
and there, as the pad-pad-pad of the collie's tireless feet pattered along the frozen road, a farm
dog would bark challenge or dart out in pursuit.
But no challenge bark checked Buff's obsessed
flight. Nor did any of the pursuing curs catch
up with him.

Now and then, along the state road, motor cars
would meet or pass him. The dog moved aside
barely far enough to miss the whirring wheels,
but did not falter in his run.

Once, as he padded through a village, some fool, catching sight of him, noted his tense pose and the arrow-like straightness of his course and raised the shout of "Mad dog!"

This asinine cry lurks ever in the back of the human throat, ready and eager to spring into life at the slightest provocation. And woe to the harmlessly running or perhaps sick dog at whom it is howled! At once the hue-and-cry is ready to start in murderous pursuit. No question is asked. Nobody stops to realise that there are probably not two actually rabid dogs in any one state in the Union in the course of any two years, and that a genuinely hydrophobic dog is no more in condition to chase and attack people than is a typhoid patient.

But in Buff's case the shout was raised too late. The tawny-and-white shape sped on through the dim moonlight and out of sight before the hue-and-cry was fairly up. And he did not so much as glance back to note the progress of the useless pursuit.

As he turned off the state road, taking the macadam byway which led towards Trent's farm, the collie dropped to a wavering halt, his sensitive nostrils pulsing. A scent had come to him, though it was still too elusive to register clearly in the eager brain.

Twenty doubtful steps Buff took along the byway, until he came to a point where a field path from a cross-road a mile away intersected it. At the intersection the scent struck him with a force that dizzied him. Nostrils to earth, he found that a man had left this path for the by-road not ten minutes earlier.

The knowledge did amazing things to the dog. For an instant he shivered as though with a physical convulsion. His breath came in long gasps. A whine in his throat shook itself forth in an eerie note that belonged to no normal beast.

Then, like a whirlwind, he was off, down the byway; nose to earth, body flat and flying. Half a mile farther on, the rush of his madly scampering feet came to the ears of a man who was plodding wearily toward the farm—a man thin and shabby, who walked as though completing an exhausting journey. In the middle of the road the man paused and glanced back. Adown the moonlit byway was dashing a tawny-and-white creature, flat to earth in its speed.

Fifty yards from the man Buff lifted his head as he galloped. The scent—any dog's strongest quality—told him he might now rely on sight, which is the weakest of a dog's senses. At what he saw, the collie gave tongue.

Not in the hideous wolf howl or in whimper did Buff speak now, but in a cry that was human and rending—a cry that tore at the listener's heartstrings by reason of its awful intensity.

Delirious—screaming, writhing, panting—Buff flung himself on the man he had tracked. He was at the end of the trail! And what he found there drove him quite insane.

Up into Michael Trent's dusty arms the dog sprang—a vibrant mass of mad ecstasy. Moaning, crying, sobbing like a human child, Buff sought to lick his master's haggard face and to pat him in a hundred places at once with the whirling paws.

Almost thrown off his balance by the impact, Trent spoke to the collie in wondering delight. And the sound of the tired voice sent Buff into a new frenzy of rapture. Dropping to earth, he whizzed round and round Trent in a bewildering gyroscopic flight, stomach to ground, tongue and throat clamorous with hoarse joy.

Presently, flinging himself at his master's feet, the dog lay there, moaning and sobbing, his swift tongue caressing the man's dusty shoes, his furry body quivering from nose to tail in hysterical bliss. There he lay while Trent leaned over and laid both calloused hands on his head, stroking him and talking to him in the pleasant, slow tones the collie loved.

"Buff!" muttered the man, swallowing hard. "*Buff!* Why, I didn't think anyone on earth cared that much about anything! Come up here, old friend! You're shaking as if you had ague. How did you find me? Have you been waiting at home for me ever since? Or have you been living with—with her?"

Buff, his paroxysm spent, crouched at Trent's feet, his silken head pressed against his master's knee, his upraised eyes scanning the man's face in adoration. From time to time he shivered and moaned.

He had come to the end of the trail—the gloriously happy end of the horrible long trail. And he understood now why his queer sixth sense had summoned him hither, from the far-off farm where for weeks he had lived so placidly. The master-call had come to him. He had obeyed it. For it had been stronger than he.

And it had led him to his god. That was all Buff knew or cared to know.

And now, still talking to his dog, still petting him, Michael Trent took up again his homeward trudge. But there was life in his step. Fatigue seemed to have fallen away from him. The ludicrous worship of a dog had somehow made life over and had changed depression to hope.

Following his old custom—immemorial among lonely men who own dogs—Trent talked to Buff as they went along, as though to another human —knowing the collie could not get the sense of one word in ten, yet glad to have this vent for his own yearning for expression.

"The start of it all is pretty hazy to me, Buff," he rambled on, in the soft monotone that was music to the dog. "I saw Hegan and Gates in the doorway. One minute I was fighting with them. The next minute I was in the smelly fo'cas'le of a tramp steamship. I was sick. And I was aching all over. I had been shanghaied. The next three months were unadulterated hell. We were bound for Honolulu by way of the Horn, Buff. And the crew was only one degree better than the captain and the mate. Let's let it go at that.

"A chap named Carney and I got to be pals. We broke ship together at San Francisco on the way back. And we made most of the transcontinental trip on brake beams. Brake beams aren't flowery beds of ease, Buff. Keep off them. Carney had got a bit of the story about me, from a man who was the mate's pal between voyages. It seems a fellow who was in prison down at Logan with Gates and Hegan helped them engineer my shanghaiing. He told them where to take me. And they loaded me on a launch of his, down the river to the harbour and sold me to the captain. He was just weighing anchor. And he was short-handed.

"Hegan and Gates were planning to keep me

out of the way and to let my stock starve and my crops go to wrack—as most likely they have, for nobody was likely to get to our out-of-the-way farm in time to prevent it. Then they were going to lay low for a few months, and after that they were coming back to Boone Lake and set fire to the house and barns. Most likely they've done it before now. Nice home-coming, hey, Buff? We're dead broke, most likely, you and I. But we've got each other, anyhow. And that's more than I dared hope for."

He was turning in at the gateway of his farm as he finished the rambling tale. Buff thrust his nose into his master's hand and whined softly. Then, in a trice the collie had stiffened to attention and darted forward through the shadows towards a patch of white that emerged from the darkness of the dooryard.

When Gates and Hegan came home to Boone Lake that day they brought with them a new possession in the shape of a mongrel bulldog of huge proportions and with a local fame for being one of the "dirtiest" fighters that ever set upon a weaker foe. Planning to carry out their amiable intent of firing Trent's house and barns late in the night, they had stationed this dog in their victim's dooryard that evening, to scare off any possible tramp or other intruder who might be intending to make the deserted house a resting place. They had no desire for such witnesses; the penalty for arson being somewhat drastic in their home state.

It was this guardian dog that came tearing forward now to repel the two intruders, as Trent and Buff turned into the dooryard. Buff, guessing his ferocious intent and resenting another and hostile dog's presence in his own beloved bailiwick, flew eagerly to meet him. An instant later the two beasts came together with a clash; and a right energetic dog fight was raging at Trent's feet.

Buff, for all his fury, fought with brain as well as brawn, against his heavier assailant.

There never yet was a bulldog that could, in the open, seize a collie that was aware of his assault and that wished to elude it.

Buff nimbly sprang aside as the bulldog rushed and let the other hurtle past him. But the bulldog did not go scatheless. As he lumbered past, a slash from Buff's curved eyetooth ploughed a long and deep red furrow along his shoulder and back. And, as he turned, Buff's slash laid open a similar cut at one side of the enemy's stomach. The collie danced out of reach of the clashing jaws that sought to grab him before he could jump back.

When the jaws clamped together the collie's throat was not there. Even as his opponent struck a second time Buff flung himself on the ground and dived for the heavy forelegs in front of him.

Buff's teeth closed on the bulldog's right foreleg. And, but for his own strong strain of collie blood, the fight must have ended then and there. For a bulldog would have gained this foreleg grip and would have hung onto it, heedless of the fact that his own spine and the back of his neck were within easy reach of the foe.

Wherefore, merely giving the forefoot an agonising bite as he went, he continued his diving rush. Under and between the bowed forelegs of the bulldog he slipped, eel-like, in swift elusiveness, slashing the other's underbody again as he went, and emerged safe on the far side of the enemy.

Back and forth over the frost-slippery, moon-lit grass raged the fight, the frantic clawing of feet and Buff's own staccato snarls and the thud of clashing bodies alone breaking the night silences. Twice the bulldog well-nigh secured his coveted throat hold—a hold that must speedily have left Buff gasping out his life through a severed jugular.

A third time the bulldog charged for the throat. Buff reared, twisting sidewise to avoid the charge and at the same time to counter on the panting and lumbering body. But he did not take account of the slipperiness of the frosty, dead grass.

The collie's hind legs slid from under him. Down he went, asprawl on his back, under this sudden loss of his precarious balance. As quick as a cat he had spun to his feet again. But the instant of wasted time had sufficed for the enemy.

The bulldog, lunging murderously for the exposed throat, missed his mark by reason of Buff's swirling motion of scrambling to his feet again. Yet this time the ravening jaws did not close on air or on fur. Instead they buried themselves in Buff's upper right foreleg, almost at the junction of leg and body.

Helpless to break free, Buff ceased to thrash about. He felt the locked jaws begin to grind, deep and deeper towards the bone. He felt his enemy's braced pressure brought to bear upon the imperilled foreleg.

Then his wolf brain told him what to do. He struck straight for the nose and upper jaw of the bulldog. He did not slash, as does a collie. He bent down and secured his grip as would a bull-dog.

The bulldog, his own hold secure in the collie's upper foreleg, was aware of a terribly painful grip on his tender nose, a grip that waxed sterner and more tense all the time, a grip also that was shutting off his breathing power.

In the anguish of choking, the bulldog let go

Buff's foreleg and shook himself furiously to get free of that encumbering hold. As he shook he gave tone, emitting a most horrendous yell of pain and rage.

Then for the first time Trent was able in the elusive moonlight and shadow bars to see how the fight was going or to intervene without peril of injuring his own dog. But as he bent down to drag the squirming bulldog away he saw he was too late. Buff's grinding jaws had found the jugular. The fight was over. The victor stood up, panting and weary, and looked down at the inert mass that had so lately been a mighty fighting machine.

Half an hour later, shaved and clean, Michael Trent set forth for Ruth Hammerton's home. Buff, wholly rested from his battle, trotted happily at his master's heels. The maid at Hammertons' gaped wordlessly at sight of the visitor.

Buff, as politeness bade him, wagged his tail and took a step towards her. The maid, by nature, was built for endurance rather than speed. Yet, recovering from her shock, she jumped at least a foot from the veranda floor; and she made a sound better fitted to a turkey whose tail feathers have been grabbed than to a decorous household servant.

After which she bolted into the house and down the hall towards the study. Trent hesitated as to whether or not he ought to follow. But Buff took matters into his own hands. At the opening of the front door he caught the scent of Hammerton's two convict visitors. And down the long hall he went like a thunderbolt.

Trent, in consternation, dashed after him. But he did not catch up with the collie until Buff halted, perforce, at the doorway which the maid's ample body was just then blocking. As he strove to wriggle past into the room Trent came alongside and seized the inexplicably excited dog firmly by the collar. This precaution saved the life of Con Hegan, who chanced to be standing nearest to the door.

It was Billy Gates who broke the brief spell. Even as Ruth started forward, with a choking little cry, towards Trent, the convict's nerve and brain suddenly collapsed. Waving a tremulous arm at the raging Buff, Gates babbled in horror:

"Take him away! For the Lord's sake, take him away! That's no dog! It's a devil! A—a ghost! I—I shot him and I buried him in a—a forty-foot well with a rope and a stone on his neck! Take him away! He's come back for me!"

At a nod from Hammerton the chief of police shoved Hegan into an adjoining room. Then, wheeling on the gibbering and helpless Gates, Trent said sternly:

"Now, talk! The whole truth, mind you, unless you want me to let this—this ghost loose at you! *Talk!*"

And Gates talked. Drunk with superstitious horror, he talked and continued to talk. Even the sight of Hammerton taking swift notes did not deter him.

As the chief of police strutted back to the lockup, propelling his handcuffed prisoners before him, he tried hard not to look at a shaded corner of the moonlit veranda—a corner wherein a maid and a man were seated very close together, with a big collie curled up in drowsy contentment at their feet.

"SOMETHING"

A DOG is only a dog. But a collie is—a collie. Says the Scotch proverb:

"A collie has the brain of a man, and the ways of a woman!"

This is the story of Dick Snowden's collie, Jock—and of—Something. You can believe the tale or not, as you choose. But if you know collies, you will think twice before you pooh-pooh it as rankly impossible. Moreover, in its chief— and strangest—happenings, it chances to be true.

It began when Dick Snowden's pretty girl-wife was lying in the centre of a huge white bed, and when she was watching the world glide past her and not much caring how soon it might glide altogether away from her.

Cuddled close to her in the enormous bed was a white-swathed bundle of tiny humanity that smelled of talcum powder and of sachet and was a week old.

The coming of Baby Marise into the ken of mankind had well-nigh cost the life of Klyda Snowden, her girl-mother. There were no complications; there was nothing the learned doctors could put a name to. But Klyda had suffered much and had been through much. She was very, very tired. So tired was she that it did not seem worth while to pick up the bulky burden of life again.

It was much easier to lie still, with half-shut eyes, and feel herself drifting lazily out of life. Dully, she knew the baby was hers, that it was the precious little daughter for whose advent she and Dick had for months been planning so happily. She knew, too, that the lean and bronzed man who spent so many miserable hours at her bedside was her worshipped husband, Dick.

Yes, she was quite sane. But she was so tired that none of the real-life things, in which usually she revelled, were worth living for. Mentally, she knew that the future was bright for her and for Dick and for their baby. Physically, she was not interested in anything but drowsing.

It was on the afternoon of the eighth day of Baby Marise's life that Dick came into the room carrying a covered wicker basket. Klyda had no interest in him or in what he was carrying— even when he set down the basket on the edge of the bed and lifted its cover. Sleepily she looked at him, ready to drop into another doze.

Into the opened basket went Dick Snowden's hand, to take out the contents. But the contents saved him the effort.

Out from the depths of the basket sprang a fluffy gold-and-white ball of dynamic energy. It wavered dizzily on the wicker edge, then catapulted clumsily to the counterpane, where it caught sight of Klyda's colourless little face set in a halo of tumbled sunlit hair.

With the awkward canter of a badly made patent toy, the ball of fluff danced sidewise up the counterpane until it reached the white little face, which it proceeded to lick ecstatically with a very small and very pink tongue.

By this time Klyda's weary brain had registered the fact that the new arrival was a two-months-old collie pup—also that it was doubtless the same collie pup which Dick had promised, a month ago, to buy for her.

The gift was one on which Klyda had set her heart; from the day she and her husband had chanced to pass by some neighbouring collie kennels and had seen a litter of month-old puppies playing with their dam in one of the wire runs. Instantly, she had taken a violent fancy to this particular pup. It was then too young to leave its mother, but Dick had secured the owner's promise to sell it to him, as soon as the youngster should be weaned.

The promise had delighted Klyda. She had named the puppy Jock and had decreed that he should be Baby's guardian and chum.

Yet, since then, so many things had happened! And now the arrival of the once-coveted pup meant nothing to Klyda at all—except that she did not like to have her wan face licked, nor to be patted at by a set of clumsy and shapeless white forepaws.

She frowned slightly and hoped Dick would take the obstreperous puppy away. But at sight of her frown the puppy evidently mistook the slight facial contortion for an invitation to play, for he braced himself on all four shapeless legs and made threatening little rushes at the frowning face, accenting his attacks with ferocious baby barks.

In spite of herself Klyda felt a vague amusement at the pup's silly antics. She reached out a weak white hand to pet him. At the touch, Jock forgot he was a lion or whatever other furious wild beast he was pretending to be. He remembered only that he was very young and very far from home and mother, and that the caress of the tired hand was sweet. With a cluck of contentment, he cuddled close to Klyda's face and curled up for a nap.

Dick, glad to have aroused his apathetic wife's interest to even so mild an extent, stooped to pick up the puppy and carry him away. But Jock was in no hurry to go. So piteously did he look to Klyda for rescue that she bade her husband leave him there for the time. Whereat, by way of showing his thanks, Jock began again to play with her hand as it lay idle on the quilt.

Up to this time everybody had moved on tip-toe about the sick-room, and had talked in under-tones. But Jock was no respecter of silence. He gambolled and barked to his heart's content. Partly amused and partly annoyed by his bump-tiousness, Klyda found herself for the first time unable to sink at will into that dreamy apathy of hers. It is hard to dream, when a tiny furry whirlwind is charging at one or is professing to believe that one's white fingers are a mortal foe to be nibbled and threatened.

Thus it was, against her own will, that Klyda Snowden was shaken from her semi-coma. After that, youth and nature combined to keep her from sinking back into it. Probably she would have gotten well, anyhow. And certainly a noisy collie pup is not to be prescribed as a temporary room-mate for a sick girl. But the fact remained that Klyda "turned the corner," that very day, and forthwith grew better.

She had not discovered a new zest in life. Her husband and her new-born child furnished that. But she had been deprived of the luxury of drift-ing away. Action and annoyance and clownish gambols had chanced to supply the needed im-petus to bring her back to normality.

Yet Dick and she always attributed her rally to the arrival of Jock. And they loved him accordingly. Instead of living in the green-painted kennel in the garden and seeing his owners for only a casual hour or so each day, he was brought up in the house and with hourly human companionship.

That sort of thing has a queerly humanising influence on a dog, especially if the dog be a thoroughbred collie.

From earliest puppyhood Jock learned to know the human voice in all its phases, and to read from experience its many shades of meaning. He learned, too, from constant hearing, the meanings of many simple words and phrases. He learned still more of human nature—all of which was wholly natural and has occurred to hundreds of house-bred collies.

From the first, Jock adopted Baby Marise as his particular deity. He would lie for hours at the foot of her crib, or would walk in sedate slowness at the side of her perambulator, in preference to a woodland race or even a romp with Dick or Klyda.

Yet between him and Dick there was a strange bond of sympathy. Dearly as the dog loved Klyda and Marise, he was closer to Dick than to either of them. He would lie with his eyes on the man's face, watching its every change; and seemed to be studying him to the very soul. Even as a puppy, Jock used to do this.

A scowl on Dick's brow would bring him forward with a rush, to offer canine sympathy or to rub his nose consolingly against his master's hand. He would go into ecstasies of joyous excitement when Dick laughed or smiled. And, as the dog grew older, he seemed able to see past mere facial expression and to read Dick's varying moods, even when those moods gave no visible sign of expression.

All of this seemed nothing short of magic to the Snowdens, though it is a common enough phenomenon to anyone who has been much with collies.

It was when Baby Marise was a harum-scarum girl of four, and when Jock was a stately giant in his early maturity, that something happened which the Snowdens never tired of talking about.

Dick started at sunrise for a day's trout-fishing along a brook which ran through a wild tract of meadow and forest, some three miles above the Snowden place. Jock, as his master set forth, galloped enthusiastically ahead, eager for the prospective walk. But Dick whistled him back. The man did not desire to have wary trout scared away by the occasional plunges of a seventy-pound collie into the brook.

"No," he said, as if talking to a fellow-human, "Not to-day, old man! Stay here and look after the place."

Crestfallen yet philosophical, Jock trotted back to the veranda and lay down, his deep brown eyes following pathetically the receding figure of his master, hoping against hope that Dick might relent and summon him to follow. Then Marise came down to breakfast with Klyda, and Jock proceeded to devote himself to their society.

It was about four o'clock that afternoon when Klyda was awakened from a nap on the porch by the sudden rising of the collie from his resting-place on the mat near her. Jock had been asleep; yet something had startled him in an instant from his repose and had changed a sedately slumbering collie into a creature of puppylike excitability. Every hair on the dog's shaggy ruff was abristle. His eyes were glinting as with pain. He burst into a salvo of frantic barking and dashed across to where Klyda lay.

Catching the hem of the astonished woman's skirt in his teeth, he tugged at her dress, backing away with a suddenness that all but threw her to the floor.

"Jock!" expostulated Klyda, recovering her balance and trying to extricate the skirt from his grip. "Jock, have you gone crazy?"

Jock's answer was to release his hold on the

skirt-hem, and to gallop off the porch and out onto the drive which led to the highway. There he halted, barked in imperious summons and darted back to Klyda. Catching her skirt again between his jaws, he sought to draw her out onto the driveway with him.

Laughing at her pet's odd behaviour, Klyda went down the steps to the drive. Instantly Jock let go of her skirt and ran fifty feet towards the main road. There, halting again, he turned and barked. As the woman still did not follow, he ran back, seized her skirt in his teeth again and tried to draw her onward.

This time Klyda did not refuse to follow. A queer notion had possessed her—a notion that Jock was not doing these unaccountable things for a mere lark or to lure her into a romp. It was not at all like the dignified collie to behave this way. Calling to her brother—who was reading, indoors—to join her, she set forth in the wake of the dog.

The moment the two humans started toward him, Jock ceased to bark in that frantic and panic-urged fashion. He wheeled and galloped off, straight across country. Every few hundred yards he would pause to make sure the others were still following, and to let them come nearer. Then he would be off again.

A wearisome walk he led the puzzled Klyda

and her grumbling brother. In a precise line he travelled, turning aside for no hillock or rock or tangle of undergrowth.

"For goodness' sake!" panted the brother, once, as he looked ruefully down at his buckskin shoes which had just plodded through a corner of swamp-land. "For goodness' sake, Klyda, let's stop this fool ramble! The idiot of a dog will probably halt in front of some oak where he's treed a cat, and he'll want us to dislodge his quarry for him. On a red-hot day like this, what's the earthly sense of following a——"

"He hasn't treed a cat," was Klyda's reply. "He hasn't treed anything. He's been with me, all day. I don't know why he is acting like this. But I know Jock, and I know he's got some good reason for being so eager for me to follow him. If you're tired——"

"Oh, I'll trail along, if you're going to!" grunted her brother. "Only, if he leads us over into the next county and then turns around and leads us back, just for fun—well, I warn you I'll guy you for the rest of your days for being so silly as to—Hello!" he broke off. "Here's where we'll have to wade!"

They had come out of the woods at the verge of a wide brook. Klyda gave a little start as she saw it, and lost her colour.

"Why, this is Snake Brook!" she cried. "Dick

and I have been here a dozen times. But we've always come by way of the road. I didn't know it was in this direction. I——"

"Well?" queried her brother. "Even at that, what's the excitement? There's nothing so very dramatic, is there, in coming upon Snake Brook? It's——"

"It's where Dick came to fish to-day," said Klyda, her pallor increasing. "Jock has led us here, and——"

"And that's the thrilling end of our quest?" interrupted her brother with a growl of disgust. "Jock got lonely for his master, and he's dragged us through marsh and brambles, all this way, just for a sweet family reunion! Lord!"

"No," contradicted Klyda, her voice not quite steady, "no! See, he hasn't crossed the brook. He's running along it, on this side. And now he's stopped again for us to follow him. Come!"

She set off at a run along the pebbly and winding margin of the brook. Jock, as she started, wheeled again and vanished into a copse of shrubbery which ran down from a steep bank to the edge of the water.

Ten seconds later the two heard the collie's voice upraised once more, this time in a quavering wolf-howl of anguish. And no longer did the undergrowth crackle at his charging progress. He had come to a halt somewhere.

"The cur's stumbled into a hornets' nest," guyed the brother, laughing loudly to subdue a prickly feeling that ran along his spine at sound of that eerie cry.

But Klyda did not answer. She was plunging headlong through the bushes, panting and gasping with her own violent efforts to reach the spot where Jock awaited her.

Out in a little clearing, beside the brook, and at the base of a ten-foot cliff-bank, she came upon the dog. He was standing guard over a body that sprawled inertly, half in the water at the cliff-foot, a splintered fishing rod at its side.

There lay Dick Snowden, his leg broken in two places by his tumble from the bank. In falling, his head had struck against a water-edge boulder. The impact had caused concussion of the brain. Nor did the victim recover consciousness until an hour after they had gotten him home.

People who did not understand collies used to smile politely and lift their brows when the Snowdens told how Jock had brought aid to the stricken master, of whose plight the dog could not possibly have known through any explainable channels.

Some of these people agreed with Klyda's brother, who always insisted there was nothing mysterious or occult about the matter. They explained that Jock had waxed lonely for his

absent master and had tried to coax Klyda into
going with him to meet the returning fisher-
man,—and that the accident to Dick had been
a mere coincidence, quite outside the dog's cal-
culations.

They did not explain how Jock knew the precise direction in which Dick had gone that day,
nor why, during Snowden's previous and succeed-
ing absences from home, the collie made no such
effort to follow him.

Klyda and Dick did not bother to argue with
these sceptics. They knew Jock; other people
did not.

"It wasn't coincidence," was all Klyda would
say when outsiders sought to convince her. "It
was—*Something*."

And so the years went on at the Snowden
home, pleasantly and uneventfully. Baby Marise
was a leggy and big-eyed girl of nine, and Jock
was in the full hale prime of latter middle age.
Dick and Klyda were sweethearts, as ever. They
and their child and their huge gold-and-white
dog formed a close corporation that made home
life very beautiful for all four of them.

Then, over the smugly complacent land, rang
a bugle-call. Half the world was sick unto death
with the Hun pestilence, and America alone could
stay the hideous disease's assault on humanity.
America alone could cure a dying world. To

achieve this Heaven-sent miracle, the lives of thousands of brave men were needed. And at the terrible blast of the bugle-call these men responded in millions.

Dick Snowden was one of them.

There were tears at the Snowden home when Dick first went thence to the officers' training-camp. There was dire loneliness after he had gone.

But there were no tears when, at the end of his last furlough, Captain Richard Snowden said good-bye to his family and embarked for France.

There were no tears, then. There was a hero-smile on Klyda's drawn lips. Baby Marise tried to smile, too. And at least she did not cry— which was very brave indeed. Jock looked long and gravely up into Snowden's forcedly gay face; and laid his splendid head against his master's khaki knee as Dick said to him:

"Good-bye, old chap! Take care of them till I come back. You're the man of the house, remember, while I'm gone."

No, there were no tears when Captain Dick Snowden sailed gallantly away to fight the grey-clad pests which were engulfing the world. But there was a deadly and bitter loneliness that swooped down on the once-merry little household and gripped it by the throat—a loneliness that deepened and grew more cruelly hard to bear as the dreary weeks sagged on.

Jock, with his queer collie sixth sense, felt acutely the changed atmosphere of the place. He sought, in a thousand unobtrusive ways, to console and cheer his mistress and Marise. And he seemed to have understood Dick's parting charge to him to assume the responsibilities of "the man of the house." Always Jock had been a fiery guardian of the home in the matter of warding off intruders. Nowadays his jealous guardianship became an obsession.

Voluntarily abandoning his lifelong nightly resting-place on the rug outside the door of Klyda's room, he took to sleeping on the veranda. Nor was his sleep heavy. A dozen times a night the wakeful Klyda could hear the big dog get to his feet and start off on a thorough patrol of the grounds.

This sentry-go accomplished, he would circle the porch and return to his doormat bed for another fitful snooze. But the very slightest sound was enough to awaken him and to bring him at once to fierce alertness. The step of a belated wayfarer on the highroad beyond,—the faintest stir of one of the sleepers within the house,— any of a hundred negligible noises of the night, —sufficed to rouse him to his duty.

In the daytime, Jock was seldom more than

arm's-length from Klyda or Marise. With cold suspicion his melancholy dark eyes would follow the motions of each casual visitor or tradesman. Yes, Jock was taking his job seriously.

On the rare occasions when a letter from France reached the place, he knew of its arrival before the mail was sorted. It would thrill him and set him to barking wildly and to scampering about the house like a joy-crazed puppy. He seemed to know the occasion was one of rapture for them all.

"The minute the letters are handed in at the door," Klyda boasted to her brother, "even before any of us have time to look them over, Jock always knows whether or not there's a letter from Dick."

"Why shouldn't he?" demanded the sceptic. "A collie has a wolf's power of scent. He can smell the touch of Dick's hand on the envelope. It's perfectly normal."

"No," denied Klyda, musingly, "it isn't normal. It's—*Something!*"

Then, late of a September night, the household was jolted from slumber by a clangour of barking from the porch.

To one who understands collies, there is as much difference in a dog's various modes of barking as in the inflections of a human voice. For example, there is the gay bark of greeting, there is the sharply imperative bark of challenge, there is the noisily swaggering bark of sheer excitement, and there is the acute and agonised bark that tells of stark emotion.

Jock's bark to-night had the timbre of that with which, long ago, he had summoned Klyda to the aid of her injured husband at Snake Brook. And the sound went through the lonely wife's soul like a knife-thrust.

She sprang out of bed and, in dressing-gown and slippers, ran out to the porch. As on that earlier day, Jock was awaiting her in fevered excitement. Catching the hem of her wrapper, he tugged. Then, dropping the wrapper, he galloped up the driveway and wheeled about to face her with a bark of summons.

To-night Klyda needed no second invitation to follow him. Bewildered, trembling, yet trusting to the collie's intuition, she stumbled along in the direction Jock led. And, leaving the driveway, he was travelling due northeast.

Well did Klyda know she was moving northeastward. For, by dint of compass and maps, she had long since figured out for herself the approximate direction of France in relation to her home. And always she faced in that direction when she knelt to pray for Dick.

For perhaps half a mile the dog continued his

progress, at first in mad eagerness, but presently in growing indecision and irresolution.

At last he stopped, sniffed the air through vertically lifted nostrils, then trotted back to Klyda. Head a-droop, tail dragging, every line of his grand body expressing the utmost miserable dejection, he crept up to Klyda and crouched before her, his head on her foot. He shuddered, as if in pain; and then whimpered softly, lifting his head for a moment and peering to the northeast.

He had failed. He had awakened with the sudden knowledge of his master's peril. He had followed the urge of the call. And all at once he had realised that for some reason he could not hope to lead his mistress to the man who so sorely needed her aid. Perplexed, heartsick, he had crawled back; helpless to do more.

Again, Klyda's brother scoffed at his sister's certainty that something was amiss with Snowden. So did all others to whom the unhappy woman told the tale. They still scoffed at the idea of any premonition on the part of the dog— but there was an awed note behind their scoffing —when, a few weeks later, a shaky scrawl was received from the absentee; a scrawl written in a base hospital:

"I am laid by the heels for a day or two by a handful of rather nasty little shrapnel-bites that Herr Fritz sprayed me with three nights ago during a reconnoitre. Nothing serious—so you're not to worry your dear self. I'll be as good as new in a week or two. The surgeon says so. He says I'll be lucky if I'm able to claim a wound-chevron on the strength of such a piker injury.

"Here is a funny bit of mental delusion that may amuse you: When I toppled over and lay there in No Man's Land,—before my men could find me and bring me in,—there was an ungodly lot of racket from the Hun batteries. It almost deafened me. But through it all I believed I could hear—as distinctly as ever I heard anything—the wild barking of old Jock.

"Wasn't that a quaint trick for a wounded man's brain to play? Jock has a pretty thunderous bark, but its echo could hardly travel three thousand miles and reach me above the roar of the boche batteries. Yet I heard it. It wasn't his usual bark, either. It sounded the way it did the time Marise fell down the well, and as it sounded when the house caught fire in the night and he roused us barely in time to put out the blaze. I must have been a bit delirious, of course. But it gave me a queer homey feeling to hear the dear old fellow's voice—even if I didn't hear it."

Klyda looked at the date on the letter. Then she subtracted three days therefrom and computed the time difference between her home and northern France. Then she turned to the little desk-calendar on which, superstitiously, she had marked with a cross the date of her awakening by Jock. After that she showed her brother the letter and the calendar. As I have said, he still scoffed. But there was something of awe in his manner.

It was a shock to Klyda to know her adored soldier was wounded. Yet it was also a joy to know that he was not only in no danger from his wound, but that he was kept, perforce, out of battle, for a time. This knowledge, and the relief from her weeks of foreboding, gave Klyda a curious sense of peace which had not been hers in many a day. Her spirits rebounded to a lightness which was almost hysterical. As the day wore on, her unnatural gaiety and her sense of nearness to Dick increased.

Early in the evening she left the house and strolled out into the white autumn moonlight. She was restless, and she wanted solitude and exercise. Jock rose from his bed on the doormat and ranged alongside her for the anticipated walk.

Crossing the stretch of moon-soaked turf, the two made their way towards a rustic summerhouse that stood on a knoll at the far end of the grounds. Here, with Dick, they had been wont to sit, daily, to watch the sunset. And to the old trysting-place, Klyda now strolled.

Jock, like herself, had been gay all day; ever since the arrival of the pencil scrawl from Dick. It was with difficulty now that he curbed his exuberant pace to keep time with hers.

They reached the summer-house on the knoll. There, Klyda stood for an instant in silence, to gaze dreamily over the moon-swept hills. The night was deathly still.

Then, of a sudden, the silences were shattered by a sound that wailed forth in hideous cadences from hill to hill; re-echoing until the placid night fairly screamed with it. Klyda gasped aloud at the horror of the plangent din, and she spun about to locate its cause.

There in the moonlight twenty feet away from her stood Jock. The dog's every muscle was tense, as if with torture. His head was flung back. From his cavernous throat was issuing a series of long-drawn howls, slow, earsplitting, raucous,—howls of mortal anguish.

"Jock!" panted Klyda in swift terror. *"Jock!"*

(At the same moment, in a base hospital near Meran-en-Laye, a nurse was drawing the top of a cotton sheet over a face whose eyes would no longer need the light of day. The nurse was saying to a fellow-worker, as she performed the grim duty:

"Poor fellow! He was doing so nicely, too, till the blood poison set in. . . . Say, Nora, did I hear a dog howling, just then, or are my nerves going bad?")

At the quick appeal in Klyda's voice Jock ceased his hideous lament and stood trembling, with head bent almost to the ground. Then, through her moment of dread, that same strange sense of nearness to her husband came back upon the woman, but fiftyfold stronger than ever before since his departure. Through no volition of her own, she heard herself whisper timidly: *"Dick?"*

As she spoke, the collie raised his head, as in joyous greeting. He came swiftly over to where his mistress stood.

But it was not towards her he was moving. Nor was it at her that his rapturously welcoming gaze was turned.

The dog was hurrying, with eyes aglint and plumy tail waving, toward a spot directly beside her. Thus had he advanced, many a time, to greet his master, when Dick had returned from brief absences and when Jock had seen him standing there with his arm thrown protectingly about his wife and his eyes smiling down into hers.

To humans, the tensely waiting woman would have seemed to be standing there in the moonlight, alone. But it was not into empty space that the advancing dog gazed so eagerly.

No one, seeing the collie then, could have doubted for an instant that Jock was looking at —*Something!*

CHUMS

ARNON FLINT had not volunteered to take the money-satchel to the bank. Indeed, he had tried hard to crawl out of the errand.

A tennis-hour, with a swim to follow, had beckoned right alluringly to him. There was no fun in missing all this and taking a hot trolley-ride into town just for the honour of acting as bearer, to the bank, of the church bazaar's satchel-ful of change and small bills.

Arnon said so, with engaging frankness, at lunch that noon, when his mother told him of the task that had been deputed to him. Whereat his father looked up gloweringly from his task of plate-clearing, and added his quota to the argument:

"As long as you eat my bread, you'll obey my orders, and your mother's, too. I don't want to hear any grumbling. You'll take that money to the bank, and you'll get a receipt for it. And you'll look sharp to get there before three, too. Let it go at that!"

For perhaps thirty seconds, Arnon wisely "let it go at that." Then human endurance broke down before equally human indignation.

"You talk a lot about my eating your bread," sniffed the boy. "But it isn't my fault I eat it. If you'd let me take a job, instead of making me get ready to go to that measly old college, I'd have been eating my own bread by this time."

"You'd be wasting another man's time and money instead of mine," retorted his father. "And you'd be back on my hands inside of a week. No, thanks. You're going to college—if ever you have sense enough to pass your entrance exams. College may make a man of you. Nothing else will. In the meantime, you'll do something for your keep, besides sulking. For instance, you'll take the bazaar's ninety-eight dollars to the bank, this afternoon. And you'll do it without any more whining."

As he stood, jammed with eight other people upon the interurban trolley-car's back platform that afternoon, Arnon morosely went over in his mind this lunch-table dialogue. He fell to chewing on the unpalatable mess of grievances that had led up to the scene. And he was hot and sick with resentment.

Some conscienceless liar once said that school-days are the happiest time in life. That same liar would make Ananias or Munchausen look like the original Truthful James. In many ways, the school-years of a growing boy are worse than a term in prison.

They are perhaps a delight to the model youth. But to the average lad they hold more torture than any grown man could endure. It is only the miraculous elastic power of youth that makes them bearable. It is the distorting and falsifying magic of retrospect that gives them their only charm.

A grown man, let us say, is in disgrace. If worst comes to worst, he can vanish; and he can start life, afresh, somewhere else, with a clean slate.

Let a boy fall into disgrace at school or at home. What road of escape is open to him? Not one. He is much more at the mercy of parent and teacher than any convict is at his warden's mercy. There are strict laws governing the treatment of prisoners by their keepers. But, within normal bounds, no law holds back a teacher or a parent— or both—from making a boy's life a continuous Hades.

Add to all this the fact that every one of youth's countless misfortunes is a hopeless black tragedy in its victim's eyes, and perhaps you will understand why boyhood is not a ceaseless delight. If any man of thirty-six were subjected to the tyranny, the terrors, the bitter dependence, the

unescapable and heavy penalties for petty faults
that encompass the average half-grown boy, he
would go insane in a night. There is no appeal,
no way out, for the boy who is in a scrape. For
a man, in such trouble, there are fifty exits.

Small wonder that so many lads yearn for a
chance to make their own way in the world, and
that they shrink in loathing from the proposed
college course which will keep them in penniless
slavery during four more endless years!

They have not yet the wit to understand that
the so-called Higher Education is often a pom-
pously windy fetish; whose chief advantage consists in the fact that it enables its possessors to
look down on its non-possessors.

This philosophy is faulty, of course. It is also
non-essential to the story; except that it throws a
light on Arnon Flint's mental processes as he
stood there, the hated money-satchel at his feet,
trying to keep his balance on the crowded rear
platform of the trolley-car.

People were forever boarding or leaving the
car. A dozen times, Arnon was shoved from
one spot to another as his fellow-standees milled
and jostled about him. Always, with his toe, he
managed to push the satchel to his new standing
place. He could not stoop to pick it up. The
platform was too crowded. He could not even

stoop down far enough to keep his eye on the bag. But he kept in constant touch with it by means of his boot-toe.

At the ball-ground gate, on the outskirts of the town, three-fourths of the passengers debarked. As the car started on, its rear platform was empty except for Arnon and the conductor and a sawdusty man in overalls.

Breathing was easier now. So was standing. A few blocks farther on, a woman got out, leaving a seat vacant on the rear bench. Arnon spied the seat and prepared to take it. As a preliminary, he bent to pick up the satchel from between his toes.

"Drop that, sonny!" exhorted the sawdusty man in overalls.

At the same moment Arnon was aware that his fingers had met around a canvas strap and not around the satchel's leathern handle. He peered down, in dull amaze.

Between his feet was a carpenter's kit. The money-bag was nowhere in sight.

The thing he had been guarding with his toes was this kit. Someone had long since taken away the satchel. It is an old trick, this "lifting" of a bag from the floor of a crowded vehicle. But to youth no misfortunes are old. All of them have the horrible charm of novelty.

The satchel was gone. And it had not been taken by mistake. For the sawdusty man's kit was the sole bit of luggage on the platform.

The satchel was gone. And with it was gone the ninety-eight dollars collected, the night before, at the church bazaar—the charity money that had been entrusted to Arnon Flint to take to bank—the money which, just then, represented Arnon Flint's honour.

Now, as any sane reader will know, the one simple and natural thing for the boy to do was to notify the police and thence to go home and tell his parents what had happened. His father was moderately well-to-do, and readily could have made up the deficit.

Yes, that would have been the one normal thing for Arnon to do:—to go home and confess. And—his first name being neither Rollo nor Percival—it is the very thing he did not do.

From across the eternal chasm which divides boyhood from middle age, the lad's right course seems absurdly simple. But to no boy, and to no one who recalls the mental agony of boyhood disgraces, will it appear so. As wisely ask an unsuspected sinner to write out a list of his misdeeds and to mail them to his wife and to the police.

Arnon had a lively imagination. He had no trouble at all in picturing the scene of his home-coming with such tidings as were his. He, who had begged to go to work,—whose father had fifty times told him he had not enough level-headedness or sense of responsibility to hold a job for one week,—he must go home and admit his father was right.

He—whose weekly spending money was just seventy-five cents—must confess he had lost ninety-eight dollars. The magnitude of the sum gripped him with panic force. A few minutes ago he had regarded the bag's contents as merely a heavy mass of small change. Now he knew it for Wealth.

The knowledge that he had committed no sin did not buoy him up in the very least. A consciousness of innocence is an excellent anchor, no doubt. But what good is an anchor after the ship has sunk?

Blindly illogical fright seized the boy as he thought of reporting the loss of such a fortune— and of the present penalty and the interminable naggings to follow. The Unknown has a host of terrors lurking at its heels. But, once or twice in a lifetime, these are outweighed by the more tangible terrors of the Known. Which accounts for suicides.

Beyond, lay the Unknown. Behind, lay the Known. Arnon Flint, in a rush of consequence-fear, chose the Unknown.

In his pocket was the best part of three dollars, the sum still left from his month's allowance received that morning. He stayed on the trolley-car until it reached the railroad station. Then he entered the station and bought a ticket for Silk City—one hundred and twenty miles to westward. Three and a half hours later, he stepped down upon the Union Station platform in Silk City.

His plan was made. There was always work for willing hands. Arnon knew there was. He knew it because he had read it—yawningly but repeatedly—in *The Boys' Uplift Magazine,* a dreary juvenile monthly for which his father had subscribed in Arnon's name.

Arnon intended to get a fair-paying job, work hard, live frugally and save that lost ninety-eight dollars as quickly as possible. When he should have saved it, he would send it home to make up the church-bazaar deficit. At the same time, he could lay pipes for his own immune home-coming. The plan was perfectly feasible. In the meanwhile, Arnon had eighteen cents in his pocket.

Now, it would be most laudable at this point to say that Arnon's search for work was at once rewarded by a good job and that his industry and talents won him swift promotion; until at last he was Silk City's merchant king. *The Boys' Up-*

lift Magazine would probably be eager to print such a yarn. But the temptation must be fought down. This is merely the true account of one unlucky boy's life in a strange city. So, back again to our story.

Eighteen cents is a wabbly foundation for a fortune. Arnon had enough sense to waste none of it in buying a night's lodging. The weather was hot. He had had plenty of experience in camping. So, after buying a big bag of broken soda-crackers and a wedge of dryish cheese for eight cents, he began to scout for a camp-site. An hour's wandering brought him to the very place for his needs.

Silk City was a "boom-burg." Thus, its east end chanced still to be unfinished. Indeed, this section was all but untouched by the hand of man. Arnon left behind him the business blocks, the tangle of residence streets, the scattered tenements and hovels; and came at last to a dreary stretch of Common whither even the hopeful development-company promoter had not yet ventured.

A corner of the Common, nearest the junction of two unpaved cross-streets, had been used as a dumping ground. Here Arnon Flint found his "house." This was an overturned piano box, one of whose sides was caved in. It was a heavy, cumbrous rickety thing. Yet, by use of all his care and strength, Arnon managed to roll and drag and shove it into a shallow sand-pit, a hundred yards from the street. Here he righted the box, planted its base as deeply as possible in the scooped-out sand at the pit's bottom and went back to the dump in search of boards to reinforce its crack-strewn roof, and for jute and straw to serve as a bed.

By sunset he had rigged up a fairly watertight abode, six feet long by four wide and five in height, with a soft, if bumpy, carpeting of straw and jute. And, as he proved by further scouting, the shack was invisible from the street.

Then he tramped to a leaking hydrant, a quarter-mile distant, washed and scoured a small and a large can (both battered but leakless) he had found on the dump; and carried home his night's supply of clean water. After which he sat down in the doorway of his piano-box shack and prepared his evening meal.

Dusk was creeping over the day. Back at home, just now, the family were sitting down to a repast of fricasseed chicken and dumplings and pie and all sorts of things.

Still, crackers and cheese and fresh water are not to be despised as an evening meal—particularly when they are spiced with adventure and reinforced by the hunger of a hustling day.

So it was not the frugality of his meal that

made the fare so hard for Arnon to eat. At first he did not know just what caused the lump in his throat and what made even the tiniest morsel of food impossible to swallow. Being only a normal boy, he had never so much as heard of psychology. Nor was there any psychologist there to prate of "reaction" and "nerve exhaustion" and of any of the dozen kindred causes which made the lad feel as he did. One of these causes alone did Arnon understand. And this one—to which he would not confess—was bitter, lonely homesickness.

He had cut himself loose from everything and everybody. He was an exile and on the threshold of a new world. For all he knew, he might also be a fugitive from justice. For, when the money's loss should be discovered, the bazaar people would probably think him a defaulter and set the police after him.

Three hours earlier Arnon had felt himself a true blend of martyr and explorer. Now he was all at once aware that he was just a lonesome and heavy-hearted boy who had no one to love him and whose only home was a smelly packing box. The lump in Arnon's throat began to swell to unbelievable size. And the eyes wherewith he gazed up over the pit-edge at the dying day, grew foolishly misted.

This would never do!

Angrily he cleared his throat and winked very fast indeed. Then he forced himself to day-dreams of the splendid job he was going to win on the morrow and of the brevity of the time that must pass before he should save up ninety-eight dollars and be able to go home. But the effort was a pitiful failure. The lump nearly strangled him. And the mist would not behave itself and keep out of his silly eyes.

Just then came the diversion that saved him from the eternal shame of crying. The dusky skyline at the edge of the shallow pit was broken suddenly by a small dark silhouette. The boy winked away his rising tears once more, and stared. There at the top, looking inquisitively down, head on one side, stood a dog—not much of a dog, perhaps, for looks or for contour or for size, but still a dog; certainly not a wolf or a lion, as the lad's worn-out nerves had at first made him think.

Presently a second dog came alongside the first. Together they blinked down at the lonely youngster. Arnon returned their gaze with keen interest. There was still light enough for him to gain a clear view of his two guests.

The first dog was a black-and-tan. At least, he was more black-and-tan than anything else. He held one forefoot gingerly in air, as though he were lame. And his left ear had evidently been chewed off, as to tip. The second dog was a pale grey—formerly white—and had longish hair. He was of the general build and specifications of a Dandy Dinmont. He and the black-and-tan were about of a height. Both were collarless, wolf-thin and of a totally disreputable aspect.

Every city has scores of such strays—forlorn mongrels that eke out a rickety living on the dumps and in garbage cans until they fall prey to dogcatcher or police or vivisector, or until a gang of pursuing boys frighten them into a blind panic and thereby start a new mad-dog scare, —a scare which wins a credit-mark for the fearless bluecoat whose pistol is emptied into the harmless and terrified little fugitive.

Yes, to a dog-fancier's eye, Arnon Flint's visitors were merely a brace of fleasome mongrels. To Arnon, though, they meant all the difference between abject loneliness and loving companionship.

Timidly the boy chirped to the dogs. Up went their ears. He groped for a chipped soda-cracker, broke it in half and held out the two pieces to them. At his gesture, the dogs instinctively shrank back—a result of the piteous experience which had taught them that a movement of the human arm is far more likely to mean a flung stone than a proffered dainty.

But it had been a barren day on the dumps. And the sight and smell of food were mighty temptations. Also, the boy was talking to them in a wondrous friendly way. And—whether they can understand words or not—dogs can read the human voice as can few humans themselves.

In Arnon's call the two strays recognised not only friendship, but appeal. They recognised the tones of a fellow-stray. Here was no little devil, coaxing them into range in order to tie a tin can or a firecracker to their stumpy tails. This lad was as much a waif as was either of them. And he craved chumship, even as did they.

Slowly, hesitatingly, mincingly, the puppies slid down the pit-bank into the hollow. Nervously, yet greedily, they nipped the offered fragments of the big soda-cracker. Ravenously they ate. Then, as their fears lessened, they fawned upon the human for more food. Arnon, as they chewed the cracker-bits, ran his fingers gently along their ears and backs, scratching their heads; all the while talking to them. At first they flinched a little from the unwonted caress. But soon they courted it.

The boy, of a sudden, found himself not only happy, but ravenously hungry. He and his two pets finished the crackers and cheese with a zest. Then all three curled up close together in the straw and went to sleep.

At sunrise Arnon awoke. Both the dogs were already astir. As he raised his head and sat looking bewilderedly about, they ran frisking up to him.

And thus began the life of the three chums— in the sand-pit's piano-box shack. It was a wonderful life for all of them. For Arnon, the dogs' presence was a veritable godsend.

The boy set forth early that first morning, to look for a job. Naturally, he did not find one. Not only do business houses cut down their working force in summer, instead of adding to it; but a boy with no references has, at best, a hard time in landing a steady position,—especially if he stammers and grows red when he is asked where he lives and the name of his father.

No, in spite of *The Boys' Uplift Magazine,* no kindly merchant was so impressed by Arnon's manliness and good manners as to offer to teach him the business from the bottom up, with a view of making him, later on, a partner.

Arnon, after a half-day's futile job-hunt, began to see how matters stood. He was sore inclined to give up the fight and to tramp all the way back to his parents' home. But at once he remembered he could not. He had responsibilities,—responsibilities he could not shirk. At the shack his two dog-chums were waiting for his return. He could not take them a hundred and

twenty miles, afoot.   He had no means of feed-
ing them on the way, even if no farm dogs should
kill them or rural poundmasters seize them.   No,
they relied on him.   And he had no right to fail
them.   He must stick.

That afternoon, by three hours of hanging
around the Union Station, he cleared up twenty
cents, carrying suit-cases and opening motorcar
doors.   He stopped at a tenement-district
grocery, on his way back to the sand-pit, and continued his journey with a very respectable armful of provisions.

As he neared the Common, Arnon quickened
not only his steps but his heartbeats. Suppose he
were wrong in his estimate of his two new friends.
Suppose they were only of the cadging, garbage-
snooping type, and had deserted the shack the
moment his back had been turned! The thought
sickened him. It was for his dogs, not for himself, he had been working that day.

He reached the sand-pit edge and halted.   At
the same instant two furry little whirlwinds burst
forth from the shack, whizzed up the steep sandy
bank and, with barks of ecstasy, hurled themselves bodily upon the returning bread-winner.

What sweeter home-coming could a heartsick
and tired exile ask? Arnon dropped his parcels,
fell on his knees and gathered his loyal little com-

rades into one expansive, squirming, yapping embrace. Through his delight at their welcome ran a thrill of joy in his own correct judgment of dog nature.

After which the entire party adjourned to the shack for supper. A glorious meal it was. During its progress, the black-and-tan revealed himself as a personage of rare education by sitting up on his hind-legs to beg for food-morsels and by rolling over, twice, in gratitude at receiving such gifts. The Dandy Dinmont had fewer accomplishments. But he showed himself a dog of great natural gifts by mastering, at the third attempt, the art of catching in his mouth a piece of cracker placed on the tip of his nose.

Arnon was quite certain that never before had two such remarkable animals come into any one boy's life. They not only learned tricks with the bewildering quickness that a mongrel always possesses and a thoroughbred so seldom acquires, but they speedily learned to look on their new master as a god and to worship him as such. Arnon named the hairy dog "Dandy" and the black-and-tan "Buck"—chiefly because the names seemed to fit like gloves.

Morning after morning, Arnon tramped Silk City, looking in vain for a steady job. Every afternoon he spent at the Union Station, rustling the hand-baggage of passengers and opening automobile doors for them; for which service he averaged from fifteen to forty cents a day. On the lean days he and his chums breakfasted and supped on crackers and cheese. On days of larger wealth they banqueted regally on bread and butter and tinned meats and ginger snaps.

For an hour, morning and night, the three romped and frolicked together and added to the marvelous list of tricks they had studied. All night, through summer heat or summer rain, they slept in the piano-box shack, cuddled into one loving triple heap. Oh, but it was a jolly life for them all!

As to the future—the winter, for instance—Arnon had no thought nor care. You see, he was only a youngster. So how could he be expected to have greater forethought than have the army of grown men who live up to every penny of their yearly income, with no constructive worry concerning joblessness or old age?

For a long, happy month, life was sweet; in the tumble-down pineboard shack. Arnon had occasional twinges of homesickness, and he had more than occasional twinges of conscience at his failure to begin saving the missing ninety-eight dollars. But, on the whole, he was having the time of his life. This was true adventure, this outcast summer routine of his. And it was a truer comradeship, too, than any he had known.

On the Fourth of July he celebrated by adorning each of his chums with a red-white-and-blue bow, culled from a length of bedraggled tricolour ribbon he had found in a gutter. On his own birthday, a week later, he spent thirty-five cents upon a truly regal spread, in honour of the event. After the sumptuous meal he treated an invisible audience to the full programme of his dogs' tricks. It was a gala night at the shack.

Next afternoon Arnon came home a half-hour later than usual, having had to carry a suit-case to a new neighbourhood, and having made a wrong turn on his way back to the Common. As he neared the sand-pit, he whistled. Then he paused to watch for the usual scurrying race of his chums up the pit-bank to meet him. But no frantic joy-barks or multiple patter of feet followed upon his whistle.

At a jump, Arnon was down in the pit. The dogs were not there.

It was twilight before his search of the region was ended. This was its end: Stammeringly he asked a passing patrolman whether he had seen two little dogs—one black, one light grey—trotting anywhere along the beat. And the policeman made curt answer:

"Nope. I didn't see 'em. But the dog-catchers was roundin' up a bunch of mutts in this

ward, 's aft'noon. Better ask at the pound. It's
down at the foot of Water Street."

"Down at the foot of Water Street" was two
miles away. Arnon Flint made the trip in
eighteen minutes—only to find the pound-pier was
closed for the night.

At grey dawn next morning after ten hours
of sleeplessness, Arnon was at the pier again,
waiting for its landward gate to swing open for
the day. After an endless delay, one of the
poundmaster's men arrived. Arnon followed him
along the pier to the enormous grated pen and
the adjoining office at the far end of the dock. In
the cage were more dogs than Arnon had ever before seen together in all his life.

*"Mongrel, puppy, whelp and hound, and curs of
low degree."*

They were crowded into the big barred inclosure—a pitiful assemblage. Some dogs were
howling, some were barking, some were fox-trot
ting feverishly back and forth, from corner to
corner, pressing close against the bars. Others,
mystically aware of their coming fate, lay, trembling convulsively from time to time; heads between forepaws, eyes abrim with dumb grief.

At the pier's outer edge, just beyond the barred
pen, an iron cage swung over the river. It hung
from a derrick. Daily, this cage was filled with
the dogs that had been longest at the pound. Then

it was dipped under water for five minutes, in full sight of the doomed survivors in the pen.

A dog-pound is not pleasant to look upon. It is little pleasanter to think upon. It is one of the needful evils of every large town—an evil that is needful to public health and to public safety, so say the city fathers. It is also needful because—though people talk much about birth-control among humans (where it cannot be enforced)—no one bothers about birth-control among dogs—where it can very easily be enforced.

Litters of dogs are allowed to grow up. The dogs are portioned among people who grow tired of them or who move away. The erstwhile pets are turned out to run the streets and to starve or to pick up a scavenger living. The grim dog-pound does the rest.

The luckless waifs are done to death by water or by gas or in the legalised hell of vivisection. May the all-pitying God of the Little People have mercy upon them! For, most assuredly, mankind will not.

Arnon stared into the thronged pen. At first, in the dim light, he could make out nothing. Then, through lips that would not steady themselves, he gave the old familiar whistle. Instantly there was a scuttling and scampering from amid the ruck of dogs. Two series of wildly eager barks cut the looser volume of howls. And Dandy and Buck came racing up to the bars that separated them from their adored master.

A minute later, a very set-mouthed and white-faced Arnon Flint stalked into the poundmaster's office. Forcing his voice raspingly through the emotion that sanded his throat, he demanded of the man in charge:

"How much does it cost to get a dog out of the pound? I've—I've got a couple of them in there."

The fat man at the desk looked up, wholly without interest. Heart-broken children, coming to plead for the return of their law-snatched pets, were no novelty at all to him. Pound-keepers have no silly sentiment. If they had, they would not be pound-keepers, but normal humans.

"Dollar apiece," he grunted. "That pays their license fee."

He turned back to his newspaper and promptly forgot the existence of the shaky and ash-faced boy. Arnon ventured one more question.

"How long," he quavered, "how long do you keep them here, before—before you———"

"Depends on how many there are," snapped the man, this time without looking up. "In summer we dowse about twenty a day."

That was all. Arnon stood gaping uncertainly,

for a moment. Then he lurched out of the office
and back to where his chums pawed at the bars,
waiting for him to take them home.

Some time later, an attendant dumped a bucket-
ful of food-scraps into the centre of the pen.
Immediately the larger and fiercer dogs fell upon
the food, crowding or scaring the smaller curs
away from it. It was all wolfed down by the
bullies of the pen before their weaker or more
timid brethren had had a mouthful.

The boy recalled now that he had crammed
most of last night's untasted supper into his
pockets, to serve him as breakfast during his
search for his chums. Quickly he emptied his
pockets; apportioning the contents between Buck
and Dandy, and harshly ordering off such larger
dogs as came snooping around for a share in
the meal.

At last he went away. There was no time to
waste, if he was to earn that two dollars for
his dogs' ransom.

Two dollars! Why, the largest sum he had
ever earned in one day at Silk City was forty-five
cents! And oftener he had not earned half that
amount. Yet the money must be gotten somehow—and soon. Then there was another handi-
cap: Out of his earnings he must buy food for
Buck and Dandy during their imprisonment, if
he did not want them to starve. Incidentally, he

himself must have food—though he wanted none
—in order to keep strong enough to work.

All day he haunted the Union Station. At sunset he was back at the pound, with a bagful of
meat-scraps for his chums. He sat beside the
bars, talking to them and putting them through
their tricks until the pier closed. Then he ran
all the way to the theatre district, in the hope of
earning a few cents more by opening the doors
of motorcars and carriages.

At the end of three days of self-starving and of
day-and-night work, he had collected ninety-four
cents. This was all he had been able to save
after buying food for his pets and a daily cracker
or two for himself. And he had sought work in
every waking hour, except such times as he set
aside for visiting the pound.

At dawn on the fourth day he found a dollar
bill in the street. An early-morning traveller
gave him twenty-five cents more for carrying a
heavy suit-case a mile to the station.

The moment the fee was paid, Arnon dashed
off for the pound. He had not only the two-
dollar ransom, but fourteen cents left over wherewith to buy the materials for a reunion feast at
the shack. His dizzy weakness and hunger were
clean forgot in the mad joy of victory.

Panting, unsteady on his legs, he rushed down
the pier. Before going into the office he paused

at the pen to tell his glorious news to the two prisoners. But his shrill whistle brought no response. He bent down, shading his eyes; and stared into the pen. Neither Buck nor Dandy was there. The souse of the derrick-cage as it smote the water, and the simultaneous crazed screams of its twenty passengers, reached his ears. And he understood.

No longer did Arnon try to fight back the babyish tears. He fell face downward on the pier and gave way to hysterical weeping.

His chums! His dear, wonderful chums! The little loyal dogs that had loved him and had comforted him so prettily in his stark aloneness and that had been so perfectly trustful in his power to save them!

A man's hand gripped Arnon's heaving shoulder and sought to raise him to his feet. The touch turned his desolate grief into a rage that was all but murderous. This pound-keeper, by one word, could have saved Dandy and Buck. And instead, he had drowned them.

With a beast snarl, the half-delirious boy was on his feet.

"You *swine!*" he screeched, as he whirled towards the man. "When I'm big enough, I'm coming back to smash every bone in your fat body! And I'm going to——"

His words caught in his throat with a click.

This was not the fat pound-office man. It was Arnon Flint's father. The boy gaped dazedly.

Yes, it was his father. But Arnon cared not one whit for that. His father could send him to jail for theft or could whale him with a horsewhip or do anything rotten he chose. It didn't matter. All that mattered was that Buck and Dandy were dead.

He glowered up into the man's face, ready for anything that might befall. Then his glower turned to a look of perplexity. His father did not glower back. Instead, Mr. Flint's face was unspeakably tender.

"Oh, my little boy!" he was saying, brokenly. "Dad's own crazy, *gallant* little boy! You're worn to a shadow! We've looked everywhere for you. It wasn't till yesterday our detectives struck the trail. And I came right on."

"I didn't steal the money," said Arnon, dully, "the bazaar money. I lost it on the trolley-car. I tried to get a job to make it up to the church, but——"

"I know, I know," broke in his father, in that same unbelievably tender and quivering voice. "Don't think any more about it. I've paid it. Why, dear lad, no one ever supposed you stole it. We knew you couldn't. Will you come back home with me, Son? Mother is pretty nearly as thin as you are, from worry over you."

"I'll come, if you like," agreed Arnon, listlessly. "It doesn't matter much, now, either way. I might as well be there as anywhere."

"Good!" approved his father. "We can just make the ten o'clock train, if we hurry. I've got a taxi waiting at the other end of the pier."

Side by side, father and son walked away from the pound. The boy's eyes were downcast. His face was haggard. His heart was dead. From time to time, as they walked, the man stole a covert glance at him, and his own face contracted as in sharp pain.

"Here's the taxi," said Mr. Flint at last. "Open the door, will you? You're nearer to it than I am."

Mechanically, Arnon turned the handle. As he pulled the taxi door ajar, two furry catapults from within the vehicle launched themselves, rapturously and yelpingly, upon him.

"You see," explained Mr. Flint, to his unhearing son, "I had quite a talk with the poundmaster before you got here, this morning. He's been noticing you, it seems. And he told me a rather pathetic little story. When I heard it I decided to make an investment in livestock. I was putting these two puppies into the taxi when you hobbled past me on your way to the pound. I——"

"*Buck!*" Arnon was sobbing, in a frenzy of bliss. "Buck! *Dandy!*"

At sound of their names, the dogs wriggled free from Arnon's embrace—just for the uproarious fun of hurling themselves once more upon him.

"Hurry up, Son!" suggested Mr. Flint, clearing his throat noisily. "Get aboard—you and the pups. We'll miss that train!"

"Not on your sweet life, we won't miss it!" exulted Arnon, scrambling into the taxi with his pets. "We've *got* to catch it. You see, I—I want my chums to—to meet Mother; just as soon as they can. They're dead sure to like her."

HUMAN-INTEREST STUFF

HAPPINESS, to Jeff Titus, had become a fine art. It had become so when he married Eve Wallace, a little wisp of a city girl who had come to the Kentucky mountain hinterland to cure a set of weak lungs—and who had not only wedded but well-nigh civilised the lanky young mountaineer.

Happiness had remained a fine art for Jeff, up there on his bare hillside farm, with Eve. It had remained so, for the most part, ever since his wedding. And now, in a single breath, happiness had taken a place among the lost arts.

The "single breath" had been supplied by a sour east wind which had smitten Eve as she stood in the shack dooryard waiting for her husband's homecoming. She was thinly clad, and she was in a perspiration from working in her flower garden. Her lungs were still weak. The east wind did the rest. By night she had a heavy cold. The third morning, pneumonia flung out its flaming red No Surrender signal on each of her fever-scorched cheeks.

And life, to Jeff Titus, all at once became a horror.

A frightened anguish gripped him by the throat and shook him to the bewildered soul; as he crouched night after night beside the slab bed where tossed and muttered the delirious little wisp of a woman who was at once his mate and his saint.

Eve was so tiny, so fragile, so good! It wasn't fair that this bullying unseen spirit of illness should torture and harry her and sap the life of her—while the man who right blithely would have been burned to a crisp to please her, sat helpless at the bedside, unable to do a thing to drive forth the damnable visitant! Jeff Titus dwelt upon the theme of his own impotence to save her; he swore venomously, and in the peculiarly hideous diction of Kentucky mountaineer blasphemy.

There were doctors, of course, in the county seat of Duneka, thirty-two miles away. But they might as well have been in Austria, for all the good they could do the sick girl. Jeff could not desert Eve to go in quest of such a physician. Nor could he send one of his mile-distant neighbours. He knew that. It would be of no use.

Those city doctors had no convenient means of getting over the thirty-odd miles of half-inaccessible trail, to his hinterland farm. Assuredly none of them was going to make the journey on foot or on mule-back, leaving his town practice for days, at the behest of a hill-billy who perhaps could not or would not pay for the sacrifice.

Meantime, Eve was growing worse, steadily worse. Even the ignorant Jeff could see that. So, apparently, could the only sharer of his day-and-night vigils—a huge and lionlike dog which lay pressed close to the far side of the bed, and which all Titus' commands could not keep out of the sick-room.

This dog, Robin Adair, was the joy of Eve's heart—or he had been, when her heart still could hold joy and not merely fever and delirium. One of Eve's ragged hill-billy admirers had given the dog to her; in the old days, when Robin was a roly-poly mass of tawny-brown fluff, no bigger than a Persian cat.

The dog had grown into a shaggy giant. A passing seed-catalogue man had told Eve he was a collie—a breed of which she had heard, in a vague fashion, as emanating from Scotland. And she had named him Robin Adair; after the hero of a Scotch song her mother had been wont to sing. He was Robin, for short. When she had married Jeff Titus, she had brought her beloved collie to live at the mountain shack.

From the moment his mistress fell ill, Robin had not once willingly stirred from her bed-side. Drinking little, eating nothing, the great dog had lain there, his sorrowing brown eyes fixed on the small white figure in the big slab bed. But of late he was beginning to vary the vigil by low-voiced whines, from time to time. And once or twice his huge body quivered as if in physical pain.

It was on the dawn of the fourth day that Robin got to his feet with a leap, and, pointing his heavy muzzle skyward, set the still room to reverberating with a yell that was nothing short of unearthly.

Jeff, starting from his daze of misery, made as though to throttle the brute that had broken in on the invalid's unresting rest. Then, remembering Eve's affection for the collie, he contented himself with picking Robin up bodily and bearing him towards the door; with the intent of putting him out of the house.

The door, before Jeff could reach it, was flung open from outside. On the threshold stood a ramrodlike figure in rusty black. The caller was the Reverend Ephraim Stair—Methodist circuit-rider for the up-State counties, and a man whose brain and heart had long since made him the blindly obeyed autocrat of his scattered mountain flock.

"What's wrong, Titus?" was his wondering greeting as his sharp old eyes flashed from the man with the big dog in his arms to the eternally whispering little form on the bed. "I heard a scream, as I was riding past, and——"

"Oh, parson!" gasped Jeff in babbling relief, dumping Robin on the puncheon floor and gripping the circuit-rider by both hands. "For Gawd's sake, *do* suthin' fer her! She acts like —like she ain't goin' to git well none!"

Loud through the mountains were the praises of Stair's medical lore. Many were the tales of sick folk he had cured; when the old women had given them up and had begun gruesomely relishful preparations for the funeral. Jeff Titus clutched at his unexpected presence, as at a lifebelt. Half in superstitious awe, he glanced at the dog whose providential screech had made the clergyman halt in his brisk ride from one county seat to the next.

Meantime, Stair had crossed to the bed, and, on his knees beside it, was examining the stricken Eve. Jeff came up behind him, standing awkwardly and with open mouth, in expectation of some miracle.

But no miracle was vouchsafed. Instead the clergyman asked one or two questions as to the illness' course, felt the patient's pulse and her torrid cheek, then ordered his host to go and fetch in his saddlebags.

"My medicine-kit is in them," he explained.

"And you can stable my horse, too. I'm going to stay."

"She—she's goin' to git on all right, now you're here, ain't she?" pleaded Titus ingratiatingly, pausing at the door.

"Get my saddlebags!" was the non-committal retort. "Jump! Then you can heat some water. Wait! Before you go, open those windows. And leave the door open. Isn't this poor child having enough trouble in breathing; without your sealing the room hermetically?"

"Sick folks hadn't oughter be let have cold air tetch 'em, I've allers heard," Jeff defended himself, nevertheless obeying. "It gives 'em——"

"It gives them life!" retorted Stair. "Now get those saddlebags!"

Next morning Eve was perceptibly worse: the breathing was more laboured; the fever blazed higher. This in spite of Stair and his ceaseless ministrations. Stark despair tore at the husband's throat.

Following Stair, as the circuit-rider left the room for a moment to wash his hands at the pump, Titus demanded fiercely:

"She's a-aimin' to die, ain't she? Spit out the truth, man! I got a right to hear it!"

"I can't say," answered Stair, taking no offence at the furious manner. "She is in the midst of the crisis now. It is the turning-point in such cases. If she rallies from that— Meanwhile we can only hope—and work. It is in God's hands. She——"

"In Gawd's hands!" mocked Jeff, wildly. "In *Gawd's* hands, hey? You're Gawd-a'mighty fond of blattin' 'bout Gawd, parson! But I take notice He ain't a-doin' nothin' fer that pore sick gal of mine, in yonder. Why ain't He? Where is He, anyhow, if He cain't——"

"He is *here,*" answered Stair very quietly. "Here, and in that delirious girl's room, back there. He is wherever His children cry out to Him in sorrow and pain—just as, in your inmost heart, you are crying to Him now. If His children are too deaf or too scared or too noisy, in their grief, to know He has come at their call, then the fault is with their own stupidity; and not with the all-pitying Father, who is carrying them through the ordeal."

He pushed past the mouthing Titus and went back to his post in the sick-room.

On the second morning Eve was in a heavy sleep. Her once-parched forehead was moist. Stair, with a jerk of his thumb, motioned Jeff out into the dooryard. On his withered face was the glow of a conqueror. Harshly, as if in doubt of his own self-control, the circuit-rider said:

"The crisis is past. She has turned the cor-

ner. I think she will live. The rest depends
on nursing—on building her up. You may thank
God, if you care to. Or if you still think He hasn't
been here——"

"If He ain't," choked Titus ecstatically, "He
sent a damn' fine substitoot:—meanin' no disre-
spec'. I—I reckon, parson—I reckon you-all
knows how small I feel; 'bout blabbin' like I did.
An'—an'—Oh, you're dead *sure* she's a-goin' to
live? There—there ain't—there ain't nothing I
c'n say! But—but——"

Incontinently Jeff Titus bolted around the side
of the house and out of sight into the woods.
When he returned, an hour later, he was carrying
a half-armful of kindling. Circumstantially and
at some length he explained to Stair that he had
spent the entire hour in looking for it. Stair
accepted the explanation in grave credulity and
forebore to glance towards the high-piled heap of
kindling in the woodshed.

At noon Eve awoke. She was very weak, very
tired, very thin and big-eyed. But she was *alive*.

And in Jeff's heart there was something that
made him yearn to howl aloud in rapture and
roll on the grass, and to join the church all over
again, and to thrash some mythical man for
speaking mythical ill of Ephraim Stair; and to
turn over his farm and his savings to foreign mis-

sions, and to get very drunk indeed, and to buy Eve a gold watch.

Being a Kentucky mountaineer, and a Titus to boot, he contented himself with grinning down upon his sick wife and grunting:

"Feel better? That's nice. Be all right, pretty soon, now. Reckon I'd best be gittin' in some more wood, b'fore it rains. So long!"

Robin Adair, like his master, knew Eve was on the way to health again. But being only a dog and not a mountaineer, Robin did not sneak out of the house to hide his emotion. He stood beside the bed, his dark eyes aglow, his furry bulk quivering all over with puppyish joy; and wagging his plumed tail, frantically, every time his mistress looked at him.

One evening a few days later the two men were smoking together in the dooryard before turning in. Eve had been made comfortable for the night and was asleep.

She had gained a little ground, but her convalescence was maddeningly slow and uncertain to Jeff. The horror of the past fortnight or so had left him nerve-shaken. In spite of all Stair's assurances, he could not throw off his fear for her safety.

"She has been through a terrible illness," patiently explained Stair for the hundredth time.

"Her body and her mind are exhausted. She lies there, like that, because she is resting. She is resting, because nature is making her rest. She is steadily getting better. Bar accidents, she is practically out of danger. Her strength is beginning to seep back, too. It would come back faster, of course, if she could rally her tired mind to some great interest in life—something that wouldn't tire or excite her too much. It would help Mother Nature along. An interest in life is a wonderful aid, in convalescence. A bit of unexpected good news, for instance——"

"Good news, hey?" mused Jeff, his bony hands supporting his leathern face as he cogitated. "Good news? H'm!"

"Yes," returned Stair, "that, or something pleasant to look forward to. When she's well enough, you might take her to Duneka, or somewhere, for a little outing. Tell her so. It may brighten her to——"

"Nope," dissented Jeff. "It wouldn't. I tried, to-day. Told her she must git well, right smart, now; so's we c'd have a ja'ntin', somewheres. She said she was so tired, she reckoned she'd jest stay quiet to home a spell. It didn't brace her, a wee peckle. Funny, too! 'Cause jest before she was took sick, she an' me was projectin', a hull lot, on a trip we was plannin' to make. She'd got her heart real sot on it—'count of suthin' she'd read into the Duneka *Chron'cle*. The fall County Fair is on, to Duneka, this week, you know. An' the *Chron'cle* told how they're lottin' on holdin' the State dawg-show there, the fourth day of the fair. That's the day after to-morror. The *Chron'cle* said there was to be reel silver cups offered fer best dawgs of a lot of breeds. Collies was one of the breeds it spoke about."

"Well?" asked Stair, in no special interest, as Jeff paused.

"Wal," went on the mountaineer sheepishly, "you-all know how much store Eve sets by Robin, here. She thinks he's jest the finest dawg on this yer planet. She was a-sayin' there couldn't be no finer dawg in the collie bunch, at the show, than what Robin is. An' she was honin' fer us to take him down there an' let him git a chance at that silver cup. Wal, whatever Eve hones fer, she's a-goin' to git—if it's gittable an' if I'm in reach to git it fer her. So I 'greed we'd take Robin to the show. She was all het up over the idee of a-gittin' that 'ere cup. An' she was a-sayin' how grand it'd be to have the paper print Robin's name as winnin' it, so's she c'd send a copy of the paper to her folks, down Looeyville way, an' all that. Wal, that's all there is to it," he ended with a loud sigh.

"Why is that all there is to it?" demanded Stair with sudden inspiration. "Why can't you take the dog down to the show yourself, if he really has a chance for the cup? That cup, and the notice in the paper, would do more to stir Eve up and to renew her interest in life than any other good news I can think of. And it'll be something to look forward to. Go ahead and do it!"

"Good! Oh, *good!*" exulted a feeble little voice in the room behind them.

Eve had waked, during their talk. And, in her tones, as she applauded the plan, rang the first interest she had shown since the beginning of her illness. Stair, listening, shut his thin lips on a belated objection that had come into his mind while the mountaineer was applauding his chance suggestion.

It had just occurred to the circuit-rider that if Robin should not be adjudged worthy of the cup, the disappointment was likely to do the invalid more harm than a week of nursing could counteract. But it was too late to voice that warning now. Eve had heard. Eve was pathetically eager over the scheme. And, kicking himself mentally for his own impulsiveness, the clergyman held his peace.

He knew nothing about dogs, from a show standpoint—and mightily he hoped Eve's estimate of her pet might be correct. But he doubted—more and more, he doubted. Collies, fit to win silver cups, do not often find their way into the mountaineer cabins in the Kentucky hinterland.

Timidly, Stair sought to wet-blanket the venture. But again he was too late. At last Eve had the desired "interest in life," an interest that threatened to bring back her fever. The dog-show virus is potent, as any exhibitor can testify. It has a mystic lure. Jeff, once he grasped the idea, was swept off his feet by it.

The fall County Fair at Duneka had begun its fourth day. That day's star feature was to be the "all breeds" dog-show, to be held in the Agricultural Building.

A gratifying number of dogs was benched in the main hall of the ramshackle structure; early on the morning of the show. Two stewards were busy receiving the fast-arriving entrants, assigning to them their places in the double aisles of wire-partitioned and straw-littered "benches," and assessing late-comers the usual extra fees for "post-entries."

To these grievously overworked functionaries, in the thick of their labours, appeared a lanky farmer of the true mountaineer type. He was clad in store-clothes that sat on his angular figure as might a horse-blanket on a washboard. By a rope, the hill-billy led a large and shaggy dog whose rough, tawny coat had been washed and brushed until it shone like bronze and fluffed out like the hair of a Circassian beauty.

"Collie dawg," announced Jeff, "owned by Miz Jeff Titus. Entered for the silver cup."

Patiently the stewards explained to him that a dog must be entered for one or more of the show's regular classes, and that the coveted silver cup was to go to the collie adjudged best in the whole show. They also informed Jeff that as his was a post-entry, it would cost him an extra fifty cents to exhibit his dog. He was told that in addition to this it would cost him a dollar for every class in which he might enter Robin.

As most of this was Greek to the puzzled exhibitor, one of the stewards asked if the dog had ever before been shown. On receiving a negative answer he took one look at the uninterested Robin and suggested he be entered for the "novice class," alone.

As soon as he could be made to understand that a collie winning, in the novice class, would stand as good a chance for the cup as would any other, Titus paid over his money and led Robin to the stall in the collie section corresponding to the number the steward had tied to the dog's collar.

After mooring Robin's rope to the ring in his wire-partitioned bench, and getting him some water, Jeff had leisure to take in his odd surroundings.

Dogs — *dogs* — DOGS! Everywhere dogs — more dogs than Jeff had known existed—dogs of all breeds and sizes, from Peke to St. Bernard. The iron-girdered roof was re-echoing with their clangour. They were barking or yapping in fifty different keys, but all with the same earnestness.

Jeff saw that each breed had a bench-section to itself. In the hall's centre, to which the bench aisles converged, were two wood-and-wire inclosures in each of which were a low central platform and a corner table and a chair. On the tables were neat piles of red and yellow and blue ribbons alongside a record-ledger. Handlers were everywhere busy making their pets ready for the judging.

Crowds of onlookers had already begun to filter through the aisles. Jeff heard someone say that the judging was about to begin, and that collies were to be among the first breeds shown.

His general curiosity sated, Titus fell to examining the dogs which were to be Robin's competitors. And at once his mountaineer scowl merged into a grin. Here, forsooth, was nothing wherewith the splendid Robin need fear comparison.

Why, of all the nineteen collies on exhibition, there was not one within three inches of Robin's height, nor one which bore any real resemblance to him. These others were strongly slender chaps, with thin heads and tapering noses and tulip ears and slant eyes. Whereas, Robin's mighty head was almost as broad and heavy as a Newfoundland's; his ears were pricked like a wolf's, and his honest brown eyes were large and round. No, most assuredly he was not in the very least like any other collie entered in the show—or in any exhibition of thoroughbreds since the birth of time.

Poor old Robin Adair was probably more collie than anything else; he may even have been a shade more than half-collie. But in his veins ran also the mixed blood of many another breed, Newfoundland predominating.

"Look over there!" Jeff heard a dapper collie-handler in a linen duster say in guarded tones to a woman who was sifting talcum powder into her gold-and-white collie pup's fluffy coat. "Over at Bench 89! What is that Thing? A dog—or a hippopotamus?"

As the woman turned to observe the luckless Robin, Jeff Titus strolled across to the man who had called her attention to the dog. His eyes were glinting flares behind their lowered lids, and his lips twisted into something which looked like a smile and wasn't. He said softly:

"Beggin' you-all's pardon, mister, what was you a-happenin' to call my dawg?"

The man in the linen duster gave one glance at the leathern face peering down so intensely into his. Then, shakily, he made reply:

"I—I wasn't speaking of your dog, sir. I was speaking of the dog in the next bench to his. I—I read the number wrong. Yours is—a—a grand—a grand—collie, sir."

He gulped, and sped down the aisles on a new-remembered errand somewhere. Jeff turned back to Robin, his mind freed of its momentary angry doubt.

The collie classes were called a few minutes later. The first to be judged were, as usual, the male puppies. Jeff, watching the performance of the entrants, saw how the judging was done. First the dogs were made to march around the ring. Then, in ones or twos, they were placed on the platform while the little tweed-clad judge studied them and felt them all over. After that, the judge wrote certain numbers in the ring-steward's book and handed to the owner of the winning dog a blue ribbon. A red ribbon went to the owner of the second best, a yellow ribbon to the third, and a white ribbon to the fourth.

Every one of the several collie classes, it seemed, must be judged in that same deliberate way; before the winners of all classes could compete for a rosette, whose acquisition meant also the winning of the silver cup. Jeff began to chafe at the needless delay which must ensue before Robin could receive his merited prize.

Then, directly after the judging of the puppies, came the novice class. Along with only two other entries, Jeff Titus led the majestically unconcerned Robin into the ring. As he passed, a titter swept the quadruple line of railbirds outside the inclosure. Jeff did not so much as look about him to locate the cause of the mirth. These fool city-folks were always laughing at nothing.

Nor did he note the glare, almost of horror, which the little tweed-clad judge bestowed upon Robin; as Eve's adored pet paced into the ring. The judge eyed him with much the expression one might expect to see in the visage of a Supreme Court justice who has been asked to hand down an official opinion on a nursery rhyme.

"Walk your dogs, please!" rasped the judge The parade started. Robin strolled uncon cernedly at his lanky master's side. As he was not a thoroughbred, his nerves were not of the hair-trigger order. The racket and the crowd and the new surroundings did not excite or terrify or make him profoundly miserable; as they did some of the high-strung collies about him. Jeff observed this calm demeanour and was proud of his dog's bearing.

The parade was halted. The judge motioned Robin's two competitors to the platform, squinted at them for a moment, ran his hand over them, examined the spring of their ribs, then their teeth, and various other details,— stood back and studied them—then handed to the owner of one a blue ribbon and to the other a red. The third-prize yellow ribbon he tossed back onto the steward's table.

The winners of the first and second prizes departed with their collies. The steward chalked up the next class on the blackboard. But Jeff Titus did not leave the ring. Eyes bulging, cheeks slowly turning from tan to brick-hue, he strode over to the judge.

"Look-a-here, you!" he rumbled in a blend of wrath and dazed incredulity. "What's the meanin' of this-yer? Are you aimin' to double-cross me? My dawg's wuth ten of them ornery critters. He's a heap bigger'n an' huskier, an' he's purtier to look at, too! What the blue blazes do you-all mean by treatin' him thisaway, you hard-biled shrimp? He——"

With much dignity the little judge turned his back on the angry Titus and started across the ring. But before he had gone two steps Jeff was once more confronting him.

"Look-a-here!" snarled Titus, again, striving to keep himself in hand. "I ain't goin' to lay down under no frame-up! You judged crooked, with my dawg. I c'n prove it. Even if you didn't have the sense to see he was the best of the hull bilin', you was bound, anyhow, to give him the yaller ribbon fer third prize. An——"

"I was bound to do nothing of the sort!" rapped out the exasperated judge. "I am here to judge collies, not dinosaurs. I refuse to countenance the claim that your dog is a collie, by giving him a third-prize ribbon; even in a class of three. So, in this class, I have deliberately withheld the third prize. Your dog is not a collie. The Lord alone knows what he is, but he's no collie. That's all. Clear out!"

For a man with heart or imagination, there is no ordeal more irksome than to judge dogs. For, in almost every division, there is some such beast as Robin Adair;—a dog loved by his owners, who know nothing of shows or of show points. A judge, in fairness to the better exhibits, must pass over these poor animals; and thereby must cause heartache and shame to their pathetic owners. It is not a pleasant task. Nor is any phase of dog-judging pleasant. It is a thankless and nerve-racking job, at best; and it has a magic quality of turning one's friends into enemies.

The little judge at the Duneka show was hardened by long practice. Also, he had all the bristling pluck of a rat-terrier. And he needed it in facing this lean giant in whose slit-eyes the murder-light was beginning to smoulder.   Jeff half extended one windmill arm in the general direction of the judge's throat.   Then he checked himself.

It was going to be bad enough to slink home with no cup, but it would be ten-fold worse to go to the hoosgow for mayhem.   He pictured sick Eve's grief over such a disgrace, and his clenched hand dropped again to his side.   Grappling with his temper, the mountaineer wheeled about and led the disqualified Robin out of the ring and back to the bench.

A sweet mess he had made of everything; he and that parson, up yonder!

They had wrought on Eve's hopes and had made her so gloriously confident that her dear dog was going to sweep all before him and win the cup!   She was lying at home, this minute, her big eyes shining with anticipation, her vivid mind picturing the triumph-scene at the show. How confidently she would be waiting for that cup!

Jeff had sought so enthusiastically to work out Stair's theory of a "good news" cure!   And how was the experiment to result?   He must go home on the morrow and tell Eve not only that he had no cup to show her, but that the judge

had actually refused Robin a third-prize ribbon, on the ground that the dog was a mongrel!
What effect was that news going to have on a
sick woman whose swift recovery depended on
her spirits?

Knowing Eve as he did, Jeff was ready to
believe it would undo most of her hard-won convalescence. And at the very least, in her weak
state, it was certain to make her cry. Jeff would
rather have faced a machine-gun nest than make
his gallant little sweetheart cry.

He began to swear, very softly but very, very
zealously. And then his resourceful mountaineer
brain unlimbered and went into action.

Presently, he arose from the bench, patted
Robin absentmindedly on the head and slouched
off towards the end of the hall, where, in a high
glass case, were displayed the prize cups and
the other trophies.

Long and minutely he scanned the glittering
prizes, especially the cup engraved "Best Collie."
And he spelled out the printed legend over the
case—which proclaimed that the cups were supplied by the long-famous jewellery firm of Pinkus
Bernstein, of Republic Street, Duneka, Kentucky.

Ten minutes later, leaving Robin to shift for
himself on his bench, Jeff was hiking towards the
business streets of the mountain metropolis. He

paused, for a space, at the bank, where he had a carefully scraped-together little account, and he drew forth a goodly share of that sum. Then he made his way to the jewellery-store. After a half-hour of dickering, he emerged from the shop, bearing a bumpy parcel.

Returning to the Agricultural Hall, he seated himself once more on the narrow bench beside the exultantly welcoming Robin, and proceeded to unwind the tissue wrappings of his package. Robin looked on in mild curiosity. His sense of smell had already told the dog that the parcel contained nothing of vital interest to him. Yet, because he had been lonely and a little worried by Jeff's long absence, Robin evinced a polite concern in the undoing of the wrappings.

The last layer of paper was removed. To the dog's view was exposed a huge and gleaming silver cup, a cup with much chasing on its polished surface and with three handles and an ebony base. It was at least double the size of the cup offered by the committee for "best collie."

"See that?" questioned Titus, holding the trophy aloft for Robin's inspection. "Forty-one dollars, that set me back. An' it'd a' been a heap more, only it was a left-over, an' had that one little gouge under the aidge. Robin, if that cup don't tickle her, suthin' terrible, I'm a clay-eater! You-all won this yer vase, to-day, Robin; by bein' 'best collie.' Jes' keep a-rememberin' that. I ain't never put nothin' over on her, b'fore. You-all knows that, Robbie. But—I reckon it's wuth doin', this yer time. She——"

He paused in his low-pitched confidence to the blinking, sympathising dog. Two men had halted just in front of him. One of them was carrying an apparatus which movie-camp memories told Jeff was a camera.

It chanced to be a moment when no less than two "Winners' Classes" were on in the show-rings. Accordingly the ring-sides were banked deep with onlookers, and this secluded section of the aisles was almost wholly stripped of specta-tors. That was why Jeff had ventured to bring forth the cup from its wrappings. The sight of the two keenly interested men set him to scowling in dire embarrassment.

The chairman of the dog-show committee was also one of the chief stockholders of the Duneka *Chronicle*. Wherefore, the dictum had gone forth to the *Chronicle* city-room that the show was to be played up, big, in both morning and evening editions. And the paper's best descrip-tive writer, one Graham, had been assigned to do some "human-interest stuff" about it, in addi-tion to the sporting editor's regulation account. Graham was a good reporter, and he had a genius for human-interest yarns. But of dogs he knew little, and of dog-shows he knew even less. Yet, gleaning such information on the subject as he could, he had set forth for the show this morning; taking along the paper's sole photographer.

After pausing near the front entrance to accustom their ears to the frightful din and to take a snapshot of the trophy-case, the two newspaper men had wandered down the first aisle into which their non-enthusiastic feet had chanced to stray. There, suddenly, Graham saw one of the "human-interest bits" for which he was always hunting.

Midway in an aisle labelled COLLIE SECTION sat a tired man, a typical mountaineer, beside a huge collie. And to the civilly interested dog the mountaineer was exhibiting pridefully a silver cup; larger than any in the trophy-case. He was talking to the dog, too, in a confidential whisper; evidently telling the collie what a splendid victory he had scored and how proud of him his master was.

Here was human-interest stuff, if ever Graham had seen it!

"Cup for best collie in the show?" asked Graham of the scowling hill-billy.

"Yep!" snapped Jeff Titus, defiantly.

"Good boy!" exclaimed Graham, seeking by

effusive geniality to break down the mountaineer's surly reserve. "He's sure one peach of a dog! What's his name? And what's yours?"

"His name," said Jeff with perilous courtesy, "is Robin—Robin Adair. He b'longs to my wife, Miz Jeff Titus—up Keytesville-way. She's sick, to home. I'm showin' him fer her. Got any more questions to pester me with, b'fore——"

"Would you mind holding up the cup, a second?" wheedled Graham, scribbling with a chewed pencil on a doubled wad of copy paper. "So! Thanks!"

Still defiantly, Jeff had held forward the cup for inspection, his free arm around the majestic Robin's shoulders. The camera clicked. Titus did not hear it, through the noise of a hundred barks and yelps. Besides, he was focusing his indignant attention on this slick-spoken opponent of his.

"Wal?" he demanded truculently. "Anything more you-all wants o' me? He's *our* dawg. An' he's good enough for *us*. If you-all don't like him none——"

"But I do!" effused Graham. "A great dog, Mr. Titus! And"—his eye running along the collie section—"he must be close to championship standard, to have beaten all of these beauties. I'd like to ask you——"

'I ain't got nothin' more to say!" growled Jeff,

half rising, and his yellow eyetooth began to show under his upcurling lip. "An' if you-all is aimin' to start trouble 'bout this yer cup——"

Graham was not aiming to start trouble. Not at all did he like the new expression, nor the voice, of this sulking hill-billy he had sought to patronise. With a signal to the photographer he moved rapidly away, continuing his progress down the aisle.

Jeff glared after him. If the man were going to inform the committee that Titus had bought a cup when he had not been able to win one, why, let him do it! Jeff wasn't going to run away. So he held his ground, feeling very wrathful, but somewhat scared. He restored the cup to its wrappings. It would be handier to carry it, that way, should he be ejected from the show on account of his fraud.

But no one ejected him. Except that people paused now and then, through the course of the day, to stare amusedly at poor Robin (and to straighten their faces in comical haste as they encountered Jeff's glower), no one molested Titus.

At four in the afternoon Jeff's raw nerves could stand the strain no longer. Untying Robin from the bench, he led him to the entrance of the hall. There he sought the superintendent of the show.

"When c'n me an' my dawg git outen here an' traipse home?" he asked.

"No dog is supposed to leave the building before ten o'clock to-night, when the show ends," replied the superintendent, adding with a cryptic glance at Robin: "But I don't think I need hold your entry to those rules. Go when you like."

The cup under his arm and Robin at his heels, Jeff departed. He had come to town on muleback, the dog running alongside. Even at the best pace he could scarce hope to get home very much before midnight. He had come to Duneka on the preceding day and had planned to stay until next morning. But, already, his imagination was afire with the thought of bursting in on Eve that very night, with the glittering trophy. So he bent his steps towards the stable where he housed his mule.

Across the fair-grounds, from the cityward gate, a bevy of barelegged newsboys was scampering, with armfuls of newspapers—copies of the *Chronicle's* first afternoon edition. One of them ran past Jeff.

Jeff's keen mountaineer eyes chanced on a dark blotch near the bottom of the swaying sheet's first page. With an unbelieving gasp, he stopped

short in his tracks and bawled to the fleeing newsboy to come back.

The boy returned, holding out the paper. Jeff
snatched it from him, riveting his incredulous
gaze upon that dark blotch on the front page.
The blotch, at close range, resolved itself into a
two-column cut—a picture of Robin, lying majestically at full length in his bench, his trustful
gaze fixed on the lank man who squatted beside
him and who held aloft an ornate silver cup!

Above the cut ran the caption:

"A PRIZE-WINNER AND HIS PRIZE."

Beneath the picture were the lines:

*"Mrs. Jeff Titus' Robin Adair; Winner of cup
for Best Collie in Show."*

Doubled, in single-column space under this,
was one of the two-stick "human-interest" stories
with which Graham was wont to strew the
Chronicle's pages. Jeff's fascinated eyes tore
themselves from the picture and caught a glimpse
of his own name midway of this explanatory yarn.
He read the sentence containing the name, then
the next line or so. Slowly and painfully he spelled
out:

Mr. Titus exhibited the dog for his wife, who
is ill at their Keytesville home. With characteris-
tic mountaineer modesty, Mr. Titus refused to
sound his splendid exhibit's praises. When con-

gratulated by throngs of admirers who paid homage to the peerless Robin Adair, Mr. Titus' sole comment on Robin's sensational victory was:

"He's good enough for us!"

Robin Adair was good enough for the judges, too, and good enough to win over one of the finest aggregations of high-bred collies ever shown in this part of the South.

The brief story switched back to the human-interest note—to the man's evident rapture in the triumph of his sick wife's pet, and his shy pride in the magnificent cup. But Jeff read no more just then.

Whirling on the impatiently waiting newsboy, he demanded thickly:

"Gimme all them newspapers you're totin'! An' then scuttle off an' fetch me a dozen more! Scat!"

Again he stared in idiotic bliss at the smudged two-column cut. What did it matter to Jeff Titus that the picture and its erroneous caption were to be "lifted out" of the next edition, and that Graham was to incur the sharpest call-down of his career, for the break he had made?

Not three copies of the *Chronicle* a week made their way to Keytesville. And, even should the next day's full account of the dog-show reach the Titus region, no mountaineer in the State would possess the technical show-lore to decipher the cryptic "summary of wins" and thus learn of Robin's defeat.

No: in the mountains, the printed word was accepted as gospel fact—by those who had education to read it. And its pictures were accepted as such by those who had not bothered to master the effete arts of reading and writing. Jeff was going to take home enough papers to go around the whole sparse neighbourhood, in addition to those which were to be mailed to Eve's people at Louisville and to any other distant kin or friends of hers. Not in the very least did Jeff Titus understand the meaning of this newspaper tribute. Nor did he bother his overwrought brain about it. He had the required "good news" for Eve. He had printed and pictured proofs thereof. If this didn't help along her tardy cure, by leaps and bounds—

"I ain't never lied to her yet, Robin!" he informed the prize-winner as they ambled homeward at dusk over the purpling miles of hilly trail. "Nor yet I don't aim to, now. We'll walk in on her, with the cup. An' when she asks, all pleased an' tickled-like, 'Why, whatever is this yer fer?' we'll jest stick a copy of the noospaper up in front of her. I'm bettin' the R'cordin' Angel is due to strain his pore ears till they ache him, if he 'lots on ketchin' *me* tellin' a lie to that Gawd-blessed gal!"

"ONE MINUTE LONGER"

WOLF was a collie, red-gold and white of coat, with a shape more like his long-ago wolf ancestors' than like a domesticated dog's. It was from this ancestral throw-back that he was named Wolf.

He looked not at all like his great sire, Sunnybank Lad, nor like his dainty, thoroughbred mother, Lady. Nor was he like them in any other way, except that he inherited old Lad's staunchly gallant spirit and loyalty, and uncanny brain. No, in traits as well as in looks, he was more wolf than dog. He almost never barked, his snarl supplying all vocal needs.

The Mistress or the Master or the Boy—any of these three could romp with him, roll him over, tickle him, or subject him to all sorts of playful indignities. And Wolf entered gleefully into the fun of the romp. But let any human, besides these three, lay a hand on his slender body, and a snarling plunge for the offender's throat was Wolf's invariable reply to the caress.

It had been so since his puppyhood. He did not fly at accredited guests, nor, indeed, pay any heed to their presence. so long as they kept their hands off him. But to all of these the Boy **was** forced to say at the very outset of the visit:

"Pat Lad and Bruce all you want to, but please leave Wolf alone. He doesn't care for people. We've taught him to stand for a pat on the head, from guests,—but don't touch his body."

Then, to prove his own immunity, the Boy would proceed to tumble Wolf about, to the delight of them both.

In romping with humans whom they love, most dogs will bite, more or less gently,—or pretend to bite,—as a part of the game. Wolf never did this. In his wildest and roughest romps with the Boy or with the Boy's parents, Wolf did not so much as open his mighty jaws. Perhaps because he dared not trust himself to bite gently. Perhaps because he realised that a bite is not a joke, but an effort to kill.

There had been only one exception to Wolf's hatred for mauling at strangers' hands. A man came to The Place on a business call, bringing along a chubby two-year-old daughter. The Master warned the baby that she must not go near Wolf, although she might pet any of the other collies. Then he became so much interested in the business talk that he and his guest forgot all about the child.

Ten minutes later the Master chanced to shift his gaze to the far end of the room. And

he broke off, with a gasp, in the very middle
of a sentence.

The baby was seated astride Wolf's back, her
tiny heels digging into the dog's sensitive ribs,
and each of her chubby fists gripping one of
his ears. Wolf was lying there, with an idiot-
ically happy grin on his face and wagging his
tail in ecstasy.

No one knew why he had submitted to the
baby's tugging hands, except because she *was* a
baby, and because the gallant heart of the dog
had gone out to her helplessness.

Wolf was the official watch-dog of The Place;
and his name carried dread to the loafers and
tramps of the region. Also, he was the Boy's
own special dog. He had been born on the Boy's
tenth birthday, five years before this story of
ours begins; and ever since then the two had
been inseparable chums.

One sloppy afternoon in late winter, Wolf and
the Boy were sprawled, side by side; on the fur
rug in front of the library fire. The Mistress
and the Master had gone to town for the day.
The house was lonely, and the two chums were
left to entertain each other.

The Boy was reading a magazine. The dog
beside him was blinking in drowsy comfort at
the fire. Presently, finishing the story he had

been reading, the Boy looked across at the sleepy dog.

"Wolf," he said, "here's a story about a dog. I think he must have been something like you. Maybe he was your great-great-great-great-grandfather. He lived an awfully long time ago —in Pompeii. Ever hear of Pompeii?"

Now, the Boy was fifteen years old, and he had too much sense to imagine that Wolf could possibly understand the story he was about to tell him. But, long since, he had fallen into a way of talking to his dog, sometimes, as if to another human. It was fun for him to note the almost pathetic eagerness wherewith Wolf listened and tried to grasp the meaning of what he was saying. Again and again, at sound of some familiar word or voice inflection, the collie would pick up his ears or wag his tail, as if in the joyous hope that he had at last found a clue to his owner's meaning.

"You see," went on the Boy, "this dog lived in Pompeii, as I told you. You've never been there, Wolf."

Wolf was looking up at the Boy in wistful excitement, seeking vainly to guess what was expected of him.

"And," continued the Boy, "the kid who owned him seems to have had a regular knack for getting into trouble all the time. And his dog was always on hand to get him out of it. It's a true story, the magazine says. The kid's father was so grateful to the dog that he bought him a solid silver collar. Solid silver! Get that, Wolfie?"

Wolf did not "get it." But he wagged his tail hopefully, his eyes alight with bewildered interest.

"And," said the Boy, "what do you suppose was engraved on the collar? Well, I'll tell you: *'This dog has thrice saved his little master from death. Once by fire, once by flood, and once at the hands of robbers!'* How's that for a record, Wolf? For *one* dog, too!"

At the words "Wolf" and "dog," the collie's tail smote the floor in glad comprehension. Then he edged closer to the Boy as the narrator's voice presently took on a sadder note.

"But at last," resumed the Boy, "there came a time when the dog couldn't save the kid. Mount Vesuvius erupted. All the sky was pitch-dark, as black as midnight, and Pompeii was buried under lava and ashes. The dog could easily have got away by himself,—dogs can see in the dark, can't they, Wolf?—but he couldn't get the kid away. And he wouldn't go without him. You wouldn't have gone without me, either, would you, Wolf? Pretty nearly two thousand years later, some people dug through the lava that covered Pompeii. What do you suppose they found? Of course they found a whole lot of things. One of them was that dog—silver collar and inscription and all. He was lying at the feet of a child. The child he couldn't save. He was one grand dog—hey, Wolf?"

The continued strain of trying to understand began to get on the collie's high-strung nerves. He rose to his feet, quivering, and sought to lick the Boy's face, thrusting one upraised white fore-paw at him in appeal for a handshake. The Boy slammed shut the magazine.

"It's slow in the house, here, with nothing to do," he said to his chum. "I'm going up the lake with my gun to see if any wild ducks have landed in the marshes yet. It's almost time for them. Want to come along?"

The last sentence Wolf understood perfectly. On the instant he was dancing with excitement at the prospect of a walk. Being a collie, he was of no earthly help in a hunting-trip; but, on such tramps, as everywhere else, he was the Boy's in-separable companion.

Out over the slushy snow the two started, the Boy with his light single-barrelled shotgun slung over one shoulder, the dog trotting close at his heels. The March thaw was changing to a sharp freeze. The deep and soggy snow was crusted over, just thick enough to make walking a genuine difficulty for both dog and Boy.

The Place was a promontory that ran out into the lake, on the opposite bank from the mile-distant village.   Behind, across the highroad, lay the winter-choked forest.   At the lake's northerly end, two miles beyond The Place, were the reedy marshes where, a month hence, wild duck would congregate. Thither, with Wolf, the Boy ploughed his way through the biting cold.

The going was heavy and heavier.   A quarter-mile below the marshes the Boy struck out across the upper corner of the lake.   Here the ice was rotten at the top, where the thaw had nibbled at it, but beneath it was still a full eight inches thick; easily strong enough to bear the Boy's weight.

Along the grey ice-field the two plodded.   The skim of water, which the thaw had spread an inch thick over the ice, had frozen in the day's cold spell.   It crackled like broken glass as the chums walked over it.   The Boy had on big hunting-boots.   So, apart from the extra effort, the glass-like ice did not bother him.   To Wolf it gave acute pain.   The sharp particles were for-ever getting between the callous black pads of his feet, pricking and cutting him acutely.

Little smears of blood began to mark the dog's course; but it never occurred to Wolf to turn back, or to betray by any sign that he was suffering.   It was all a part of the day's work—a cheap price to pay for the joy of tramping with his adored young master.

Then, forty yards or so on the hither side of the marshes, Wolf beheld a right amazing phenomenon. The Boy had been walking directly in front of him, gun over shoulder. With no warning at all, the youthful hunter fell, feet foremost, out of sight, through the ice.

The light shell of new-frozen water that covered the lake's thicker ice also masked an air-hole nearly three feet wide. Into this, as he strode carelessly along, the Boy had stepped. Straight down he had gone, with all the force of his hundred-and-twenty pounds and with all the impetus of his forward stride.

Instinctively, he threw out his hands to restore his balance. The only effect of this was to send the gun flying ten feet away.

Down went the Boy through less than three feet of water (for the bottom of the lake at this point had started to slope upward towards the marshes) and through nearly two feet more of sticky marsh mud that underlay the lake-bed.

His outflung hands struck against the ice on the edges of the air-hole, and clung there.

Sputtering and gurgling, the Boy brought his head above the surface and tried to raise himself by his hands, high enough to wriggle out upon the surface of the ice. Ordinarily, this would

have been simple enough for so strong a lad.
But the glue-like mud had imprisoned his feet
and the lower part of his legs; and held them
powerless.

Try as he would, the Boy could not wrench
himself free of the slough. The water, as he stood
upright, was on a level with his mouth. The air-
hole was too wide for him, at such a depth, to get
a good purchase on its edges and lift himself
bodily to safety.

Gaining such a finger-hold as he could, he
heaved with all his might, throwing every muscle
of his body into the struggle. One leg was pulled
almost free of the mud, but the other was driven
deeper into it. And, as the Boy's fingers slipped
from the smoothly wet ice-edge, the attempt to
restore his balance drove the free leg back, knee-
deep into the mire.

Ten minutes of this hopeless fighting left the
Boy panting and tired out. The icy water was
numbing his nerves and chilling his blood into
torpidity. His hands were without sense of
feeling, as far up as the wrists. Even if he could
have shaken free his legs from the mud, now, he
had not strength enough left to crawl out of
the hole.

He ceased his uselessly frantic battle and stood
dazed. Then he came sharply to himself. For,
as he stood, the water crept upward from his

lips to his nostrils. He knew why the water seemed to be rising. It was not rising. It was he who was sinking. As soon as he stopped moving, the mud began, very slowly, but very steadily, to suck him downward.

This was not a quicksand, but it was a deep mud-bed. And only by constant motion could he avoid sinking farther and farther down into it. He had less than two inches to spare, at best, before the water should fill his nostrils; less than two inches of life, even if he could keep the water down to the level of his lips.

There was a moment of utter panic. Then the Boy's brain cleared. His only hope was to keep on fighting—to rest when he must, for a moment or so, and then to renew his numbed grip on the ice-edge and try to pull his feet a few inches higher out of the mud. He must do this as long as his chilled body could be scourged into obeying his will.

He struggled again, but with virtually no result in raising himself. A second struggle, however, brought him chin-high above the water. He remembered confusedly that some of these earlier struggles had scarce budged him, while others had gained him two or three inches. Vaguely, he wondered why. Then turning his head, he realised.

Wolf, as he turned, was just loosing his hold

on the wide collar of the Boy's mackinaw. His cut forepaws were still braced against a flaw of ragged ice on the air-hole's edge, and all his tawny body was tense.

His body was dripping wet, too. The Boy noted that; and he realised that the repeated effort to draw his master to safety must have resulted, at least once, in pulling the dog down into the water with the floundering Boy.

"Once more, Wolfie! *Once more!*" chattered the Boy through teeth that clicked together like castanets.

The dog darted forward, caught his grip afresh on the edge of the Boy's collar, and tugged with all his fierce strength; growling and whining ferociously the while.

The Boy seconded the collie's tuggings by a supreme struggle that lifted him higher than before. He was able to get one arm and shoulder clear. His numb fingers closed about an up-thrust tree-limb which had been washed down stream in the autumn freshets and had been frozen into the lake ice.

With this new purchase, and aided by the dog, the boy tried to drag himself out of the hole. But the chill of the water had done its work. He had not the strength to move farther. The mud still sucked at his calves and ankles. The big hunting-boots were full of water that seemed to weigh a ton.

He lay there, gasping and chattering. Then, through the gathering twilight, his eyes fell on the gun, lying ten feet away.

"Wolf!" he ordered, nodding towards the weapon. "Get it! *Get* it!"

Not in vain had the Boy talked to Wolf, for years, as if the dog were human. At the words and the nod, the collie trotted over to the gun, lifted it by the stock, and hauled it awkwardly along over the bumpy ice to his master, where he laid it down at the edge of the air-hole.

The dog's eyes were cloudy with trouble, and he shivered and whined as with ague. The water on his thick coat was freezing to a mass of ice. But it was from anxiety that he shivered, and not from cold.

Still keeping his numb grasp on the tree-branch, the boy balanced himself as best he could, and thrust two fingers of his free hand into his mouth to warm them into sensation again.

When this was done, he reached out to where the gun lay, and pulled its trigger. The shot boomed deafeningly through the twilight winter silences. The recoil sent the weapon sliding sharply back along the ice, spraining the Boy's trigger finger and cutting it to the bone.

"That's all I can do," said the Boy to himself.

"If anyone hears it, well and good. I can't get at another cartridge. I couldn't put it into the breech if I had it. My hands are too numb."

For several endless minutes he clung there, listening. But this was a desolate part of the lake, far from any road; and the season was too early for other hunters to be abroad. The bitter cold, in any case, tended to make sane folk hug the fireside rather than to venture so far into the open. Nor was the single report of a gun uncommon enough to call for investigation in such weather.

All this the Boy told himself, as the minutes dragged by. Then he looked again at Wolf. The dog, head on one side, still stood protectingly above him. The dog was cold and in pain. But, being only a dog, it did not occur to him to trot off home to the comfort of the library fire and leave his master to fend for himself.

Presently, with a little sigh, Wolf lay down on the ice, his nose across the Boy's arm. Even if he lacked strength to save his beloved master, he could stay and share the Boy's sufferings.

But the Boy himself thought otherwise. He was not at all minded to freeze to death, nor was he willing to let Wolf imitate the dog of Pompeii by dying helplessly at his master's side. Controlling for an instant the chattering of his teeth, he called:

"Wolf!"

The dog was on his feet again at the word; alert. eager.

"Wolf!" repeated the Boy. *"Go! Hear me? Go!"*

He pointed homeward.

Wolf stared at him, hesitant. Again the Boy called in vehement command, *"Go!"*

The collie lifted his head to the twilight sky with a wolf-howl hideous in its grief and appeal —a howl as wild and discordant as that of any of his savage ancestors. Then, stooping first to lick the numb hand that clung to the branch, Wolf turned and fled.

Across the cruelly sharp film of ice he tore, at top speed, head down; whirling through the deepening dusk like a flash of tawny light.

Wolf understood what was wanted of him. Wolf always understood. The pain in his feet was as nothing. The stiffness of his numbed body was forgotten in the urgency for speed.

The Boy looked drearily after the swift-vanishing figure which the dusk was swallowing. He knew the dog would try to bring help; as has many another and lesser dog in times of need. Whether or not that help could arrive in time, or at all, was a point on which the Boy would not let himself dwell. Into his benumbed brain crept the memory of an old Norse proverb he had read in school:

"Heroism consists in hanging on, one minute longer."

Unconsciously he tightened his feeble hold on the tree-branch and braced himself.

From the marshes to The Place was a full two miles. Despite the deep and sticky snow, Wolf covered the distance in less than nine minutes. He paused in front of the gate-lodge, at the highway entrance to the drive. But the superintendent and his wife had gone to Paterson, shopping, that afternoon.

Down the drive to the house he dashed. The maids had taken advantage of their employers' day in New York, to walk across the lake to the village, to a motion-picture show.

Wise men claim that dogs have not the power to think or to reason things out in a logical way. So perhaps it was mere chance that next sent Wolf's flying feet across the lake to the village. Perhaps it was chance, and not the knowledge that where there is a village there are people.

Again and again, in the car, he had sat upon the front seat alongside the Mistress when she drove to the station to meet guests. There were always people at the station. And to the station Wolf now raced.

The usual group of platform idlers had been dispersed by the cold. A solitary baggageman was hauling a trunk and some boxes out of the express-coop on to the platform; to be put aboard the five o'clock train from New York.

As the baggageman passed under the clump of station lights, he came to a sudden halt. For out of the darkness dashed a dog. Full tilt, the animal rushed up to him and seized him by the skirt of the overcoat.

The man cried out in scared surprise. He dropped the box he was carrying and struck at the dog, to ward off the seemingly murderous attack. He recognised Wolf, and he knew the collie's repute.

But Wolf was not attacking. Holding tight to the coat-skirt, he backed away, trying to draw the man with him, and all the while whimpering aloud like a nervous puppy.

A kick from the heavy-shod boot broke the dog's hold on the coat-skirt, even as a second yell from the man brought four or five other people running out from the station waiting-room.

One of these, the telegraph operator, took in the scene at a single glance. With great presence of mind he bawled loudly:

"MAD DOG!"

This, as Wolf, reeling from the kick, sought

to gain another grip on the coat-skirt. A second kick sent him rolling over and over on the tracks, while other voices took up the panic cry of "Mad dog!"

Now, a mad dog is supposed to be a dog afflicted by rabies. Once in ten thousand times, at the very most, a mad-dog hue-and-cry is justified. Certainly not oftener. A harmless and friendly dog loses his master on the street. He runs about, confused and frightened, looking for the owner he has lost. A boy throws a stone at him. Other boys chase him. His tongue hangs out, and his eyes glaze with terror. Then some fool bellows:

"Mad dog!"

And the cruel chase is on—a chase that ends in the pitiful victim's death. Yes, in every crowd there is a voice ready to raise that asinine and murderously cruel shout.

So it was with the men who witnessed Wolf's frenzied effort to take aid to the imperilled Boy.

Voice after voice repeated the cry. Men groped along the platform edge for stones to throw. The village policeman ran puffingly upon the scene, drawing his revolver.

Finding it useless to make a further attempt to drag the baggageman to the rescue, Wolf leaped back, facing the ever larger group. Back went his head again in that hideous wolf-howl.

Then he galloped away a few yards, trotted back, howled once more, and again galloped lakeward.

All of which only confirmed the panicky crowd in the belief that they were threatened by a mad dog. A shower of stones hurtled about Wolf as he came back a third time to lure these dull humans into following him.

One pointed rock smote the collie's shoulder, glancingly, cutting it to the bone. A shot from the policeman's revolver fanned the fur of his ruff, as it whizzed past.

Knowing that he faced death, he nevertheless stood his ground, not troubling to dodge the fusillade of stones, but continuing to run lakeward and then trot back, whining with excitement.

A second pistol-shot flew wide. A third grazed the dog's hip. From all directions people were running towards the station. A man darted into a house next door, and emerged carrying a shotgun. This he steadied on the veranda-rail not forty feet away from the leaping dog, and made ready to fire.

It was then the train from New York came in. And, momentarily, the sport of "mad-dog" killing was abandoned, while the crowd scattered to each side of the track.

From a front car of the train the Mistress and the Master emerged into a bedlam of noise and confusion.

"Best hide in the station, Ma'am!" shouted the telegraph operator, at sight of the Mistress. "There is a mad dog loose out here! He's chasing folks around, and——"

"Mad dog!" repeated the Mistress in high contempt. "If you knew anything about dogs, you'd know mad ones never 'chase folks around,' any more than diphtheria patients do. Then——"

A flash of tawny light beneath the station lamp, a scurrying of frightened idlers, a final wasted shot from the policeman's pistol,—as Wolf dived headlong through the frightened crowd towards the voice he heard and recognised.

Up to the Mistress and the Master galloped Wolf. He was bleeding, his eyes were bloodshot, his fur was rumpled. He seized the astounded Master's gloved hand lightly between his teeth and sought to pull him across the tracks and towards the lake.

The Master knew dogs. Especially he knew Wolf. And without a word he suffered himself to be led. The Mistress and one or two inquisitive men followed.

Presently, Wolf loosed his hold on the Master's hand and ran on ahead, darting back every few moments to make certain he was followed.

"Heroism—consists—in—hanging—on — one —minute—longer," the Boy was whispering de-

liriously to himself for the hundredth time; as
Wolf pattered up to him in triumph, across the
ice, with the human rescuers a scant ten yards
behind.

THE FOUL FANCIER

IN the sixth round of his fight with Kid Feltman, the end came. And it was not at all the end that anybody but Dan Rorke and Keegan, his manager, looked for.

For the outclassed and battered and wabbling Rorke won.

Two minutes earlier, no one in the Pastime Athletic Club auditorium would have bet a cancelled lottery ticket on Rorke's chances. And the result left the crowd as puzzled as was the raging Feltman himself.

No; Rorke did not see one sweet face in the throng—a face that nerved him to superhuman effort and victory. Nor did he spur himself to a Herculean last stand that won him the fight. That was not Dan Rorke's way. And most assuredly it was not the way of his manager and mentor, Red Keegan. The victory was won by subtler and less hackneyed methods.

Here, in brief, was the procedure:

At the end of the fifth round Dan had slumped back to his corner, dizzy and gone. Red Keegan's practised eye summed up his condition as it had summed up his chances during the past two rounds. And he whispered:

"Time's come for it, Danny boy! He's too many for you."

Danny boy needed no further amplifying of the order. Twenty times in the gym, under Keegan's shrewd tutelage, he had rehearsed what now he was about to do.

Rorke rose sluggishly, groggily, staggeringly, to the summons for the sixth round. He swayed drunkenly towards the centre of the ring. Seeing which, the crowd screeched to Feltman to sail in and finish him. Obligingly, Feltman prepared to obey the behest of his patrons. He took no chances of a possible trick by laying himself open. But, with all the zest that could include caution, he went for his worn-down opponent.

Rorke met the onslaught right gamely. He called on all his waning strength for one last desperate rally. And the crowd did homage to his gameness by howling approval.

Feltman was a wise man. He knew this false burst of power could not last. Sooner than waste himself in fighting back he covered and waited for the momentary flash to burn out.

But the cheering of the fickle crowd was too much for him. And after an instant of blocking and retreating he met the pathetically brief rally, foot to foot.

There was a flurrying exchange of close-quarters blows, Rorke spinning about so that his back was towards the referee. And, as he spun, Rorke screamed out in mortal agony. His gloved hands flew heavenward, pawing the air.

He sank to the canvas floor, doubled up like a jack-knife; his hands clutching spasmodically at his abdomen some two or three inches below the belt.

Feltman stepped back in astonishment. He had not struck below the belt. He could not account for Rorke's posture of anguish. But for the fallen man's face both Feltman and the perplexed referee would have branded the squirming and groaning antics as a pure fake. But there was nothing fakelike in the face that twitched above the writhing body. Rorke's swarthy visage had gone green white. It had the ghastly hue of death.

On the instant Red Keegan was leaning over the ropes, shaking his fist in Feltman's face, and squalling shrilly:

"*Foul!* Did y'see that, Mister Referee? Y'saw it! Y'couldn't miss seeing it! Foul! Look at the poor lad, will you? He's *dying!*"

The referee, Honest Roy Constantin, lived up to the record that had given him his nickname.

Rorke was rolling about the floor in torment. His face was better indorsement of his condition than would have been fifty doctors' certificates. Only by a foul could such agony have been caused.

Not alone was Rorke's manager claiming it, but fifty voices from boxes and bleachers were taking up the yell in the wontedly sheeplike fashion of fight fans. Honest Roy himself had been behind Rorke at the moment the blow was struck. But he had seen that Feltman was leading for the body. And he could deduce the rest.

While Kid Feltman frothed at the mouth with impotent fury, Honest Roy Constantin thereupon awarded the fight to Rorke—on a flagrant foul. And the whole thing was done on the strength of Rorke's facial aspect. If Constantin had chanced to be an actor instead of a poolroom czar he would never have been taken in by so simple a trick. For even in those days it was a common ruse on the stage.

Dan Rorke, at the outset of the round, had drawn in a deep breath; and he had held it. This, together with his wild exertions, had turned his complexion to a purple red. Then, suddenly, as he fell, he had relaxed his muscles and his breath; and had at once taken another breath and had rolled his eyes upward. The receding blood had left his face a chalky green. Long rehearsed acting had done the rest. After that first frenzied

glare at the referee he had let his head droop
and had hidden his slowly incarnadining cheeks
from further view. The one glimpse of his
corpse-like face was enough for Honest Roy.

"You see, Danny," apologised Keegan, when
he had half carried his principal to the dressing
room, "it was the only way out. We either mis-
judged that Feltman bird wrong or else we over-
played the big improvement you've been making
these past few months. One or the other. It
don't matter which. The way it lays, you ain't
good enough—not yet—to go up against a top-
notcher like him. I seen that before you'd been
in the ring two rounds. He was a-eating you
up. It was either pull the good old foul claim
or stand for a knock-out. I didn't dast give you
the office for any funny business. Not with
Honest Roy refereeing. He's a crank on square
fighting, Roy Constantin is. He'd 'a' spotted
any of our best ones. So I had to frame it, other
way round. But it was a close call, at that!"

When Red Keegan picked Dan Rorke out of
the night-shift puddler crew at the Pitvale Steel
Works he did so after a long psychological study.
This study dealt much with the young middleweight's rugged strength and gameness and his
natural skill as a fighter. But it concerned itself equally with Rorke's innate gifts for more
subtle things; among the rest, a certain crude

ability for acting. Then he had moulded the ignorant boy according to his own wily plans.

As a man, Keegan was not a marked success. As a crooked diplomatist, he had sparks of genius. Too fragile and too timid to hit a blow himself, he was a born ring general. And it was his joy and his talent to study out more foul tactics than occur to the normal fighter's bovine brain in the course of a life-time.

None of these manœuvres came under the head of "rough stuff" or even of "coarse work." There was a finesse to them all. They could be pulled —rightly learned by the right man—under the very nose of the average referee.

Not once, but six times, had Dan Rorke gone into the ring, coached by Keegan, and bested men who were his superiors. He had done it by a succession of crafty and murderous fouls, which the referee failed to bring home to him.

Twice, by unobtrusive butting, in the course of a clinch, he had ripened his half-stunned antagonist for an easy knock-out. Again, he had driven his specially shod heel down on the instep of Spider Boyce with such scientific force as to make the sufferer drop his guard long enough to let in a haymaker to the jaw. Surreptitious kneeing was another of his arts.

All these tricks seem broad and obvious in the telling. So would a full description of the method whereby a conjurer hauls a kicking rabbit out of an empty hat. It is all in the way it is done. And, thanks to Red Keegan's tireless rehearsing and to his own peculiar talents, Rorke did it in a way to defy casual detection.

When an overkeen referee happened to be the third man in the ring there were other tactics to fall back on. In such event and with a too formidable opponent, there were still divers means for wooing victory—the claim of foul and the white-faced anguish, for example. Twice before, in other sections of the fight map, had Rorke and Keegan worked this bit of acting.

As a result Dan Rorke was rising fairly fast in his profession. He was not of championship timber. He would never develop into such a contender; nor does one real-life fighter in fifty. But he was good enough to do all manner of things to dozens of fairly good men in the rank and file of the middleweight army. And the dollars were drifting in.

To Dan Rorke himself—fresh from the puddling gang, and seeing the fight game only through Red Keegan's gimlet eyes—there was nothing wrong or even doubtful in his own methods. He took his orders from Keegan; and his share of the cash profits. He did not bother his thick head about ethics.

It was a week after the Rorke-Feltman battle,

and while Kid Feltman was still making the sporting world ring with his cries of trickery and his clamour for a return match. Rorke and his manager had gone back to their home town of Pitvale; not only for a needed rest, but to let certain unjust and cruel accusations blow over. Rorke, some months earlier, had been installed in the biggest room of the manager's Pitvale bungalow; and had settled thus in the first semblance of a home he had ever known since his graduation from the orphan asylum, twelve years agone. Behind the bungalow was the rickety barn which served as his training quarters.

Dan's old fellow toilers of the Pitvale Steel Works had bet loyally on their former associate in his fight with the redoubtable Feltman. Even though their paladin had won on a foul, still he had won, and they had cashed in on their bets. Gratitude welled high in their souls. And it took a practical form.

On the morning of the eighth day after the match, a delegation of five puddlers invaded the Keegan bungalow at breakfast time; escorting among them a big young collie dog, gold and white in hue, classic in outline, kingly in bearing.

The pup had belonged to the foreman of the night shift, who was taking a job somewhere out West and could not carry his pet along. So the boys had bought him cheap; and now presented him in due and ancient form to Dan Rorke, as a pledge of their hero worship.

In all his twenty-four years Rorke never before had had a dog of his very own. Such luxuries had not been encouraged at the orphan asylum, nor at any of the steel-works boarding houses where he had since lived.

Now, at sight of the splendid beast, the friendship of a normal man for a good dog woke within him. In spite of Keegan's sour protests, the pup was installed in the bungalow as a permanent member of the household. In honour of the champion who just then was the idol of Rorke's profession, the newcomer received the historic name of "Jeff."

An instant and perfect liking sprang up between Jeff and his middleweight master. From the first the two were inseparable. For some reason best known to himself, the young collie accepted the fighter as his one and eternal lord; and lavished on him a single-hearted devotion he had never granted to his former uninterested owner.

To Rorke the dog was a revelation. His starved heart went out to the collie's staunch friendliness. His sluggish imagination was stirred to unguessed depths by the dog's flashes of cleverness and of gay loyalty. His vanity—

and something deeper—was touched to the quick by the deathless worship in his pet's eyes.

If Dan Rorke strayed through the town, for the sake of giving the Pitvalians the privilege of gazing on their foremost citizen, Jeff was always trotting gravely at his side. If he suppled his hard muscles by a ten-mile hike through woodland and over mountain, the collie's plumed tail was ever just ahead, as pacemaker for the trip.

At meals Jeff stretched himself out on the floor beside Rorke's chair, scorning to beg, but eagerly receptive of such food bits as were tossed to him. At night the dog slept outside Rorke's door, a keenly alert sentinel over his master's rest.

Once, down on Main Street, a Rorke fan swatted the fighter applaudingly on the back. In practically the same instant the swatter was on his own back in the street, with Jeff's teeth menacing him. The collie had misunderstood the motive of the blow, and, after the manner of his kind, had sprung to his demigod's defence.

This sealed once and forever Rorke's love for Jeff. The dog had risked dire punishment to ward off a fancied danger from him. It was wonderful—tremendous! Dan told of it, for the next six weeks, whenever he could find anyone to listen to his marvelious yarn. And he added so many unconscious details in the repeated telling that late comers in the succession of listeners were left with a vague impression that Jeff had beaten off fully a dozen armed men who had assailed the fighter.

Keegan used to groan in spirit whenever Dan pointed out Jeff to some chance caller and began the oft-told saga. One dog man earned Rorke's lifelong hatred and the many-adjectived appellation of liar by his tactlessness in saying:

"Why, most any good purp will do as much as that; if he thinks someone's trying to hurt the feller that owns him."

Dan Rorke was calmly certain that no other dog on earth would have had the pluck and the loyalty to do it. And gradually Jeff became to him a sort of fetish for everything that was noblest. Which perhaps was quite as natural as that a high-bred collie should deem Dan Rorke worthy of adoration.

On a slippery and slushy morning in early spring, some six months after dog and man formed their lifepartnership, Dan started through a corner of Pitvale for his daily hike. He had just won a foul-incrusted battle and had not yet signed up for another. In the interval before hard training should set in, he was keeping in shape by means of these daily tramps and by a little gym work.

He and Jeff came abreast of Vining's livery stable, and were about to swing past it when out through the open doorway flashed something tawny and big and ponderous. In other words, Vining's vile-tempered old mongrel English mastiff had caught scent of the approaching collie and had dashed forth to do battle with the stranger.

That was a cute trick of Vining's dog. He was a terror in the neighbourhood; this huge mastiff with the quarter streak of St. Bernard and the temper of a sick wildcat. And for years he had maintained his repute as local bully.

Even now, when age and weight were beginning to slow him down, he still revelled in the prospect of springing out upon some unwary and less warlike dog as it passed the stable; and doing his industrious best to kill it.

As it chanced, this was a street seldom used by Rorke. And Jeff and the mastiff had never before met. Jeff, mincing along on fastidious white toes through the slush, close behind his master, had no warning of the attack. The first hint of danger came when, out of the ever-watchful corner of his slanting dark eye, he chanced to see the whizzing brindled bulk bearing down upon him. There was no time to get out of the way; even had Jeff been of the breed that gets out of the way when peril shows its shining face. To the average dog, there would have been no chance to prepare for the impact. But the best type of collie is not an average dog. In his brain, though never in his heart, he harks back to his wolf ancestors.

It was this ancient wolf strain, now, that made the sedately pacing Jeff spin sidewise as though on a pivot; letting the mastiff fly past him, the flaring jaws missing his head by an inch.

The mastiff whirled, almost in mid-air, and came back to the assault. But as he charged a second time Jeff was not there. The collie had not run; he had merely side-stepped. And in the same motion his white eyetooth scored a deep furrow in the side of the charging foe.

Dan Rorke had swung aloft his walking stick to stop the unequal fight and rescue his chum, for he had heard of the brindled monster's prowess. But at this move from Jeff he let his striking arm drop, idle, and he sputtered aloud in stark admiration:

"Footwork, b'gee! And countering, too! Lord, but Jim Corbett might 'a' been proud of that stunt!"

Again the mastiff was charging in; lurching craftily, to drive his nimbler foe into the angle of door and wall, and thus to corner him and render his footwork useless. Jeff saw through the ruse, but he saw too late to escape.

Now, the collie was a scant eighteen months old. His chest and shoulders had not yet gained the proportions that would be theirs in another two years. Moreover, this was his first battle. Left to himself, he would never have sought trouble; for he was a friendly and frolicsome youngster who had met with nothing but kindliness in all his brief life.

But his every muscle and joint was as lithe as oiled whipcord. There was not a fleck of loose flesh on his wiry sixty-six-pound body. And behind his conscious brain burned not only the battle prowess but the uncanny shrewdness of his ancient vulpine forbears.

Back in the wilderness days, the wolf that could not hold his own in warfare and be ready for all surprises, was the wolf that died exceeding young and left no progeny. The wolf that won the right to have descendants was the wolf brave enough and quick-witted enough to transmit his life-saving traits to those descendants.

All this a thousand years ago; and Dan Rorke's pet collie was profiting by it.

When the mastiff charged him Jeff acted on pure instinct. Having shown his resentment at the effort to chew him up, he was now quite content to let the quarrel rest where it was. But apparently this dog mountain who had attacked him would not have it so. In fact, the mastiff had cornered him. And the only road to safety was to go through a foe nearly twice as big as himself.

This looked like an impossible task, yet Jeff tackled it. His hind quarters were wedged between the open door and the street wall. In front was the mastiff. The big dog was not charging now. No need to waste speed and rashness on a helplessly cornered victim. Head down, legs crouched, the mastiff crept on his waiting prey. There was a hideous menace in the crawlingly savage advance.

Up went Dan Rorke's stick again. Dan had gripped the weapon by the ferrule and he was measuring the distance between its clubbed handle and the giant mongrel's head. But, as before, he did not strike; for there was no need.

The mastiff gathered himself for a death spring. But Jeff sprang without waiting to gather himself. Jeff did not spring aloft, as did the other. He dived under the rearing forelegs, slashing one of them to the bone as he sped.

The mastiff snapped murderously at his whizzing foe, as Jeff passed under him. His ravening teeth closed on nothing but a bunch of golden ruff hair instead of reaching their goal in the collie's vertebræ. And the mouthful of fur was his sole asset from the encounter.

Roaring aloud with rage and with the pain of his flesh wounds, the mongrel bounded out of the corner and made for his escaped victim. Now Jeff had fought his way out of the trap at no worse loss than a bunch of neck hair. The whole world lay before him as an avenue of retreat. No domestic animal but the greyhound can pass a strong young collie in a footrace. And assuredly this unwieldy mastiff could never have hoped to overhaul him.

But a queer change had come to the friendly youngster during that ugly moment in the corner. He, who had always been on jolly terms with everyone, had been set upon in unprovoked fashion while he was minding his own business. He had been threatened with death; for a less clever dog than Jeff could not have failed to read red murder in the mastiff's bloodshot eyes.

More, a wad of his fur had been yanked out in most painful fashion. And, for the first time in his eighteen pleasant months of life, hot wrath surged up in the collie's friendly heart. This giant was not going to treat him so and get away with it scot-free. The battle yell of his wolf ancestors burst from Jeff's furry throat.

As the mastiff turned he faced a wholly different antagonist from the astonished puppy he had set upon in the corner. Ruff abristle, head down, snowy fangs glinting from under his upwrithing lip, young Jeff flew to meet him like a fluffy catapult. And a truly epochal fight was on.

The mastiff went at his work with veteran ferocity and method, born of fifty death fights. But he had run up against something unique in his long experience. Jeff was not there. Or rather, Jeff was everywhere at once and nowhere in particular. He was in and out and over and under; never wasting time in seeking for a permanent hold, but nipping, tearing or slashing, and then striking at almost the same instant for some totally different part of the mongrel's big body.

The mastiff reared and thrashed about, ever striving to pin his eel-like adversary under him; to crush him down by dint of vast weight; to pinion him while the heavy foam-flecked jaws should find their death-hold. But Jeff had an annoying fashion of not staying in any one place long enough to be annihilated. And at every impact his white teeth were leaving their red mark.

"It's—it's Corbett and Sullivan, all over again!" blithered Dan Rorke, his expert eye following each move, his soul afire with prideful ecstasy at his untried chum's marvellous war genius. "Will you look at that footwork!" he exhorted high heaven and the fast-gathering knot of spectators.

Then his triumph song became a grunt.

The mastiff, in one of his mad lunges, had found his mark. His jaws closed on Jeff's fur-padded shoulder; and he hung on. With one wrench of his bull head he bore the slighter dog to earth and began to grind his jaws into the shoulder he had seized.

For a moment Jeff writhed and flung himself about impotently in the fearsome grip. In that instant of futile heaving his eyes sought and met Rorke's. And in the flashing gaze there was no tinge of fear or of appeal. It was as though he tried to assure the man that he had fought his best and that he was sorry he could do no better.

But before Dan's stick could go up there was a new flurry of fur and flesh, and Jeff's sharp teeth had sunk in agonising style deep into one of the mongrel's thick pads. The pain was so sudden and acute that the mastiff loosed his merciless shoulder grip, to lunge for the collie's head. And in that brief instant Jeff was not only on his feet and free, but was back at the assault with all his primal zest.

The mastiff, bleeding and almost breathless, reared for another attack. His cut hind foot clawed at a film of ice on the slippery pavement. He lost his balance and fell floundering on his back in the slush. For a second he lay there, stunned, for his head had hit the edge of the open door as he fell, and his brindled throat was exposed and defenceless.

"Now's your chance, Jeff!" chortled Rorke deliriously. *"Finish* him!"

But the collie did not take the chance. As the mongrel tumbled backward, Jeff had darted in at him. But, when he saw the huge brute prone and helpless on the ground, the collie for some innate sportsmanly reason forbore to fly at the inviting throat and rip out the jugular.

Instead, looking down in grave wonder at the sprawling and kicking mastiff, Jeff took a step backward and stood, ears cocked, head on one side, slender body still braced for action, waiting for the fallen dog to rise.

Dan gasped. Then he swore aloud.

The worn-out mongrel staggered to his feet, all the fight knocked out of him by the stunning head blow and by loss of blood. Jeff danced forward afresh to the fray. But, tail between legs, the mastiff turned and limped off into the stable. His back and the slipping hind legs offered rare chance for the victor to clinch his hard-won conquest. But Jeff only stared in mild interest after his beaten enemy. Then, limping a bit from his shoulder wound and panting fast from his fierce exertions, he trotted over to Dan Rorke and thrust his wet muzzle into his master's hand as if in quest of sympathy or praise.

He got both.

Fairly crowing with exultation Dan dropped

his stick and flung both arms about his scarred
pet in a breath-taking bear hug.

"Gee, but you're the real thing, Jeffie!" he
carolled, fondling the inordinately happy dog.
"Of all the pups that ever happened you're—
you're that pup! Say"—appealing to the crowd
—"did you birds ever see the like of this feller's
footwork? Did you? And did you see how he
wouldn't pitch into that big stiff when he was
down and out? Some white man, I'll say! Come
on home, Jeff! That shoulder of yourn will
stand some patching. C'mon, Champ! Gee,
but I sure named you after the right man!
There ain't anything double your weight can
lay a glove on you!"

Red Keegan pattered home excitedly from a
morning visit to the Pitvale Hotel. In his hand
he was brandishing a telegram that had been received at the hotel telegraph desk while he was
there. He made his way on hurrying feet to
the barn back of the bungalow, which served
his fighters as a gym, and where, at this time
of day, Rorke was reasonably certain to be
dawdling with the punching bag.

He came upon Dan, kneeling beside his collie
and washing out lovingly a deeply ragged cut in
the dog's right shoulder. At sight of the manager Rorke broke forth into a gleeful recital of
the bout between Jeff and the mastiff. But he

had scarcely gotten through the first sentence when Keegan cut him short.

"That c'n wait!" decreed the manager, waving the telegram. "This can't. Listen! I've cinched Feltman, at last. For right here in Pitvale. Main bout for the Athaletic Carn'val, next month. Four thousand dollars! Biggest purse ever! Those carn'val guys don't seem to care how they spend it. And they count on your being a star attraction, here in Pitvale. Remember we figgered they'd do that."

"Uh-huh," assented Rorke, unimpressed. "But say, Red, you'd ought to 'a' seen the way Jeff lit into him, after he'd fought his way out of that corner! He——"

"Shut up!" commanded Keegan, with the exquisite courtesy of his kind. "Here we're landing the biggest thing we've ever pulled off, and you go gassing 'bout a measly dog fight! I tell you——"

"Well," retorted Dan, nettled at his manager's tone and still more at his total dearth of appreciation for Jeff, "I don't see as there's anything to put on a silk shirt for, in the bunch of news you've lugged home with you. When I fought Feltman, back in August, you and Bud Curly would 'a' had to carry me out'n the ring, heels forward, if we hadn't been able to swing that white-in-the-face claim of foul. I've gone ahead some since then, I know that, but I don't figger I've gone ahead far enough to stop Kid Feltman. And we can't try the same white-face stunt a second time on him. He'll be watching for it. So will the ref'ree, whoever he is. You act like you'd brang home a gold mine, Red. Looks to me like you'd carted back a hornets' nest. How's the purse going to be split? A lad like Feltman'll want to——"

"Danny," interposed Keegan with weary scorn, "you talk even foolisher'n you look. And you look foolisher'n any other man the Lord ever bothered to pin a face onto. I told you, a month ago, the way I was aiming to work this thing. If you've got more int'rest in how you're bandaging that cur's shoulder than in the way we're due to make a killing, there's no use going over it all again to you. I remember, last time, you were so busy teaching Jeff to speak for bones that you didn't more'n half listen to me. And now I s'pose I got to say it all over again."

He sighed. It was the sigh of a martyr. But Dan did not answer. With worried tenderness he was twining about Jeff's hurt shoulder a festoon of witch-hazel-soaked bandage. With patience—an ostentatious and grunt-punctuated patience—Keegan waited until the first-aid task was ended and the bandaged collie was curled up at his master's feet. Then he spoke.

"Feltman's been after that return fight with us," he began with laboured detail and as if talking to a mental defective, "till he's got so he'd pretty near be willing to get into the ring with you blindfold and with both hands tied behind him. Maybe you know that, if you know anything. Which you don't. He's itching to square himself for that won-on-foul of ours. And I've been letting him itch, till he wouldn't gag on terms. But, at that, it's a miracle we've landed him. Anyone with a grain of sense ought to see through it.

"First, I juggle the carn'val crowd into making him and his manager stand for Sol Kampfmuller as ref'ree. If there's anything Sol knows less about than ref'reeing a fight I'd like to know what it is. Being sporting ed'tor of the *Chronicle* here, he thinks he knows it all, and that what he don't know he suspects. I've seen him ref'ree two fights. Why, that poor Ocity wouldn't know a foul if it was printed out for him on a raised map! Anyone could get by with murder, with him as ref'ree. It's 'most a shame to try the real classy stunts on him. Any raw work'd do.

"Feltman's nearer a topnotcher than ever you'll get to be in fifty years, but he's a numbwit. You could hit him with an axe in the ring, before he'd find out he was being fouled. So there's your comb'nation—a chucklehead ref'ree and a fair-fighting guy who don't know how to watch out for fouls. And then there's you, who I've learned to be the best lad at slick fouling in the whole business.

"Why, it's too easy! It's a crime. You c'n cripple or dizzy him in the very first round if you've a mind to. And as often after that as you need. Then, keep remembering that four-thousand-dollar purse, with eighty per cent for the winner. And even a minus-brain like yours ought to be able to figger out the answer. We'll start you training, to-morrow. I've a couple of corking new ones I've worked out lately. One of 'em's a killer. And both of 'em smooth enough to get past most any ref'ree, let alone Sol Kampf-muller and that carn'val crowd. We'll work 'em out and brush up on a few of the old ones too. So——"

"Funny thing!" spoke up Rorke, his hand on the dog's head. "Funny think 'bout Jeffie, here! He had a dandy chance to rip the throat out of that Vining dog; and he wouldn't do it, just because the dog was down and couldn't help him-self! What d'you think of that, Red? Just because the other dog was down. No ref'ree to penalise him for fouling, either. He just step-ped back, kind of politelike, and——"

"For the love of Mike!" groaned the irate

manager, "will you stop jawing about that bum cur and——"

"Then," pursued Rorke serenely, "when Vining's dog turned tail and sneaked away, Jeff had the chance of his life to tear in and do all sorts of damage. But he didn't. Wouldn't fight foul —the grand little cuss!"

Rorke fell silent. The manager stared at him in lofty and wordless contempt, but Dan did not see him. Still patting Jeff's head aimlessly and brooding over the couchant dog with puckered half-shut eyes, he sat there. Dan Rorke was thinking; and thought, to him, was as difficult as it was rare. Presently he spoke again— in a rumbling, ruminating mutter.

"Wouldn't fight foul, Jeff wouldn't," he repeated. "Fought like a bearcat, so long as the scrap was even. But not a foul stunt from first to last. Wouldn't win on a foul. He couldn't tell but what that big mutt would get up and tear him in half, like he'd just come plenty close to doing. But Jeff wouldn't tackle him while he was down. Wouldn't——"

"Say!" put in Keegan. "I'm going to the house to write a letter and then send off a wire. Keep right on talking, please, all the while I'm gone. Keep on telling about that dog fight. Then, by the time I get back, maybe the most of it will have got out'n your system and you can think of real things again. So long."

Dan Rorke did not obey his manager's elephantinely sarcastic request to go on talking of the dog fight in Keegan's half-hour absence. But he did the next thing—he went on thinking about it. At least his wontedly sluggish thoughts fixed themselves on one detail of the fray, clinging to it like leeches and sending forth ramifications into the far and unused recesses of his brain.

These thoughts were not put into words. But their gist may be translated roughly into English, somewhat as follows:

Jeff had fought without training or precept. He had followed his own instincts. He had fought according to his nature. Thus, he had fought fair. He had fought clean. Not only had he disdained to make use of any crooked advantage, but he had risked defeat and possible death sooner than to foul.

Jeff was a dog.

Dan Rorke was a man.

How did Dan Rorke win his fights? Three out of four of them he won by clever fouling. He fought crooked. That was how he made his living—by tactics his own dog would not stoop to.

The collie looked on Dan as the greatest person under the sun. Yet the dog fought square and Dan fought foul. What was the answer?

It was a joke in fistic circles that Dan Rorke was the dirtiest fighter in that section of America; and that he managed to get away with it by sheer craftiness.

Dan had felt—still felt—a thrill of admiration for Jeff for fighting so fair. Wasn't it possible that the fight public might give that same sort of admiration to a man who was known to fight fair? Going a tottering mental step farther, wasn't it just barely possible that all reg'lar folks had that same little thrill of admiration for a fellow who was on the level in everything? It was a funny idea, of course, but——

Then again it was great to have someone, even a dog, look up to anybody as Jeff looked up to his master; and to think that master was the best man alive. What sort of mangy hypocrite was Dan Rorke to make his living crookedly, by super-fouling, while Jeff thought he was a saint?

The dog fought clean. The man fought dirty. Was the man lower than the dog? It was a rotten thought. But it had a whole lot of sense to it. If Jeff, here, could risk death sooner than fight foul, what was the reason why Dan Rorke——

At this point in the argument Dan stopped

and started all over, from the beginning. He was on the third complete review of it when Red Keegan came bustling back.

"Well," queried the manager briskly, "have you told yourself enough about the dog fight, so's you c'n remember it a while without telling it again?"

"I—I guess so," mumbled Dan uncertainly.

And he made excuse to get out of the way. He was still thinking; thinking hard and with a growing unhappiness. His thoughts were not yet crystallisable into words.

But next morning, after a night of less continuous slumber than he could recall in many a year, he dressed and started down to breakfast with a brand-new and granite-hard resolve in his tired mind. For once in his life he had solved a problem—had solved it all himself.

As he opened the door of his bedroom Jeff leaped eagerly up from his nightly vigil post across the outer threshold. Stiff as he was from his shoulder hurt, the dog gambolled gleefully round his master, patting at Dan's knees with his flying white paws, wriggling himself into an ecstatic interrogation mark, and whimpering with delight at the wonderful fact that his adored demigod was once more with him after ten whole hours of absence.

Thus, the world over, do the average run of

collies give morning salute to the man or woman they have accepted as their deity. And, as ever, the greeting warmed Dan Rorke's long-loveless heart. He stooped over and patted the silken head.

The collie growled in horrific menace and caught Dan's big hand between his mighty jaws as if to crush it. But the jaws did not exert the pressure of a fraction of an ounce on the firm flesh they had so playfully imprisoned. And the throaty growls were belied by a furious wagging of the plumed tail.

This was Jeff's favourite game with his master. With no one else would he deign to play.

Dan rumpled the dog's soft ears, and looked with a queer new timidity into the deep-set dark eyes of his chum. At the unquestioning joyous devotion he saw there, he felt a tiny twinge of relief. Something he had let himself fear, in the long night's meditations, had not yet begun to happen. There was still time, plenty of time.

And, his resolve firmer than ever, he ran down to the breakfast room, where Red Keegan was already seating himself at the table.

"*Chron'cle's* got a spread on your match with Feltman!" was the manager's morning salutation. "First page; and again, under Kampf-muller's sign'ture, on the sporting page. We've got a good start, all right. Now——"

"If it isn't too late," said Dan hesitantly, "I kind of wish you'd cancel the match. I don't honest think I c'n stop Kid Feltman; for all you say I've gone ahead this half year. And it's more'n an even bet he c'n stop me inside the limit. So I've been thinking it over, and I guess you'd best call it off; or get 'em to subst'toot some easier guy than Felt——"

"Good Lord!" snorted Keegan. "Do you set there and tell me you don't even remember from yesterday the layout for that fight? Of all the——"

"Yep," answered Rorke, sullenly playing with his food and glancing down for encouragement at the collie lying on the floor beside him. "Yep. I remember it all right, all right, Red. I remember it. But it won't work. That's why I——"

"Won't *work?*" thundered Keegan, glaring across at his embarrassed star. "Why the blue hell won't it work? It's the prettiest set-up we've ever handled. There ain't a flaw to it. Won't work, hey? Why the——"

"Because," replied Dan sheepishly, yet firm as stone, as he glowered back at his manager, "because that set-up of yours calls for a heap of fancy fouling. And—and I'm—I'm off fouling. Off it for keeps. That's——"

Red Keegan broke in on the halting announcement with a sound that a turkey might have produced had its tail feathers been pulled violently at the moment it chanced to be gobbling. The result was a noise that brought Jeff to his feet with a jump; his tulip ears cocked, his eyes aglow with excited inquiry; a series of staccato barks racketing from his furry throat.

"Lay down, Jeffie!" ordered Dan. "He ain't going to bite me. He's only——"

"Are you plumb crazy, Dan?" sputtered the manager. "Or is it a bum little joke? Off fouling, hey? What's going to keep you from the hungry house if——"

"If clean scrapping won't keep me fed," answered Rorke, "I'll go get back my job in the puddling gang. Anyhow, it goes like I said. I'm off fouling. Now go ahead and swear!"

But Red Keegan did not go ahead and swear. Profanity was a very present help to the nerves, in the event of stepping on a tack or mashing one's thumb with a hammer or on hearing that one's wife had eloped. But this matter lay too deep for swearing.

Blusteringly, then flatteringly, then coaxingly and at last with the tremolo stop pulled far out, he pleaded with Dan. He painted in glowing colours the middleweight's comfortable rise from the ranks and the golden future that awaited him under Keegan's guidance, if only he would have the intelligence to stick to his manager's tuition and not get fool ideas that he could fight on the square well enough to keep himself warm. He foretold a future of failure and gutter poverty should the fool hold to this suicidal new plan.

To all of which Dan Rorke answered not a word; but sat glumly frowning at the spotty table-cloth and occasionally letting his fidgety hand rest for a second on Jeff's head. When at last Keegan had run down and was bereft equally of breath and vocabulary and emotion, Dan began to speak. He did not look at the puffingly apoplectic manager, but rambled on as if addressing the hole in his napkin.

"A feller told me once," he began, "that there's mighty little a collie dog don't know. And I've seen enough of Jeff, here, to find out that's so. Jeff c'n tell when I'm blue and when I'm tickled, just by looking at me. It—it'd be funny, wouldn't it, if he c'd get to telling, by looking at me, that I'm not on the square? A dog with Jeff's breeding and Jeff's sense would sure be too high-toned to pal with a crook, if he knowed it. And he knows a lot of things I'd never s'posed a animal c'd know."

He looked down again at the collie as if for moral support. At the worry in his master's glance, Jeff's dark eyes took on a glint of eager concern. He laid one white little forepaw on Dan's muddy boot, and whined softly, far down in his throat. Thus encouraged, Rorke went on:

"That's only one end of it. Here's another: A man's pretty low down in the list, ain't he, if he can't even fight as square as his dog c'n fight? A clean dog's sure got a right to a clean master. Them folks yesterday was all praising Jeff. They wasn't praising him so much for licking the big feller as for licking him, *clean;* and for not fouling when he had a chance to. I c'd see that myself. Well, I sh'd think folks would feel that way about a man that fights clean. Anyhow," he finished defiantly, "no poor dog's going to have the right to say he's a whiter man than what I am. I been thinking it all over. And that's the answer. I'm off fouling. Like I said."

For the next twenty-four hours the bungalow and the gym were vibrant with the sounds of argument and vituperation. Keegan exhausted his every battery. And—like most men who think slowly and seldom—Dan Rorke grew more and more firmly set in his queer resolution, the more he discussed it.

Even stolid Bud Curly, his sparring partner and general handy man round the gym, was moved to bewilderment by the once-docile fighter's firmness in resisting the all-powerful boss.

Only once, in a day and night of abusive exhortation on Red's part, did Dan lose for an instant his sullen calm. That was when Keegan grumbled:

"It's all the damn' dog's fault. It's him that's turned you loony. I've got a good mind to shoot him. Then maybe you'll——"

"You shoot that dog," flared Rorke, striding up to the little manager, his thick fingers working convulsively, "and, by the good Lord, I swear I'll break your neck over my knee; if I go to the chair for it. That goes for *you*, too, Curly! If you think I'm bluffing, you'd best change your mind—unless you're sick of staying alive. It goes!"

To Bud Curly's surprise the irascible Red did not retort. Instead, he stood looking long and earnestly at the raging fighter. Then he said with conciliatory calm:

"Nobody wants to hurt the purp, Dan. Climb down off the ceiling. And if you're so dead set on playing the fool—well, I s'pose I'll have to trail my bets along with yours. You can't lick Feltman on the square. But it won't be my fault if you don't put up the best fight of your life ag'in him. It's too late to cancel the match now. All me and Curly c'n do is to train you to the minute and trust to luck for the rest."

Glad to have won his sorry point, Dan settled

down with grim energy to the task of training. He knew how slight were his chances of victory. Yet he was ready to meet the suddenly reconciled Keegan halfway, by training at his level best.

Feltman and a little retinue came to Pitvale, in order to be on the ground, and to avoid travel before the fight. They set up training quarters scarce two blocks away from Keegan's bungalow.

For nearly a month the two rivals wrought at their preparations for the battle. Once or twice on hike or sprint they chanced to meet in street or highroad. And such well-rehearsed chance meetings, with their mutual scowling frigidity, served Kampfmuller as splendid "grudge-fight" copy for the *Chronicle*.

The fight was to be held in the Pitvale Coliseum, a vast and barnlike structure originally built for state conventions and for summer Chautauqua lectures. It was scheduled for ten o'clock on the night of April second.

On the morning of April second Dan Rorke awoke from a ten-hour sleep, ran under the shower, rubbed down, slipped into his clothes, and started for breakfast with the appetite of a longshoreman. His nerves as well as his physique had profited by his hard and wise training.

If he was due to end the day in defeat, at

least the thought of it had not marred his night's rest or his appetite.

Outside his bedroom door he paused as usual for his morning frolic with Jeff. But Jeff was not there.

In all their long months of chumship this was the first morning that Jeff had not been on hand to greet with noisy delight his new-awakened master. And the dog's absence perplexed Rorke.

Downstairs he went, hoping to find the collie waiting for him in the dining-room. The room was empty. Whistling for the missing Jeff, Dan went out on the tiny front porch. No dog was in view. But he saw Keegan and Bud working with scrambly haste at a far end of the yard, piling shovelfuls of fresh dirt into what looked like a new-dug hole under the yard's one fruit tree.

Before Dan could call out, Curly happened to look up from his toil; and caught sight of him as he stood on the porch steps. Curly nudged Keegan and said something out of the corner of his mouth. The two exchanged nervous whispers; then Red dropped his spade and came hurrying towards the house, a labouredly artificial smile of greeting on his bothered face.

"Seen Jeff, anywhere?" asked Rorke, his puzzled eyes still on Curly, who was now patting the crumbly earth smooth over the filled excavation.

"Sure, I've seen him!" babbled Keegan with forced joviality, and looking anywhere rather than at Dan. "He was frisking round here just a minute ago. Must 'a' run down street, a ways. He'll be back soon. Come on in and eat! Sleep all right? I wasn't expecting you down for another ten minutes."

He had mounted the steps and almost forcibly was propelling Dan indoors.

"Looking for Jeff?" hollowly queried Bud Curly, coming up the steps behind him. "He's all right. Good old Jeff's all right. He was playing round in the gym just now."

Dan Rorke was the least subtle of men; and his brain was too small to hold suspicion. But a five-year-old child would have been keenly aware of the guilt and furtiveness in the manner of the two. Dan stopped short. He looked from one to the other of them; then at the fresh earth under the fruit tree.

"Red, you told me Jeff went down street!" he accused. "And now Bud says he's out in the gym. Which of you is lying? And why is either of you lying? And what were you burying out there? Speak up, one of you; or I'll go there and dig till I find out!"

He spoke with rising excitement. As he finished he made as if to start across the yard towards the tree.   Both men seized him and both began speaking at once.

"Jeff's all right!" insisted Red.   "And we was just spading up the earth to make that tree grow better.   It's too spindly.   And——"

"Yes," declared Bud in the same breath, "Jeff's feeling fine.   He'll be back pres'n'ly.   We was trying to see could we bury some garbage out yonder, 'stead of bothering to burn it. We——"

"Jeff is dead!" interrupted Dan, his voice all at once lifeless and flat.   "You been burying him. You don't want me to know.   He——"

The two others fidgeted guiltily.   Then, clearing his throat, Keegan said:

"I wanted to keep it from you, till after to-night, Danny.   I'm sorry.   Sorry, right down to the ground.   But since you've guessed that much of it I'd best tell you the whole thing.   Buck up and take it like a he-man, son.   After all, he was only just a dog. I'll buy you another one and——"

"There ain't any other one!" denied Rorke chokingly.   "There was only just Jeff!   Him and me.   And he was the chum I— What happened to him?" he demanded fiercely, swallowing very hard and trying to keep his voice steady and his eyes dry.   "Spill it!"

"Then take it!" cried Keegan harshly.   "Take

it straight, like a he-man had ought to take rotten news. This morning, when I went apast your door, there lay Jeff. He was stone-dead. I picked him up and brang him down on the porch. I knowed how it'd queer your nerve to find out he was gone. So I aimed to bury him and tell you he'd just strayed off, like; and that he would come home by and by. When I got him out on the porch I noticed he was all strained backward. And I'd seen dogs poisoned by strychnia before. There ain't any other poison that makes 'em look that way. He——"

"Poisoned!" yelled Dan in blind fury, catching at the word. "I'll find the swine that did it, if it takes every cent I got. And when I once get hold of him——"

"I beat you to it, Danny," continued Red's sorrowing tones. "I got Curly, here, to start digging a grave; and I piked down to Reuter's drug store. I had a sneaking s'spicion, already. Reuter was just opening up for the day when I got there. I asked him who had bought strychnia of him lately. The only strychnia he's sold in the past week was what he sold to a man yesterday; a feller who had a doctor's p'scription for it, and said he wanted it to poison cats that kep' him awake by yowling under his window. He got Reuter to tell him how to fix it up in a piece of meat——"

"Who was he?" broke in Rorke, his eyeteeth showing, his deep voice a half-coherent growl. "Who——"

"The doctor that gave the man the p'scription," said Keegan slowly, "was that old down-and-out M. D. slob that Feltman has for a handy man. The feller that bought the poison and asked Reuter how to fix it was—Kid Feltman. He——"

The manager got no further. Dan Rorke was out of the door and down the steps at one bound. It was only as he stopped to yank madly at the gate latch that Red and Curly overtook him and threw themselves bodily on the raging man. Even then it was a matter of minutes before their combined strength and Bud's wrestling grip, from behind, could quell him.

"Let me go!" he snarled, straining and biting at the detaining arms. "I'll settle with him before Jeff's cold! I'll——"

"You'll settle with him a heap better'n by trying to beat him up now, with his handlers and them to keep you from doing it," promised Keegan. "There's better ways. Lots better ways. You listen to me, Danny boy!"

Momentarily spent with his own fury, Rorke suffered himself to be dragged indoors. There Keegan faced him and said:

"You want to square yourself with Feltman —and more'n square yourself? Good. Then here's the way: Feltman's always hated you, ever since he lost to you that time. He's told fifty folks he'd get even. He's seen, and he's heard, how much store you set by Jeff. So he poisoned him to get back at you. Now here's how you'll get back at *him*: You was going to fight him clean. And he'd 'a' most likely won. So that ain't the way to fight him, if you want to settle with him for poor Jeff. The way to do is to sail in with every foul that can git past Kampfmuller. And a hay load of 'em c'n git past that ivory mine. Foul him from the start, with the murderingest set of fouls I've ever learned you. Cripple him so he'll be in the hosp'tal a year. Foul him into a dead one; and then punch his head off'n him and win as early in the fight as you want to. Git the idee? Foul him to death if you like. It's no worse'n he treated Jeff. The ring's the place to finish him. Not now, where you'd likely land up in the hoosgow before you'd more'n half hit him. Go to it!"

Dan grunted avid assent. And after breakfast careful rehearsing of old foul tactics and a study of new ones began.

As Dan Rorke, stripped and eager, sat in his hot dressing room under the auditorium that night, waiting for the summons to enter the ring, he had his first minute of solitary reflection throughout the whole Keegan-infested day. His manager was upstairs, wrangling with the carnival treasurer. Curly had gone to the ring to watch the wind-up of the second preliminary bout.

Dan was alone. In his heart still raged black hate and a craving for revenge. And he was sick with grief over his chum's murder.

While he sat there, the faint challenge bark of a dog—a collie, perhaps—from nowhere in particular, drifted to him through the ill-boarded dressing-room walls. At the sound Dan started violently.

"Jeff?" he whispered under his breath.

As if in answer to his call, the room all at once seemed athrob with the presence of his loved dog. In superstitious awe Dan peered about him. Then he straightened his bent body. And to an unseen Something he began to speak.

"We're going to pay up the bill in a few minutes now, Jeffie!" he promised. "Watch me!"

The foolish words started a new train of thoughts in the tormented brain. Watch him? The clean-fighting dog watch his master put up the foulest fight of his career? With the vision came sharp revulsion.

"Watch me, Jeff!" he repeated aloud. "Watch me do it! Watch me do it, square! *Square,* Jeffie, boy!"

While the odd exaltation was still upon him

Keegan and Curly came back to the dressing room to escort him to the arena.

The Pitvale Athletic Carnival crowd that night witnessed the bloodiest and most spectacularly ferocious battle in the annals of the local ring.

From the sound of the gong Dan Rorke was at his antagonist, forcing the fight at every point. Never once for the fraction of a second did he abandon the aggressive. Feltman showered upon him an avalanche of scientific punishment. But it failed to slow down that homicidal attack.

To Red Keegan's goggle-eyed dismay and despite his dumfounded inter-round pleas, Rorke fought as clean as a Galahad. Not once would he make use of even the safest foul. Not once would he seek to elude the dull referee by using the easiest of Keegan's carefully taught ruses.

He fought like a wild beast, but he fought like a fair one. Buoyed up by his insane hate for his enemy and by his stark craving for vengeance, he was as a man in delirium. The hideous punishment meted out to him had no visible effect on his maniac strength or speed. His madness did not preclude the use of all the skill he could muster, but it made him impervious to pain and to shock.

Round after round the fight slashed on, while

the crowd screamed and pounded in delight and while Red Keegan and Curly watched their madman with anguished eyes. Willing to take the heaviest blow, if only he might land as heavy a smash in return, Dan tore away at his foe.

Four times he was knocked down. Once he was unconscious for five seconds. But borne ever onward by that wild urge of revenge he came flying back to the combat with undiminished fury.

Flesh and blood could not stand the fearful tax indefinitely. Through all his mania Rorke began dimly to realise that there was a trifle less crushing vehemence in his own punches and less whirlwind speed in his onslaught. With every atom of will and of rage and of resolve in his whole cosmos, he scourged himself to renewed effort. The welter of blows avalanched upon him, unfelt.

Over and over in his hot brain he was saying:

"Watch me do it, Jeff! Watch me do it, *square!*"

And he fought on.

As Dan reeled back to his corner at the end of the hammer-and-tongs ninth round he heard, as from miles off, Keegan's voice whispering to him:

"Try out the good old stunts, Danny! 'Tain't too late, even yet. He's groggy. Try em. Curly tells me he's making a joke of how he killed Jeff. Says he kicked the poor purp yesterday, too, when he met him in the street. He——"

Dan heard no more. The minute's rest was over almost before it began. His ears ringing with the tale of the kick, he plunged back into the fight.

Feltman met him in midring; a horribly battered and staggering Feltman, who sought to improve on his minute's rest by feinting with the left and then aiming a great right swing for the head.

The swing did not land. Disregarding the feint, Rorke had bored in. The swing passed beyond him, while his two fists were greedily busy with infighting at his tired adversary's body. Across the ring and to the ropes, with all his ebbing force, he hammered Feltman. Against the ropes he drove him. Then, as Feltman rebounded from the impact, Dan flung every remaining sinew of strength into a cross-body right for the jaw.

It was a reckless blow, except as a counter. And Feltman saw it coming in time. But his worn-out guard would not obey the dazed brain's mandate quickly enough to block the mighty punch. Rorke's rage-driven right fist caught his opponent flush on the point of the chin. And Feltman sprawled prone on his face.

Quietly, non-dramatically, he lay there, dead to the world while the referee counted. At the count of eight Feltman tried instinctively to get up. But he succeeded only in rolling over on his back.

Cut to ribbons, bleeding, bruised, aching and all but blinded, Dan Rorke suffered the exultant Keegan and Bud to guide him down to his dressing room. He had won. He had thrashed the man who had poisoned Jeff. This much his dizzy senses told him.

But Feltman was still alive. And Jeff was dead. Dan's heart was like cold lead beneath his bruised ribs. His sensational victory was as ashes and dust to him. He was deaf to Keegan's hysterical adulation. Nothing mattered.

Bud Curly swung open the dressing-room door. Over the threshold swept a whirlwind of gold and white, barking rapturously and flinging itself upon Rorke's bleeding chest.

(Long afterwards Dan listened with a foolish grin on his swollen face while Keegan confessed the truly Keeganesque trick whereby he had sought to lure back his man to an acceptance of the sure-to-win foul tactics; of the hiding of Jeff in a neighbour's cellar for the day; and the spiriting of him into the dressing room after the fight began; of the coaching of Curly into indorsing the tale of poison and of Bud's part in the mock grave digging,—a digging timed nicely to coincide with Dan's appearance on the porch.)

All this, much later. But, for the instant, the only thing Dan Rorke knew was that his dead pet—or its ghost, it did not matter which—had come back to him; and that everything was once more tremendously worth while and that the world was a gorgeous place to do one's living in.

Forgetful of hurts and of weakness, he gathered the ecstatically squirming collie into his battered bare arms and babbled sobbingly:

"I did it, square, Jeff. I did it, square! You—you *saw* me do it, SQUARE "

THE GRUDGE

THIS is the strange yarn of three dogs. If the dogs had been humans, the story would have been on stage and screen long ago.

Frayne's Farms is the alliterative name for the hundred-acre tract of rich bottom land; in the shadow of the Ramapo Mountains,—a range that splits North Jersey's farm country for some twenty odd miles.

Back in these mountains are queer folk; whose exploits sometimes serve as a page story for some Sunday newspaper. Within forty miles of New York City as the crow flits, the handful of mountaineers are well-nigh as primitive as any South Sea Islanders. They are as a race apart; and with their own barbarous codes and customs.

Down from the mountains, in the starvingly barren winter time, every few years, a band of huge black mongrel dogs used to swoop upon the Valley, harrying it from end to end in search of food; and leaving a trail of ravaged henroosts and sheepfolds in their wake.

These plunderers were the half-wild black dogs of the mountaineers;—dogs blended originally from a tangle of diverse breeds; hound predominating; and with a splash of wolf-blood in their rangy carcases.

When famine and cold gripped the folk of the mountains, the dogs were deprived of even such scanty crusts and bones as were their summer portion. And, under the goad of hunger, the black brutes banded for a raid on the richer pickings of the Valley.

At such times, every able-bodied farmer, from Trask Frayne to the members of the Italian garden-truck colony, up Suffern-way, would arm himself and join the hunt. Rounding up the horde of mongrels, they would shoot fast and unerringly. Such few members of the pack as managed to break through the cordon and make a dash for the mountains were followed hotly up into the fastnesses of the grey rocks and were exterminated by trained huntsmen.

The mountaineers were too shrewd to make any effort to protect their sheep-slaying and chicken-stealing pets from the hunters. Much as they affected to despise the stolid toilers of the Valley, yet they had learned from more than one bitter and long bygone experience that the Valley men were not safe to trifle with when once righteous indignation drove them to the warpath.

For years after such a battle, the Valley was

wholly free from the marauding black-dog pack
Not only did the dogs seem to shun, by experience, the peril of invading the lowlands; but their
numbers were so depleted that there was more
than enough food for all of the few survivors, in
the meagre garbage of the mountain shacks.
Not until numbers and forgetfulness again joined
hands with famine, did the pack renew its Valley
forays.

When this story begins, a mere two years had
passed since the latest of the mongrel hunts.
Forty farmers and hired men, marshalled and
led by young Trask Frayne, had rounded up not
less than seventy-five of the great black raiders
at the bank of the frozen little Ramapo river,
which winds along at the base of the mountain
wall, dividing the Valley from the savage hinterland.

The pack's depredations had beaten all records,
that season. And the farmers were grimly
vengeful. Mercilessly, they had poured volley
after volley into the milling swarm of free-
booters. Led by a giant dog, ebony black and
with the forequarters of a timber wolf, the handful of remaining pillagers had burst through the
cordon and crossed the river to the safety of
the bleak hills.

It was Trask Frayne who guided the posse of
trackers in pursuit. For the best part of two

days the farmers kept up the hunt. An occasional far-off report of a shotgun would be
wafted to the Valley below, in token of some
quarry trailed to within buckshot range.

The gaunt black giant leading the pack seemed
to be invulnerable. No less than five times during that two-day pursuit some farmer caught
momentary sight of him; only to miss aim by
reason of the beast's uncanny craftiness and
speed.

Trask Frayne himself was able to take a hurried shot at the ebony creature as the fugitive
slunk shadowlike between two hillock boulders.

At the report of Trask's gun, the huge mongrel had whirled about, snarling and foaming at
the mouth and had snapped savagely at his own
shoulder; where a single buckshot had just
seared a jagged groove. But, before Frayne
could fire a second shot, the dog had vanished.

Thus the hunt ended. Nearly all the black
dogs of the mountaineers had met the death
penalty. It was the most thorough and success-
ful of the historic list of such battles. The raiders were practically exterminated. Many a year
must pass before the pack could hope again to
muster numbers for an invasion. And the Valley breathed easier.

Yet, Trask Frayne was not content. He knew
dog-nature, as it is given to few humans to know

it. And he could not forget the wily black giant
that had led the band of mongrels. The Black
was a super-dog, for cunning and strength and
elusiveness. That had been proven by certain
ultra-devastating features of the raid; as well
as by his own escape from the hunters.

And the Black still lived;—still lived, and with
no worse reminder of his flight than a bullet-cut
on one mighty shoulder. Such a dog was a
menace; so long as he should continue alive.

Wherefore, Trask Frayne wanted to kick himself for his own ill-luck in not killing him. And
he was obsessed by a foreboding that the Valley
had not seen the last of the Black. He could
not explain this premonition.

He could not explain it, even to himself. For
Valley history showed that each battue served as
a wholesome lesson to the black dogs for years
thereafter. Never, between forays, was one of
them seen on the hither side of the Ramapo.
Yet the idea would not get out of Frayne's head.

Trask had hated the necessary job of destroy-
ing the mongrels. For he loved dogs. Nothing
short of stark need would have lured him into
shooting one of them. His own two thoroughbred collies, Tam-o'-Shanter and Wisp, were
honoured members of the Frayne household.

Dogs of the same breed differ as much in char-
acter as do humans of the same race. For ex-

ample, no two humans could have been more widely divergent in nature than were these two collies of Trask's.

Tam-o'-Shanter was deep-chested, mighty of coat, tawny; as befitted the son of his illustrious sire, old Sunnybank Lad. Iron-firm of purpose and staunchly loyal to his master, Tam was as steady of soul as a rock. Whether guarding the farm-buildings or rounding up a bunch of scattered sheep that had broken bounds, he was calmly reliable.

He adored Trask Frayne with a worship that was none the less all-absorbing because it was so undemonstrative. And he cared for nothing and nobody else on earth—except Wisp.

Wisp had been the runt of a thoroughbred litter. He was slender and fragile and wholly lovable; a dainty little tricolour, scarce forty pounds in weight. Not strong enough for heavy work, yet Wisp was a gallant guard and a gaily affectionate house dog—the cherished pet and playfellow of the three Frayne babies. Also, he was Tam's dearest friend.

The larger collie, from puppyhood, had established a protection over Wisp; ever conceding to him the warmest corner of the winter hearth, the shadiest spot in the dooryard in summer, the best morsels of their joint daily meal. He would descend from his calm loftiness to romp with the frolicsome Wisp;—though the sight of stately Tam, trying to romp, was somehow suggestive of Marshal Joffre playing pat-a-cake.

In short, he loved Wisp, as he loved not even Trask Frayne. More than once, in the village, when a stray cur misunderstood Wisp's gay friendliness and showed his teeth at the frail little dog, Tam so far departed from his wonted noble dignity as to hurl himself upon the aggressor and thrash the luckless canine into howling submission.

He was Wisp's guardian, as well as his dearest comrade. Once in a very great while such inseparable friendships spring up between two collies.

One morning in June, Trask set forth for Suffern with a flock of sixty sheep. The day was hot; and the journey promised to be tiresome. So, when the two collies had worked the sixty out from the rest of the Frayne bunch of sheep and had started them, bleating and milling, toward the highroad, Trask whistled Wisp back to him.

"Home, boy!" he ordered, patting the friendly uplifted head and playfully rumpling the collie's silken ears. "Back home, and take care of things there, to-day. It's a long hot trip for a pup that hasn't any more stamina than you have. Wispy.

Tam and I can handle them, all right. Chase back home!"

The soft brown eyes of the collie filled with infinitely pathetic pleading. Wisp understood the meaning of his master's words as well as might any of the Frayne children. From birth he had been talked to; and his quick brain had responded; as does every clever collie's.

Wisp knew he had been bidden to stay at home from this delightful outing. And every inch of his body as well as his eloquent eyes cried aloud in appeal to be taken along. Yet, when, once more, Frayne petted his head and pointed towards the dooryard, the good little chap turned obediently back.

As he passed Tam, the two dogs touched noses; as if exchanging speech of some sort;—as perhaps they were. Then, disconsolately, Wisp trotted to the house and curled up on the door-mat in a small and furry and miserably unhappy heap. There he was still lying, his sorrowful eyes fixed on his master and on his busily-herding chum; as the huddle of sheep were guided out of the gateway into the highroad beyond.

Glancing back, Frayne smiled encouragingly at the pathetic little waiting figure at the door. Tam, too, paused, as he manœuvred the last silly sheep into the highroad; and stood beside Frayne, for a second, peering back at his chum. Under their momentary glance, Wisp made shift to wag his plumy tail once; by way of affectionate farewell.

Long afterward, Trask Frayne could summon up memory of the daintily graceful little dog, lying so obediently on the doormat and wagging such a brave goodbye to the master who had just deprived him of a jolly day's outing. Possibly the picture remained in Tam-o'-Shanter's memory, too.

It is to be hoped so. For never again were Frayne or Tam to see their lovable little collie chum.

Dusk was sifting down the valley from beyond the mountain wall that afternoon, when Trask Frayne turned once more into the gateway leading to his farm. At his side trotted Tam. It had been a hard day, both for dog and man. At best, it is no light task to marshal a flock of sixty bolting sheep along miles of winding road. But when that road is infested with terrifying motor-cars and when it goes past two or three blast-emitting stone-quarries and a railway, the labour is spectacular in spots and arduous at all times.

But, at last, thanks to Tam, the sheep had reached Suffern without a single mishap; and had been driven skilfully into the herd-pens. The seven-mile homeward tramp had been, by contrast, a mere pleasure-stroll. Yet, both the collie and his master were glad of the prospect of rest and of supper.

Frayne, reviewing the labour of the day, was pleased with his own foresight in making Wisp stay at home. He knew such an ordeal, in such weather, would have tired the delicate collie half to death.

Coming up the dusky lane from the house to meet the returning wanderers was a slender, white-clad woman. As he saw her, Frayne waved his hat and hurried forward at new speed. Thus, always, after one of his few absences from home, his pretty young wife came up the lane to welcome him. And, as ever, the sight of her made him forget his fatigue.

Yet, now, after that first glance, worry took the place of eagerness, in Frayne's mind. For his wife was advancing slowly and spiritlessly; and not in the very least with her wonted springy walk.

"The heat's been too much for her!" he muttered worriedly to Tam. "It's been a broiling day. She ought to have——"

But Tam was no longer beside him. The big collie had started ahead, toward the oncoming woman.

Usually, when Mildred Frayne came thus to greet her returning husband, Wisp was with her.

The little dog would bound ahead of his mistress, as Frayne appeared; and come galloping merrily up to him and Tam. Tam, too, always cantered forward to touch noses with his chum.

But, by this evening's dim light, Frayne could not see Wisp. Nor did Tam rush forward as usual. Instead, he was pacing slowly toward Mildred, with head and tail adroop.

As Tam had turned in at the gate beside his master, the collie had come to a convulsive halt. His nostrils had gone upward in a series of eagerly suspicious sniffs. Then, his shaggy body had quivered all over, as if with a spasm of physical pain. At that moment, Mildred's white-clad figure had caught his wandering eye. And he had moved forward, downcast and trembling, to meet her.

It was Tam,—long before Trask,—who discovered that Mildred was weeping. And this phenomenon, for the instant, turned his attention from his vain search for Wisp and from the confusingly menacing scents which had just assailed his nostrils.

Departing from his lifelong calm, the big dog whined softly, as he came up with Mildred; and he thrust his cold muzzle sympathisingly into her loose-hanging hand. Within him stirred all his splendid race's pitiful yearning to comfort a human in grief. So poignant was this craving that it almost made him forget the increasingly keen scents which had put him on his guard when he came in through the gateway.

"Hello!" called Trask, cheerily, as he neared his wife. "Tired, dear? You shouldn't have bothered to walk all this way out to meet me. After a rotten day like this, you ought to be resting. . . . Where's Wisp? Is he 'disciplining' me for making him stay home? I——"

Then he, too, saw Mildred was crying. And before he could speak again, she had thrown her arms around his neck; and was sobbing out an incoherent story, broken by an occasional involuntary shiver. Holding her close to him and asking eagerly futile questions, Trask Frayne, bit by bit, drew forth the reason for her grief.

Harry and Janet, the two older children, had gone down to the river, that noon, to fish, off the dock, for perch. Mildred, at an upper window where she was sewing, had watched them from time to time. For the river was high and rapid from recent rains.

But Wisp was with them; and she had experience in the little collie's sleepless care over the youngsters. More than once, indoors, Wisp had thrust his own slight body between a Frayne child and the fire. Again and again, at the dock, he had interposed his puny bulk and had shoved with all his force; when one or another of the babies ventured too close to the edge.

To-day, as she looked up from her sewing, she had seen the trio leave the dock and start homeward. Janet had been in the lead; swinging the string of perch and sunfish and shiners they had caught. They had skirted a riverside thicket on their way to the home-path.

Out from the bushes had sprung a gigantic lean dog, jet black except for a zig-zag patch of white on one shoulder. The wind had been strong in the other direction. So no scent of the dog had reached Wisp, who was dawdling along a bit to the rear of the children.

The black had made a lightning grab at the carelessly swung string of fish; and had snatched them away from Janet. As he turned to bolt back into the thicket with his stolen feast, Harry had caught up a stick and had charged in pursuit of the string of laboriously-caught fish. The child had brought his stick down with a resounding thwack on the head of the escaping beast.

The blow must have stung. For, instantly, the Black dropped the fish and leaped upon the tiny chap. All this in a single second or less.

But, before the mongrel's teeth could reach their mark, Wisp had flashed past the two startled children and had launched his weak body straight at the Black's throat.

Down went the two dogs in a tearing, snarling heap.

Mildred, realising how hopelessly unequal was the contest, had run to the aid of her beloved Wisp. Fleeing downstairs, she had snatched Trask's gun from its peg above the mantel, had seized at random a handful of shells; and ran out of the house and towards the river, loading the gun as she went.

By the time she came in sight, the Black had already recovered the advantage he had lost by Wisp's unexpected spring. By dint of strength and of weight, he had torn himself free of Wisp's weak grip, had flung the lighter dog to earth and had pinned him there. Right gallantly did little Wisp battle in the viselike grasp of the giant. Fiercely he strove to bite at the rending jaws and to rip free from the crushing weight above him.

But, as ever, mere courage could not atone for dearth of brute strength and ferocity. Undeterred by his foe's puny efforts or by the fusillade of blows from Harry's stick and from Janet's pudgy fists, the Black had slung Wisp to one side and had lunged once more at him.

This time he found the mark he sought:—the back of the neck, just below the base of the brain. He threw all his vast jaw-power into one terrific bite. And little Wisp's frantic struggles ceased.

The valiant collie lay inert and moveless; his neck broken.

Maddened by conquest, the Black tossed the lifeless body in air. It came to ground on the edge of the river. There, from the momentum of the toss, it had rebounded into the water. The swift current had caught it and borne it downstream.

Then, for the first time, the Black seemed to realise that both frantically screaming children were showering futile blows on him. With a snarl he turned on Harry. But, as he did so, Mildred's flying feet brought her within range. Halting, she raised the gun and fired.

She was a good shot. And excitement had not robbed her aim of steadiness. But excitement had made her catch up a handful of cartridges loaded lightly with Number Eight shot; instead of anything more deadly.

The small pellets buzzed, hornetlike, about the Black's head and shoulders; several of them stinging hotly. But at that distance, the birdshot could do no lasting damage. Nor did any of it chance to reach one of his eyes.

With a yell of pain he wheeled to face the woman. And she let him have the second barrel. Memories of former clashes with gunners seemed to wake in the brute's crafty brain. Snarling, snapping, shaking his tormented head, he turned and plunged into the narrow river; gaining the farther bank and diving into the waterside bushes before Mildred could think to reload.

The balance of the day had been spent in a vain search of the bank, downstream, for Wisp's lost body; and in trying to comfort the heartbroken children. Not until she had gotten the babies to bed and had soothed them to sleep did Mildred have scope to think of her own grief in the loss of the gentle dog who had been so dear to her.

"He—he gave his life for them!" she finished her sobbing recital. "He knew,—he *must* have known,—that he had no chance against that horrible monster. And Wisp had never fought, you know, from the day he was born. He knew that brute would kill him. And he never hesitated at all. He gave his life for the children. And— and we can't—can't even say a prayer over his grave!"

But Trask Frayne, just then, was not thinking of prayers. Deep down in his throat, he was cursing:—softly, but with much venom. And the nails of his hard-clenched fists bit deep into his palms.

"Black, with a white scar on the shoulder?" he said, at last, his own harsh voice not unlike a dog's growl. "Hound ears, and the build of a timber-wolf? Almost as big as a Dane; and bone-thin? H'm! That's my buckshot-scar on his shoulder,—that zig-zag white mark. To-morrow morning, I'm going hunting. Up in the mountains. Want to come along, Tam?"

But, as before, Tam was not there, when his master turned to speak to him. The collie had waited only long enough to note that the task of comforting the weeping Mildred had been taken over by more expert powers than his. Then he had trotted off towards the house; not only to solve the problem of these sinister scents which hung so heavy on the moist night air, but to find his strangely-absent chum, Wisp.

Circling the house, he caught Wisp's trail. It was some hours old; but by no means too cold to be followed by a collie whose scenting powers had once tracked a lost sheep for five miles through a blizzard. With Wisp's trail was mingled that of two of the children. And it led to the river-path.

True, there were other trails of Wisp's, that the sensitive nostrils caught. But all of them were older than this which led to the water. Therefore, as any tracking dog would have known, Wisp had gone riverward, since he had been near the house. And down the path, nose to ground, followed Tam-o'-Shanter.

He did not move with his wonted stolidity.

For, over and above the mere trail scent, his nostrils were assailed by other and more distressingly foreboding smells;—the smells he had caught as he had entered the gate;—the smells which grew ranker at every loping step he took.

In half a minute he was at the bank. And before that time, he had abandoned the nose-to-earth tracking. For now all around him was that terrible scent.

Back and forth dashed and circled and doubled Tam. And every evolution told him more of the gruesome story.

Here among the bushes had lain a strange animal; an unwashen and pungent and huge animal; apparently sleeping after a gorge of chicken or lamb. Here, along the path, had come the children, with Wisp behind them. Here the strange dog had leapt forth; and here,—alongside that string of forgotten and sun-blown fish on the ground,—Wisp and the stranger had clashed.

The dullest of scents could have told the story from that point:—the trampled earth, the spatters of dried blood, the indentation in the grass, where Wisp's writhing body had striven so heroically to free itself from the crushing weight above it and to renew the hopeless battle.

Wisp was dead. He was slain by that huge and rank-scented creature. His body had touched the river-brink, fully five feet from the scene of the fight. After that it had disappeared. For running water will not hold a scent.

Yes, Wisp was dead. He had been murdered. He had been murdered,—this adored chum of his,—by the great beast whose scent was already graven so indelibly on Tam's heartsick memory.

There, at the river-edge, a few minutes later, Trask Frayne found Tam-o'-Shanter; padding restlessly about, from spot to spot of the tragedy; whimpering under his breath. But the whimper carried no hint of pathos. Rather was it the expression of a wrath that lay too deep for mere growling.

At his master's touch, the great collie started nervously; and shrunk away from the caress he had always craved. And his furtively swift motion, in eluding the loved hand, savoured far more of the wolf than of the trained house dog. The collie, in look and in action, had reverted to the wild.

Tam trotted, for the tenth time, to the spot at the river-shore, where the Black had bounded into the water. Impatiently,—always with that queer little throaty whimper,—he cast up and down along the bank, in quest of some place where Wisp's slayer might perhaps have doubled back to land.

Presently, Trask called to him. For the first

time in his blameless life, Tam hesitated before obeying. He was standing, hock-deep, in the swirling water; sniffing the air and peering through the dusk along the wooded banks on the far side of the stream.

Again, and more imperatively, Frayne called him. With visible distaste, the collie turned and made his way back towards his master. Frayne had finished his own fruitless investigations and was starting homeward.

Half-way to the house he paused and looked back. Tam had ceased to follow him and was staring once more at the patches of trampled and dyed earth. A third and sharper call from Trask brought the collie to heel.

"I don't blame you, old boy," said Frayne, as they made their way towards the lighted kitchen. "But you can't find him that way. To-morrow you and I are going to take a little trip through the mountains. I'd rather have your help on a hunt like that than any hound's. You won't forget his scent in a hurry. And you know, as well as I, what he's done."

On the way to the house, Frayne paused at the sheepfold; and made a careful detour of it. But the inspection satisfied him that the fence (built long ago with special regard to the mountainpack's forays) was still too stout to permit of any dog's breaking through it. And he passed on to the house; again having to summon the newly-furtive collie from an attempt to go back to the river.

"He won't pay us another visit to-night, Tam," he told the sullen dog, as they went indoors. "He's tricky. And if he's really on the rampage, here in the Valley, he'll strike next in some place miles away from here. Wait till to-morrow."

But once more Tam did not follow his over-lord's bidding. For, at dawn of the morrow, when Trask came out of the house, shotgun in hand, the dog was nowhere to be found. Never before had Tam forsaken his duties as guardian of the farm to wander afield without Frayne.

The jingle of the telephone brought Trask back into the house. On the other end of the wire was an irate farmer.

"I'm sending word all along the line," came his message. "Last night a dog bust into my hencoop and killed every last one of my prize Hamburgs and fifty-three other chickens, be-sides. He worked as quiet as a fox. 'Twasn't till I heard a chicken squawk that I came out. That must have been the last of the lot; and the dog had got careless. I had just a glimpse of him as he sneaked off in the dark. Great big cuss he was. As big as a house. Looked some-thing like a wolf by that bum light; and some-thing like a collie, too. Last evening I got news that Gryce, up Suffern-way, lost a lamb, night before, from some prowling dog. D'you s'pose the dogs from the mountains is loose again?"

"One of them is," returned Frayne. "I'm going after him, now."

He hung up the receiver, and, gun under arm, made his way to the scow lying at the side of the dock. Crossing the river, he explored the bank for a half mile in both directions. Failing to find sign or trail of the Black, he struck into the mountains.

It was late that night when Trask slouched wearily into his own house and laid aside his gun.

"Any trace of him?" asked Mildred, eagerly.

"Not a trace," answered Frayne. "I quartered the range, farther back than we ever hunted before. And I asked a lot of questions at that God-forsaken mountaineer settlement, up there. That's all the good it did. I might hunt for a year and not get any track of the beast. Those mountaineers are all liars, of course. Not one of 'em would admit they'd ever seen or heard of the dog. If I'd had Tam with me, I might have caught the trail. To-morrow, I'll see he goes along. He——"

"Tam?" repeated Mildred, in surprise. "Why, wasn't he with you? He hasn't been home all day. He——"

"Hasn't been home? Do you mean to say he didn't come back?"

"No," said his wife, worriedly. "When I got up this morning and found you both gone, I thought of course you'd taken him along, as you said you were going to. Didn't——"

"He wasn't anywhere around when I started," replied Frayne. "He's—he's never been away for a whole day, or even for a whole hour, before. I wonder——"

"Oh, do you suppose that horrible brute has killed Tam, too?" quavered Mildred, in new terror.

"Not he," Trask reassured her. "Not he, or any other mortal log. But," he hesitated, then went on, shamefacedly, "but I'll tell you what I *do* think. I believe Tam has gone hunting, on his own account. I believe he's trailing that mongrel. If he is, he has a man's size job cut out for him. For the Black is as tricky as a weasel. Tam thought more of Wisp than he thought of anything else. And he was like another animal when he found what had happened, down yonder. Take my word for it, he is after the dog that murdered his chum. Whether he'll ever get him, is another matter. But, if he really is after him, he'll never give up the hunt, as long as he has a breath of life left in him. Either he'll overhaul the cur or—well, either that or we'll never see him again. There's no sense in my poking around in the mountains without him. All we can do is wait. That and try to find Tam and chain him up till he forgets this crazy revenge-idea."

But even though the Fraynes did not see their cherished collie when they arose next morning, they did not lack for news of him. In the middle of a silent and doleful breakfast a telephone ring summoned Trask from the table.

"That you, Frayne?" queried a truculent voice. "This is Trippler,—at Darlington. I got rotten news for you. But it's a whole lot rottener for *me*. Last night my cow-yard was raided by a dog. He killed two of the month-old Jersey calves and pretty near ripped the throat out of one of my yearlings. I heard the racket and I ran out with my gun and a flashlight. The cow-yard looked like a battlefield. The dog had skipped. Couldn't see a sign of him, anywheres.

"But about half an hour later he came back. He came back while I was redding up the yard and trying to quiet the scared critters. He came right to the cow-yard gate and stood sniffing there as bold as brass; like he was trying to catch the scent of more of my stock to kill. I heard his feet a-pattering and I turned the flashlight on him.

"He was *your* dog, Frayne! That big dark coloured collie dog of yours. I saw him as plain as day. I upped with my gun and I let him have it. For I was pretty sore. But I must have missed him, clean. For there wasn't any blood near his footprints, in the mud, when I looked. He just lit out. But I'm calling up to tell you you'll have a big bill to pay on this; and——"

"Hold on," interrupted Frayne, quietly. "I'll be up there, in twenty minutes. Good-bye."

As fast as his car could carry him, Trask made his way up the Valley to Darlington, and to the Trippler farm. There an irately unloving host awaited him.

"Before you go telling me the whole story all over again," Trask broke in on an explosive recital, "take me over to the exact spot where you saw Tam standing and sniffing. The ground all around here is soaked from the shower we had last evening. I want to see the tracks you were speaking of."

Muttering dire threats and whining lamentations for his lost calves, Trippler led the way to the cow-yard; pointing presently to a gap in the privet hedge which shut off the barns from the truck garden. Frayne went over to the gap and proceeded to inspect the muddy earth, inch by inch.

"It was here Tam stood when you turned the light on him?" he asked.

"Right just there," declared Trippler. "And I c'n swear to him. He——"

"Come over here," invited Trask. "There are his footprints. As you said. And I'd know them anywhere. There's no other dog of his size with such tiny feet. He gets them from his sire, Sunnybank Lad. Those are Tam's footprints, I admit that. I'd know them anywhere;—even if they didn't show the gash in the outer pad of the left forefoot; where he gouged himself on barbed wire when he was a pup."

"You admit it was him, then!" orated Trippler. "That's all I need to hear you say! Now, how much——?"

"No, no," gently denied Frayne. "It isn't anywhere near all you need to hear. Now, let's go back into the cow-yard. As I crossed it, just now, I saw dozens of dog-footprints, among the hoof-marks of the calves. Let's take another look at them."

Grumblingly, yet eager to add this corroboratory evidence, Trippler followed him to the wallow of churned mud which marked the scene of slaughter. At the first clearly defined set of footprints, Trask halted.

"Take a good look at those," he adjured. "Study them carefully. Here, these, for instance;—where the dog planted all fours firmly for a spring. They're the marks of splay feet,

a third larger than Tam's; and not one of them
has that gash in the pad;—the one I pointed out
to you, back at the gap. Look for yourself."

"Nonsense!" fumed Trippler, albeit a shade
uneasily, as he stood up stiffly after a peering
study of the prints. "Anyhow," he went on, "all
it proves is that there was two of 'em. This big
splay-footed cuss and your collie. They was
working in couples, like killers often does."

"Were they?" Frayne caught him up. "Were
they? Then suppose you look carefully all
through this welter of cow-yard mud; and see
if you can find a single footprint of Tam's. And
while you're looking, let me tell you something."

As Trippler went over the yard's mud with
gimlet eyes, Trask related the story of Wisp's
killing; and his own theory as to Tam.

"He's trailing that black dog," he finished.
"He struck his scent somewhere, and followed
him. He got here a half-hour too late. And
then when you fired at him he run off, to pick
up the trail again. But I doubt if he got it.
For, the Black would probably be cunning enough
to take to the river, after a raid like this. He'd
have sense enough to know somebody would
track him. That brute has true wolf-cunning."

"Maybe—maybe you're right," hesitated
Trippler, after a minute search of the yard had
failed to reveal a footprint corresponding with

Tam's. "And the county's got to pay for 'any damage done to stock by an unknown dog.' That's the law. I'm kind of glad, too.. You see, I like old Tam. Besides, I c'n c'llect more damages from the county than I c'd c'llect from a lawsoot with a neighbour. What'll we do now? Fix up a posse; like we did, the other times?"

"No," replied Trask. "It would do no good. The Black is too clever. And in summer there are too many ways to throw off the scent. Tam will get him,—if anyone can. Let's leave it to him."

But other farmers were not so well content to leave the punishment of the mysterious raider to Tam. As the days went on, there were more and more tidings of the killer. Up and down the Valley he worked; never twice in succession in the same vicinity.

Twice, an hour or so after his visits, men saw Tam prowling along the mongrel's cooling tracks. They reported to Frayne that the collie had grown lean and gaunt and that his beautiful coat was one mass of briar and burr; and that he had slunk away, wolf-fashion, when they called to him.

Frayne, himself, caught no slightest sight of his beloved dog; though, occasionally, in the mornings, he found empty the dish of food he had set out on the previous night. Trask was working out the problem, for himself, nowadays, deaf to all requests that he head another band of hunters into the mountains. He was getting no sleep to speak of. But he was thrilling with the suspense of what sportsmen know as "the still hunt."

Every evening, when his chores and his supper were finished, Frayne went to the sheepfold and led thence a fat wether that had a real genius for loud bleating. This vocal sheep he would tether to a stake near the river-bank. Then he himself would study the trend of the faint evening breeze; and would take up a position in the bushes, somewhere to leeward of the sheep. There, gun across knees, he would sit, until early daylight.

Sometimes he dozed. Oftener he crouched, tense and wakeful, in his covert; straining his eyes, through the gloom, for the hoped-for sight of a slinking black shadow creeping towards the decoy. Not alone to avenge the death of Wisp and to rid the Valley of a scourge did he spend his nights in this way. He knew Tam; as only a born dogman can know his dog. He missed he collie, keenly. And he had solid faith that on the death of the Black, the miserable quest would end and Tam would return to his old home and to his old habits.

So, night after night, Frayne would keep his vigil. Morning after morning, he would plod home, there to hear a telephoned tale of the Black's depredations at some other point of the Valley. At first his nightly watch was kept in dense darkness. But, soon the waxing moon lightened the river-bank; and made the first hours of the sentry duty easier.

Frayne began to lose faith in his own scheme. He had an odd feeling that the Black somehow knew of his presence in the thicket and that Frayne's Farms was left unvisited for that reason. Trask's immunity from the Black's depredations was the theme of much neighboured talk, as time went on. Once more was revived Trippler's theory that Tam and the Black were hunting in couples and that the collie (like so many dogs which have "gone bad") was sparing his late master's property.

On all these unpleasant themes Trask Frayne was brooding, one night, late in the month; as he sat in uncomfortable stillness amid the bushes and stared glumly out at the occasionally-bleating wether. He had had a hard day. And the weeks of semi-sleeplessness were beginning to tell cruelly on him. His senses had taken to tricking him, of late. For instance, at one moment, this night, he was crouching there, waiting patiently for the full moon to rise above the eastern hills, to brighten his vigil. The next moment,— though he was certain he had not closed his eyes,

—the moon had risen and was riding high in the clear heavens.

Frayne started a little, and blinked. As he did so, his disturbed mind told him he had not awakened naturally, but that he had been disturbed by some sound. He shifted his drowsy gaze towards the tethered sheep. And at once all slumber was wiped from his brain.

The wether was lying sprawled on the ground, in a posture that nature neither intends nor permits. Its upflung legs were still jerking convulsively, like galvanised stilts. And above it was bending a huge dark shape.

The moon beat down mercilessly on the tableau of the slain sheep, and of the Black, with his fangs buried deep in the twisting throat.

Now that the longed-for moment had at last come, Trask found himself seized by an unaccountable numbness of mind and of body. By a mighty effort he regained control of his faculties. Slowly and in utter silence he lifted the cocked gun from his knees and put its butt to the hollow of his shoulder.

The Black looked up, in quick suspicion, from his meal. Even in the excitement of the instant, Frayne found scope to wonder at the brute's ability to hear so noiseless a motion. And his sleep-numbed finger sought the trigger.

Then, in a flash, he knew why the Black's great

head had lurched so suddenly up from the interrupted meal. From out a clump of alder, twenty feet to shoreward of the river-bank orgy, whirled a tawny shape. With the speed of a flung spear it sped; straight for the feasting mongrel. And, in the mere breath of time it took to dash through the intervening patch of moonlight, Frayne recognised the newcomer.

The Black sprang up from beside the dead sheep, and faced the foe he could no longer elude. Barely had he gained his feet when Tam was upon him.

Yet the mongrel was not taken unaware. His crafty brain was alert and the master of his sinewy body. As Tam leaped, the black dog reared to meet him. Then, in practically the same gesture, the Black shifted his direction, and dived beneath the charging collie, lunging for the latter's unprotected stomach. It was a manœuvre worthy of a wolf; and one against which the average dog must have been helpless.

But the Black's opponent was a collie. And, in the back of his brain, though never in his chivalric heart, a collie is forever reverting to his own wolf ancestors. Thus, as the Black changed the course of his lunge, Tam, in mid-air, changed his. By a violent twist of every whalebone muscle, Tam whirled himself side-

wise. And the Black's ravening jaws closed
on nothing.

In another instant,—even before he had
touched ground,—Tam had slashed with his
curving eyeteeth. This is another trick known
to practically no animal save the wolf and the
wolf's direct descendant, the collie. The razor-
like teeth cut the Black's left ear and cheek as
cleanly as might a blade.

But, in the same motion, the Black's flying
head had veered; and his jaws had found a hold
above Tam's jugular. Again, with the normal
dog, such a hold might well have ended the fight.
But, the Providence which ordained that a collie
should guard sheep on icy Highland moors also
gave him an unbelievably thick coat, to fend off
the weather. And this coat serves as an almost
invulnerable armour; especially at the side of the
throat. The Black's teeth closed upon a quantity
of tangled fur; but on only the merest patch of
skin and on none of the under flesh at all.

Tam ripped himself free, leaving a double
handful of ruff between the Black's grinding
jaws. As the mongrel spat out the encumbering
gag of fur, Tam's curved fang laid bare the
scarred shoulder once grazed by Trask Frayne's
buckshot. And, in a rolling, fighting heap, the
two enemies rolled over and over together on the
dew-drenched grass.

Frayne's gun was levelled. But the man did not dare fire. By that deceptive light, he had no assurance of hitting one dog without also killing the other. And, chafing at his own impotence, he stood stock-still, watching the battle.

Both dogs were on their feet again; rearing and rending in mute fury. No sound issued from the back-curled lips of either. This was no mere dogfight, as noisy as it was pugnacious. It was a struggle to the death. And the dogs realised it.

Thrice more, the Black struck for the jugular. Twice, thanks to Tam's lightning quickness, he scored a clean miss. The third time, he annexed only another handful of hair.

With his slashes he was luckier. One of Tam's forelegs was bleeding freely. So was a cut on his stomach, where the Black had sought to disembowel him. And one side of his muzzle was laid open. But the collie had given over such mere fencing tactics as slashing. He was tearing into his powerful and wily foe with all the concentrated fury of his month's vain pursuit of vengeance.

The Black dived for the collie's forelegs, seeking to crack their bones in his mighty jaws and thus render his foe helpless. Nimbly, Tam's tiny white forefeet whisked away from the peril of each dive. In redoubled fury he drove for the throat. And the two clashed, shoulder to shoulder.

Then, amid the welter, came the final phase of the fight. The Black, as the two reared, lunged again for the collie's hurt throat. Tam jerked his head and neck aside to avoid the grip. And, as once before, the Black changed the direction of his lunge. With the swiftness of a striking snake, he made the change. And, before the other could thwart or so much as divine his purpose, he had secured the coveted hold, far up on Tam's left foreleg.

No mere snap or slash, this; but a death grip. The Black's teeth sank deep into the captured leg; grinding with a force which presently must snap the bones of the upper leg and leave the collie crippled against a practically uninjured and terrible antagonist. The rest would be slaughter.

Tam knew his own mortal peril. He knew it even before Trask Frayne came rushing out from his watching-place, brandishing the gun, club fashion. The collie did not try to wrench free and thereby to hurry the process of breaking his leg or of tearing out the shoulder-muscles. He thought, as quickly as the mongrel had lunged.

Rearing his head aloft, he drove down at the Black. The latter was clinging with all his might to the collie's foreleg. And, in the rapture of having gained at last a disabling grip, he ignored the fact that he had left an opening in his own defence;—an opening seldom sought in a fight, except by a wolf or a wolf's descendant.

It was for this opening that Tam-o'-Shanter struck. In a trice his white teeth had buried themselves in the exposed nape of the Black's neck.

Here, at the brain's base, lies the spinal cord, dangerously within reach of long and hard-driven fangs. And here, Tam had fastened himself.

An instant later,—but an instant too late,— the Black knew his peril. Releasing his grip on the collie's leg, before the bone had begun to yield, he threw his great body madly from side to side, fighting crazily to shake off the death-hold. With all his mighty strength, he thrashed about.

Twice, he lifted the seventy-pound collie clean off the ground. Once he fell, with Tam under him. But the collie held on. Tam did more than hold on. Exerting every remaining atom of his waning power, he let his body be flung here and there, in the Black's struggles; and he concentrated his force upon cleaving deeper and deeper into the neck-nape.

This was the grip whereby the Black, a month agone, had crushed the life out of friendly little Wisp. And, by chance or by fate, Tam had been enabled to gain the same hold. Spasmodically, he set his fangs in a viselike tightening of his grip.

At one instant, the Black was whirling and writhing in the fulness of his wiry might. At the next, with a sickening snapping sound, his giant body went limp. And his forequarters hung, a lifeless weight, from his conqueror's jaws.

Tam relaxed his hold. The big black body slumped to earth and lay there. The collie, panting and swaying, stood over his dead enemy. The bitterly long quest was ended. Heavenward went his bleeding muzzle. And he waked the solemn stillnesses of the summer night with an eerie wolf howl, the awesome primal yell of Victory.

For a few seconds Trask Frayne, unnoticed, stared at his dog. And, as he looked, it seemed to him he could see the collie change gradually back from a wild thing of the forests to the staunch and adoring watchdog of other days. Then the man spoke.

"Tam!" he said, quietly. *"Tam!* Old friend!"

The exhausted victor lurched dizzily about, at sound of the voice. Catching sight of Trask, he trembled all over.

He took a dazed step towards Frayne. Then,

with something queerly like a human sob, the collie sprang forward; and gambolled weakly about the man; licking Trask's feet and hands; springing up in a groggy effort to kiss his face; patting his master's chest with eager forepaws; crying aloud in an ecstasy of joy at the reunion.

Then, all at once, he seemed to remember he was a staid and dignified middle-aged dog and not a hoodlum puppy.   Ceasing his unheard-of demonstrations, he stood close beside Frayne; looking up into Trask's eyes in silent worship.

"You've done a grand night's work, Tam," said Frayne, seeking to steady his own voice. "And your hurts need bathing.   Come home."

His plumed tail proudly wagging, his splendid head aloft, Tam-o'-Shanter turned and led the way to the house he loved.

THE SUNNYBANK COLLIES

H ERE, at "Sunnybank," — at Pompton Lakes, in New Jersey,—we raise thoroughbred collies. For many years we have been breeding them. For many years longer, I have been studying them.

The more I study them, the more I realise that there is something about a collie—a mysterious, elusive something—that makes him different from any other dog. Something nearer human than beast. And, for all that, he is one hundred per cent dog.

There is much to learn from him; much to puzzle over; as perhaps the following discursive yarns about a few members of the long line of Sunnybank collies may show.

Greatest of them all was Lad. One would as soon have thought of teaching nursery rhymes to Emerson as of teaching Lad "tricks." Beyond the common babyhood lessons of obedience and of the Place's simple Law, he went untaught. And he taught himself; being that type of dog. For example:—

The Mistress had been dangerously ill, with pneumonia. (In my book, *Lad: A Dog,* I tell how Laddie kept vigil outside her door, day and night, until she was out of danger; and how he celebrated her convalescence with a brainstorm which would have disgraced a three-months puppy.) Well, on the first day she was able to be carried out of doors, the Mistress lay in a veranda hammock, with Lad on the porch floor at her side.

Friends—several instalments of them—drove to the Place to congratulate the Mistress on her recovery; and to bring gifts of flowers, fruit, jellies, books. All morning, Lad lay there, watching the various relays of guests and eyeing the presents they laid in her lap. After the fifth group of callers had gone, the big collie got up and trotted off into the forest. For nearly an hour he was absent.

Then he came back; travelling with difficulty, by reason of the heavy burden he bore. Somewhere, far away in the woods, he had found, or revisited, the carcase of a dead horse—of an excessively dead horse. From it he had wrenched two ribs and some of the vertebræ.

Dragging this horrible gift along, he returned to the veranda. Before any of us were well aware of his presence (the wind setting in the other direction) he had mounted the steps and, with one mighty heave, had lifted the ribs and vertebræ over the hammock edge and laid them in the lap of his dismayed Mistress.

Humans had celebrated her recovery with presents. And he, watching, had imitated them. He had gone far and had toiled hard to bring her an offering that his canine mind deemed all-desirable.

It was carrion; but it represented, to a dog, everything that a present should be.

Dogs do not eat carrion. They merely rub their shoulders in it; on the same principle that women use perfumes. It is a purely æsthetic pleasure to them. And carrion is probably no more malodorous to a human being than is the reek of tobacco or of whisky or even of some $15-an-ounce scent, to a dog. It is all a matter of taste and of education.

Noting that his gift awoke no joy whatever in its recipient's heart, Lad was monstrous crest-fallen. Nor, from that day on, did he ever bring carrion to the Place. He even abstained hence-forth from rubbing his shoulders in it. Evident-ly he gathered, from our reception of his present, that "it is not done."

When Lad was training his little son, Wolf, to become a decent canine citizen, he was much annoyed by the puppy's trick of watching his sire bury bones and then of exhuming and gnawing them himself. Lad did not punish the puppy for this. He adopted a shrewder and surer way of saving his buried treasures from theft.

Thereafter, he would bury the choice bone deeper in the ground than had been his habit. And, directly above it, just below the surface of the earth, he would inter a second and older bone; a bone that had long been denuded of all meat and was of no further value to any dog.

Wolf, galloping eagerly up to the spot of burial, as soon as Lad moved away, would dig where his father had dug. Presently, he would unearth the topmost and worthless bone. Satisfied that he had exhausted the possibilities of the *cache*, he dug no deeper; but left the new and toothsome bone undiscovered.

By the way, did it ever occur to you that a dog is almost the only animal to bury food? And did you ever stop to think why? The reason is simple.

Dogs, alone of all wild animals (dogs and their blood-brethren, the wolves), used to hunt in packs. All other beasts hunted alone or, at most, in pairs. When prey was slain, the dog that did not bolt his food with all possible haste was the dog that got the smallest share or none at all. When there was more food than could be devoured at one meal, he had the sense to lay up provision for the next day's dinner.

He knew, if he left the carcase lying where it was, it would be devoured by the rest of the hungry pack. So he buried as much of it as he could, to prevent his brethren from finding and eating it.

Thus, the dog, alone of all quadrupeds, still bolts his food in huge and half-chewed mouthfuls; and the dog buries food for future use. These two traits are as purely ancestral as is the dog's habit of turning around several times before settling himself to sleep for the night. His wild ancestors did that, to crush the stiff grasses and reeds into a softer bed and to scare therefrom any lurking snakes or scorpions.

Lad's "talking" was a byword, at Sunnybank Only to the Mistress and myself would be deign to "speak." But, to us, he would sometimes talk for five minutes at a time. Of course, there were no actual words in his speech. But no words were needed to show his meaning.

His conversation used to run the full gamut of sounds, in a way that was as eerie as it was laughable. He could—and did—express every shade of meaning he chose to.

Indignation or disgust was voiced in fierce grumbles and mutters, that were run together in sentence lengths. Sympathy found vent in queer crooning sounds, accompanied by swift light pats of his absurdly tiny white forepaws.

Grief was expressed in something too much like human sobs to be funny. And so on through every possible emotion,—except fear. The great dog did not know fear.

No one, listening when Lad "talked," could doubt he was seeking to imitate the intonation and meanings of the human voice.

Once, the Mistress and I went on a visit of sympathy to a lugubrious old woman who lived some miles from Sunnybank, and who had been laid up for weeks with a broken arm. The arm had mended. But it was still a source of mental misery to the victim. We took Lad along, on our call, because the convalescent was fond of him. We had every cause, soon, to wish we had left him at home.

From the instant we entered the old woman's house, a demon of evil mirth seemed to possess the dog. Outwardly, he was calm and sedate, as usual. He curled up beside the Mistress, and, with head gravely on one side, proceeded to listen to our hostess' tale of the long and painful illness. But, scarcely had the whiningly groaning accents framed a single sentence of the recital, when Lad took up the woful tale on his own account.

His voice pitched in precisely the same key as the speaker's, he began to whine and to mumble. When the woman paused for breath, Lad filled in the brief interval with the most heartrendingly lamentable groans; then continued his plaint with her. And all the time, his deep-set, sorrowful eyes were fairly a-dance with mischief, and the tip of his plumy tail was quivering in a tense effort not to betray his sinful glee by wagging.

It was too much for me. I got out of the room as fast as I could. I escaped barely in time to hear the hostess moan:

"Isn't it wonderful how that dog understands my terrible suffering? He carries on, just as if it were his own agony!"

But I knew better, in spite of Lad's affirmative groan. In personal agony, Lad could never be lured into making a sound. And when the Mistress or myself was unhappy, his swift and heart-broken sympathy did not take the form of lamentable ululations or of such impudent copying of our voices.

It was just one of Lad's jokes. He realised as well as we did that the old lady was no longer in pain and that she was a chronic calamity howler. That was his way of guying the mock-sufferer. Genuine trouble always stirred him to the depths. But, his life long, he hated fraud.

Lad's story is told in detail, elsewhere; and I have here written overlong about him. But his human traits were myriad and it is hard for me to condense an account of him.

Then there was Bruce,—hero of my dogbook of the same name. Bruce's "pedigree name" was Sunnybank Goldsmith; and for many years he brought local dog-show fame to the Place by an unbroken succession of victories. A score of cups and medals and an armful of blue ribbons attest his physical perfection.

But dog-shows take no heed of a collie's mentality, nor of the thousand wistfully lovable traits which make him what he is. When we carved on Bruce's headstone the inscription, *"The Dog Without a Fault,"* we referred less to his physical magnificence than to the soul and the heart of him.

He was wholly different from Lad. He lacked Lad's d'Artagnan-like dash and gaiety and uncanny wisdom. Yet he was clever. And he had a strange sweetness of nature that I have found in no other dog. That, and a perfect "one-man-dog" obedience and goodness.

Like Lad, he was never struck or otherwise punished; and never needed such punishment. He and Laddie were dear friends, from the moment they met. And each was the only grown male dog with which the other would consent to be on terms of cordiality.

Bruce had a melancholy dignity, behind which lurked an elusive sense of fun.

For his children—he had many dozens of them

—he felt an eternal disgust; even aversion. Let visitors start to walk towards the puppy-yards, and Bruce at once lowered his head and tail and slunk away. When a group of the puppies, out for a gallop, caught sight of their sire and bore down gleefully upon him, Bruce would stalk off in utter gloom. Too chivalric to hurt or even to growl at any of the scrambling oncoming babies, he would none the less take himself out of their way with all possible haste.

But, on occasion, he could rise to a sense of his duties as a parent. As when one of the young dogs was left tied for a few minutes to a clothesline, three summers ago. The youngster gnawed the line in two and pranced merrily away on a rabbit hunt, dragging ten feet of rope with him.

When I came home and saw the severed clothesline, I knew what must be happening, somewhere out in the woods. The dangling rope was certain to catch in some bush or stump. And the puppy, in his struggles, would snarl himself inextricably. There, unless help should come, he must starve to death.

For twenty-four hours, two of the men and the Mistress and myself scoured the forests and hills for a radius of several miles. We looked everywhere a luckless puppy would be likely to entangle himself. We shouted ourselves hoarse.

in hope of an answering cry from the lost one.

After a day and a night of this fruitless search, the Mistress and I set off again; this time taking Bruce along. At least, we started off taking him. After the first hundred yards, he took us. Why I bothered to follow him, I don't yet know.

He struck a bee line, through woods and brambles, travelling at a hand gallop and stopping every few moments for me to catch up with him. At the end of a mile, he plunged into a copse that was choked with briars. In the centre of this he gave tongue, with a salvo of thunderous barks. Twice before, I had searched this copse. But, at his urgency, I entered it again.

In its exact centre, hidden from view by a matted screen of briars and leaves, I found the runaway. His rope had caught in a root. He had then wound himself up in it, until the line enmeshed him and held him close to earth. A twist of it, around his jaws, had kept him from making a sound. He was half dead from fright and thirst.

Having found and saved the younger dog, Bruce promptly lost all interest in him. He seemed ashamed, rather than pleased, at our laudations.

On such few times as we went motoring without him, Bruce was always on hand to greet us on our return. And his greeting took an odd

form. Near the foot of the drive was a big
Forsythia bush. At sight of the approaching
car, Bruce invariably rushed over to this bush
and hid behind it. At least he bent his head until a branch of the bush hid it from view.

Then, tail a-quiver, he would crouch there;
not realising that all of him except his head was
in plain sight to us. When at last the car was
almost alongside, he would jump out; and stand
wagging his plumed tail excitedly, to note our
surprise at his unforeseen presence. Never did
this jest pall on him. Never did he have the faintest idea that his head was the only part of his
beautiful self which was not clearly visible.

Bruce slept in my bedroom. In the morning,
when one of the maids knocked at the door to
wake me, he would get to his feet, cross the room
to the bed, and lay his cold muzzle against my
face, tapping at my arm or shoulder with his
paw until I opened my eyes. Then, at once, he
went back to his rug and lay down again. Nor,
if I failed to climb out of bed for another two
hours, would he disturb me a second time.

He had waked me, once. After that, it was
up to me to obey the summons or to disregard
it. That was no concern of Bruce's. His duty
was done!

But how did a mere dog know that the knock
on the door was a signal for me to get up? Never

by any chance did he disturb me until he heard that knock.

He was psychic, too. Rex, a dog that I had had long before, used to sleep in a certain corner of the lower hall. He slept there for years. He was killed. Never afterward would Bruce set foot on the spot where Rex had been wont to lie. Time and again I have seen him skirt that part of the floor, making a semi-circular detour in order to avoid stepping there. I have tested him a dozen times, in the presence of guests. Always the result was the same.

Peace to his stately, lovable, whimsical soul! He was my dear chum. And his going has left an ache.

Wolf is Lad's son—wiry and undersized; yet he is as golden as Katherine Lee Bates' immortal "Sigurd." He inherits his sire's wonderful brain as well as Laddie's keen sense of humour.

Savage, and hating strangers, Wolf has learned the law to this extent: no one, walking or motoring down the drive from the gate and coming straight to the front door, must be molested; though no stranger crossing the grounds or prowling within their limits need be tolerated.

A guest may pat him on the head, at will; and Wolf must make no sign of resentment. But all my years of training do not prevent him from snarling in fierce menace if a visitor seeks to pat his sensitive body. Very young children are the only exceptions to this rule of his. Toddling babies may maul him to their hearts' content; and Wolf revels in the discomfort.

Like Lad, he is the Mistress' dog. Not merely because he belongs to her; but because he has adopted her for his deity.

When we leave Sunnybank, for two or three months, yearly, in midwinter, Wolf knows we are going; even before the trunks are brought from the attic for packing. And, from that time on, he is in dire, silent misery. When at last the car carries us out of the gate, he sits down, points his muzzle skyward, and shakes the air with a series of raucous wolf-howls. After five minutes of which, he sullenly, stoically, takes up the burden of loneliness until our return.

The queer part of it is that he knows—as Lad and Bruce used to know—in some occult way, when we are coming home. And, for hours before our return, he is in a state of crazy excitement. I don't try to explain this. I have no explanation for it. But it can be proven by anyone at Sunnybank.

The ancestral herding instinct is strong in Wolf. It made itself known, first, when a car was coming down the drive towards the house, at a somewhat reckless pace, several years ago. In the centre of the drive, several of the collie pups were playing. When the car was almost on top of the heedless bevy of youngsters, Wolf darted out, from the veranda, rushed in among the pups and shouldered them off the drive and up onto the bank at either side. He cleared the drive of every one of them; then bounded aside barely in time to escape the car's front wheels.

He was praised for this bit of quick thought and quicker action. And the praise made him inordinately proud. From that day on, he has hustled every pup or grown dog off the drive, whenever a car has come in sight through the gateway.

When the pups are too far scattered for him to round them up and shove them out of harm's way, in so short a time, he adopts a still better mode of clearing the drive. Barking in wild ecstasy, he rushes at top speed down the lawn, as though in pursuit of some highly alluring prey. No living pup can resist such a call. Every one of the youngsters dashes in pursuit. Then, as soon as the last of them is far enough away from the drive, Wolf stops and comes trotting back to the house. He has done this, again and again. To me, it savours of human reasoning.

In the car, Wolf is as efficient a guard as any policeman. When the Mistress drives alone, he sits on the front seat beside her. If she stops in front of any shop, he is at once on the alert. At such times, a woman acquaintance may come alongside for a word with her. Wolf pays no heed to the newcomer.

But let a *man* approach the car; and Wolf is up on his toes, and ready for trouble. If the man lays a hand on the automobile, in the course of the chat, Wolf is at his throat. When I am driving with the Mistress, he lies on the rear seat and does not bother to act as policeman; except when we leave the car in his keeping.

People, hereabouts, know this trait of Wolf's and his aversion to any stranger. And they forbear to touch the car when talking with us. Last year, a friend came alongside, while we were waiting, one evening, for the mail to be sorted. Wolf had never before seen this man. Yet, after a single glance, the dog lost his usual air of hostility. There was a slight tremble in our friend's voice as he said to us:

"My collie was run over to-day and killed. We are mighty unhappy, at our house, this evening."

As he spoke, he laid his hand on the door of the car. Wolf lurched forward, as usual. But, to our amazement, instead of attacking, he whimpered softly and licked the man's face. Never before or since, have I seen him show any sign of friendly interest in a stranger—not even to this same man, when they chanced to meet again, a few months later.

Bruce's son, Jock, was the finest pup, from a dog-show point of view—and in every other way —that we have been able to breed. Jock was physical perfection. And he had a brain, too; and abundant charm; and a most intensely haunting personality. He had from earliest puppyhood, all the steadfast qualities of a veteran dog; and at the same time a babylike friendliness and love of play.

Nor did he know what it was to be afraid. Always, in presence of danger, he met the menace with a furious charge, accompanied by a clear, trumpet-bark of gay defiance. Once, for instance, he had been lying beside my chair on the veranda. Suddenly he jumped to his feet, with that same gay, fierce bark.

I turned to see what had excited him. A huge copperhead snake had crawled up the vines to the porch floor and had wriggled on; to within a foot or two of my chair.

Jock was barely six months old. Yet he flew to the assault with more sense than would many a grown dog.

All dogs have a horror of copperheads, and Jock was no exception. By instinct, he seemed to know what the snake's tactics would be. For he strove to catch the foe by the back of the neck, before the copperhead could coil.

He was a fraction of a second too late.   Yet he was nimble and wise enough to spring back out of reach, before the coiling serpent could strike.   Then, with that same glad bark of defiance, he danced about his enemy, trying to take the snake from the rear and to flash in and get a neck grip before the copperhead could recoil after each futile strike.

I put an end to the battle by a bullet in the snake's ugly head.   And Jock was mortally offended with me, for hours thereafter, for spoiling his fun.

When he was eight months old, I took the little chap to Paterson, to his first (and last) dog show.   Never before had he been off the Place or in a house.   Yet he bore himself like a seasoned traveller; and he "showed" with the perfection of a champion.   He won, in class after class; annexing two silver cups and several blue ribbons.   His peerless sire, Bruce, was the only collie, in the whole show, able to win over him, that day.

Jock beat every other contestant.   He seemed to enjoy showing and to delight in the novelty and excitement of it all.   He was at the show for only a few hours; and it was a triumph-day for him.

Yet cheerfully would I give a thousand dollars not to have taken him there.

For he brought home not only his many prizes but a virulent case of distemper; as did other dogs that attended the same show.

Of course, I had had him (as well as all my other dogs) inoculated against distemper, long before; and such precautions are supposed to be effective. But the disease got through the inoculation and infected him.

He made a gallant fight of it—oh, a *gallant* fight!—the fearless little thoroughbred! But it was too much for him. For five weeks, he and I fought that grindingly losing battle.

Then, in the dim grey of a November dawn, he lifted his head from my knee, and peered through the shadows towards one black corner of the room. No one, watching him, could have doubted that he saw Something—lurking there in the dark.

Sharply, he eyed the dim room-corner for an instant. Then, from his throat burst forth that glad, fierce defiance-bark of his—his fearlessly gay battle shout. And he fell back dead.

What did he see, waiting for him, there in the murk of shadows? Perhaps nothing. Perhaps "the Arch-Fear in visible shape." Who knows?

In any case, whatever it was, he did not fear it. He challenged it as fiercely as ever he had challenged mortal foe.   And his hero-spirit went forth to do battle with it—unafraid.

God grant us all so gallant an ending!

His little mother, Sunnybank Jean, had never cast Jock off, as do most dog-mothers when their pups are weaned.   To the day I quarantined him for distemper, she and her son had been inseparable.

A week after Jock's death, Jean came running up to me, shaking with glad eagerness, and led me to the grave where the puppy had been buried. It was far off, and I had hoped she would not be able to find it.   But she had been searching, very patiently, whenever she was free.

And now, when she had led me to the grave, she lay down close beside it.   Not despondently; but wagging her plumed tail gently, and as if she had found at last a clue in her long search. Scent or some other sense told her she was nearer her baby than she had been in days.   And she was well content to wait there until he should come back.

All of which is maudlin, perhaps; but it is true.

Perhaps it is also maudlin to wonder why a sane human should be fool enough to let himself care for a dog, when he knows that at best he is due for a man's size heartache within a pitifully brief span of years.   Dogs live so short a time; and we humans so long!

This rambling tale of my dogs leaves no room to tell at length of the collie who was never allowed in the dining-room until the after-dinner coffee was served; and who came the length of the hall and up to the table the moment the maid brought in the coffee cups (how he timed it to the very second, none of us knew; yet not once did he miss connections by the slightest fraction of a minute).

Nor does it permit the tale of the collie pup who was proud of his stunt in learning to take the morning paper off the front steps and carry it into the dining-room; and whose pride in the accomplishment led him presently to collect all the morning papers from all the door steps within the radius of a mile and deposit them happily at my feet.

Nor can I tell of the collie that caught and followed the trail of my footsteps, through the rain, along a crowded city street; in and out of a maze of turnings; and came up with me inside of three minutes. Nor of a long line of other collies, some of whom showed human intelligence; and some, intelligence that was almost more than human.

Not even of the clown pup that was so elated over "rounding up" his first bunch of sheep that he proceeded to round up chickens and cats and every living and round-up-able creature that he could find; nor of the collie who, taught to fetch my hat, was wont to romp up to me in the presence of many outsiders; bearing proudly in his teeth an assortment of humble, not to say intimate and humiliating, garments.

*　　*　　*

Comedian dogs, spectacular dogs, gloriously human dogs, Sunnybank collies of every phase of heart and brain and soul—one common and pathetically early tragedy has waited or waits for you all! Among you, you have taught me more of true loyalty and patience and courtesy and divine forgiveness and solid sanity and fun and a hundred other worth-while lessons, than all the masters I have studied under.

*　　*　　*

I wonder if it is heretical to believe that when at last my tired feet shall tread the Other Shore, a madly welcoming swirl of exultant collies—the splendid Sunnybank dogs that have been my chums here—will bound forward, circling and barking around me, to lead me Home!

Heretical or otherwise, I want to believe it. And if I fail to find them there, I shall know I have taken the Wrong Turning and have reached a goal other than I hoped for.

THE END